Our Humble Helpers

Our Humble Helpers

by

Jean-Henri Fabre

TRANSLATOR'S PREFACE

IN ITS purpose and style this book closely resembles the same author's "Story-Book of Science," and it belongs to the same series. To many readers, however, it is likely to prove even more interesting than its predecessor, inasmuch as the domestic animals are more familiar and hence more interesting to many persons than the ant, the spider, the plant-louse, the caterpillar, and other examples of insect life discussed in the earlier work. Particularly at this time, when not a few of us, both old and young, are turning our attention, however inexpertly, to farming in a small way, in order to make the most of nature's food resources within our reach, we like to become a little better acquainted with the denizens of the farmyard and the four-footed helpers in the field. The pig and the hen, the goose and the turkey, the ox and the ass, the horse and the cow, the sheep and its canine keeper—these and many other old friends of ours in the animal kingdom are made to enliven the following pages by the genius and skill of him who knew and loved them all as few naturalists have known and loved their dumb fellow-creatures.

Faithfulness to the spirit of the French original has throughout been striven for rather than a blind subservience to the letter. May the attempt to render at least a little of the charm of that original be found not wholly unsuccessful!

Contents

CHAPTER I

THE COCK AND THE HEN

UNDER THE big elm tree in the garden Uncle Paul has called together for the third time his usual listeners, Emile, Jules, and Louis. After the story of the Ravagers, which destroy our harvests, and that of the Auxiliaries, which protect them, he now proposes to tell the story of our Humble Helpers, the domestic animals. He thus begins:

"The cock and the hen, those invaluable members of our poultry-yards, came to us from Asia so long ago that the remembrance of their coming is lost. At the present day they have spread to all parts of the world.

"Is it necessary to describe the cock to you? Who has not admired this fine bird, with its bright look, its proud bearing, its slow and sedate walk? On its head a piece of scarlet flesh forms a scalloped crest; under the base of the beak hang two wattles resembling pieces of coral; on each temple, by the side of the ear, is a spot of dull white naked skin; a rich tippet of golden red falls from the neck over the shoulders and breast; two feathers of a greenish metallic luster form a graceful arch of plumage in the upper part of the tail. The heel is armed with a horny spur, hard and pointed; a formidable weapon with which, in fighting, the cock stabs his rival to death. His song is a resonant peal that makes itself heard at all hours, night as well as day. Hardly does the sky begin to brighten with the twilight of dawn when, erect on his perch, he awakens the nocturnal echoes with his piercing *cock-a-doodle-doo*, the reveille of the farm."

"That," said Emile, "is the song I like so much to hear in the morning when I am about half-way between sleeping and waking."

"It is the cock's crowing," put in Louis, "that wakes me up in the morning when I have to go to market in the next town."

"The cock is the king of the poultry-yard," resumed Uncle Paul. "Full of care for his hens, he leads them, protects them, scolds and punishes them. He watches over those that wander off, goes in quest of the vagrants, and brings them back with little cries of impatience, which, no doubt, are admonitions. If necessary, a peck with the beak persuades the more refractory. But if he finds food, such as grain, insects, or worms, he straightway lifts up his voice and calls the hens to the banquet. He himself, however, magnificent and generous, stands in the midst of the throng and scratches the earth to turn up the worms and distribute here and there to the invited guests the dainties thus unearthed. If some greedy hen takes more than her share, he recalls her to a sense of her duty to the community and reprimands her with a peck on the head. After all the others have eaten their fill he contents himself with their leavings.

"Plainer in costume, the hen, the joy of the farmer's wife, trots about the poultry-yard, scratching and pecking and cackling. After laying an egg she proclaims her joy with an enthusiasm in which her companions take such a share that the whole establishment bursts into a general lively chorus in celebration of the happy event. She has a habit of squatting down in a dusty and sunny corner where she flutters her wings with much content and makes a fine shower fall between her feathers to relieve the itching that torments her. Then with outstretched leg and wing she sleeps away the hottest hours of the day; or, without disturbing her voluptuous repose, spying a fly on the wall, she snaps it up with one quick dart of her beak. Like the cock, she swallows fine gravel, which takes the place of teeth and serves to grind the grain in her gizzard. She drinks by lifting her head skyward to make each mouthful go down. She sleeps on one leg, the other drawn up under her plumage and her head hidden under her wing."

"These curious particulars of the hen's habits," said Jules, "are quite familiar to us all; we see them every day with our own eyes. One only is new to me: hens, you say, swallow little grains of sand which take the place of teeth for grinding the food in the gizzard. I don't know what the gizzard is, and I don't see how little stones that have been swallowed can be used as teeth."

"A short digression on the digestive organs of birds," replied Uncle Paul, "will give you the information you ask for.

"Birds do not chew their food; they swallow

PELICAN

it just as they seize it, or nearly so. The beak, lacking teeth, is for that very reason unsuited for the work of grinding. It merely seizes; it strikes, picks up, digs, pierces, breaks, tears, according to the kind of food adapted to the bird's needs. A solid horn covers the bony framework of the two mandibles and makes their edges sharp and very well fitted for dismembering if necessary, but not for triturating.

"Rapacious birds that feed on live prey have the upper mandible short, strong, hooked, and terminating in a sharp point, sometimes with serrate edges. With this weapon the hunting bird kills its prey, and tears it to pieces while holding it with its vigorous talons armed with sharp, curved nails.

"Fish-eating birds that tear the fish to pieces in order to swallow it have the hooked beak of the rapacious birds; those that swallow the fish whole have a straight beak with long, wide mandibles. Some throw it into the air to catch it in their beak a second time, head first, and swallow it without any difficulty in spite of the fin-bones, which lie flat from front to back while the fish is passing through the narrow gullet. A great fishing bird, the pelican, has in its lower mandible a large membranous pouch, a sort of fish-pond, where it stores the fish as long as the catch lasts. Thus stocked up, it seeks a quiet retreat on some ledge of rock by the water-side and takes out, one by one, the fish packed away in its pouch, to feed on them at leisure."

"The pelican seems to me a wise fisher," remarked Emile. "Without losing a minute in swallowing, it begins by filling the bag under its beak. The time will come later for looking over the catch and enjoying the fish at leisure. I should like to see it on its rocks with its bag full."

"And that other one," said Jules, "that throws the fish it has caught into the air so as to catch it again head first and not strangle when swallowing it—is not that one just as clever?"

"Each kind has its special talent," replied Uncle Paul, "which it uses with the tool peculiar to the bird, the beak. If the story of the auxiliaries, related some time ago, is still fresh in your minds, you will remember that insect-eating birds have the beak slender and sometimes very long, to dig into the fissures of dead wood and bark; but those that catch insects on the fly, as the swallow and the fern-owl, have the beak very short and exceedingly wide, so that the game pursued is caught in the open gullet and becomes coated with a slimy saliva which holds it fast. Finally, I will remind you of the granivorous birds—the sparrow, linnet, greenfinch, chaffinch, and many others. All these birds, whose chief food consists of grain, have the beak short, thick, pointed; adapted, in fact, to the picking up of seeds from the ground, freeing them from their husks, and breaking their shells to obtain the kernel. By virtue of its strong mandibles, the beak of the hen belongs to this last category, although at the same time its rather long, sharp, and slightly hooked extremity indicates carnivorous tastes. Such a beak calls not only for seeds, but also for small prey, such as insects and worms."

CHAPTER II

THE GIZZARD

"Nearly all the higher or mammiferous animals," Uncle Paul continued, "such as the dog, cat, wolf, horse, have only one digestive pouch—a stomach—where the alimentary substances are dissolved and made fluid, so as to enter the veins and be turned into blood, by which all parts of the body are nourished. But the ox, goat, and sheep—the cud-chewers, in short—have four digestive cavities, which I will tell you about later. I will tell you how, in the pasture, these animals hastily swallow almost unchewed grass and put it by in a large reservoir called a paunch, from which it comes up again afterward in a season of repose, to be rechewed at leisure in small mouthfuls.

"Well, birds are fashioned in a similar way, as far as eating is concerned. Not being able to chew, as they have no teeth, they swallow their food without any preparation, nearly as the beak has seized it, and amass a quantity of it in a spacious stomach, just as the ox does in his paunch. From this reservoir the food passes, little by little, into two other digestive cavities, one of which immerses it in a liquid calculated to dissolve it, and the other grinds and triturates it better than the best pair of jaws could do. There takes place a kind of chewing, it is true, only the food, instead of returning to the beak, where teeth are lacking for its thorough mastication, continues its journey, and on the way comes to the triturating machine. Birds, then, are generally provided with three digestive cavities.

"The first is the crop, situated just at the base of the neck. It is a bag with thin and flexible walls, its size proportioned to the resistant nature of the food eaten. It is very large in birds that feed on grain, especially the hen, and is medium-sized, or even wholly wanting, in those that live on prey, which is much easier to digest than dry and hard seeds. In the crop, the food swallowed in haste remains hours and even days, as in a reservoir; there it softens somewhat, and is then submitted to the action of the other digestive pouches. The crop corresponds in a certain sense to the bag in which the pelican stores up his fishing; it represents also the first stomach of the ox and the other cud-chewers or ruminants.

"Next to the crop is a second enlargement, called the succenturiate ventricle, of small capacity but remarkable for a liquid of a bitter taste that oozes in fine drops through its walls and moistens the food as it passes. This liquid is a digestive juice; it has the property of dissolving the alimentary substances as soon as trituration has done the greater part of the work. The food does not remain in this second stomach; it merely passes through to become impregnated with the digestive juice.

"The third and last stomach is known as the gizzard. It is rounded and is slightly flattened on both sides, like a watch-case, and is composed—especially in birds that live on grain—of a very thick, fleshy wall, lined on the inside with a kind of hard and tenacious leather which protects the organ from attrition. Finally, it is to be noted that at the same time the bird is swallowing grain it takes care also to swallow a little gravel, some very small stones which, away down in the gizzard, will perform the office of teeth."

"I know what the gizzard is," volunteered Emile. "When they are cleaning a chicken to cook, they take out of the body something round that they split in two with a knife; then they throw away a thick skin all wrinkled and stuffed with grains of sand, and the rest is put back into the chicken."

"Yes, that is the gizzard," said Uncle Paul. "Let us complete these ideas got from cooking. The bird, not having in its beak the molars necessary for grinding, as in a mill, the seeds that are hard to crush, supplies its gizzard with artificial teeth, which are renewed at each repast; that is to say, it swallows little pebbles. The grain, softened in the crop and moistened with the digestive juice during its passage through the succenturiate ventricle, reaches the gizzard mixed with the little stones that are to aid the triturating action. The work then performed is easy to understand. If you pressed in your palm a handful of wheat mixed with gravel, and if your fingers, by continual movement, made the two kinds of particles rub vigorously against each other, is it not true that the wheat would soon be reduced to powder? Such is the action of the gizzard. Its strong, fleshy walls contract powerfully and knead their contents of sand and seeds without suffering damage themselves from the friction, because of the tough skin that lines their inside and protects them from the roughness of the gravel. In such a mill the hardest kernels are soon reduced to a sort of soup.

"To make you understand the prodigious power of the gizzard, I cannot do better than relate to you certain experiments performed by a learned Italian, the abbot Spallanzani. A century ago the celebrated abbot, while pursuing his researches on the natural history of animals, caused a number of hens to swallow some little glass balls. 'These balls,' he said, 'were sufficiently tough not to break when thrown forcibly on to the ground. After remaining three hours in the hen's gizzard they were for the most part reduced to very tiny pieces with nothing sharp about them, all their edges having been blunted as if they had passed through a mill. I noticed also that the longer these little glass balls remained in the stomach, the finer the powder to which they were reduced. After a few hours they were broken into a multitude of vitreous particles no larger than grains of sand.' "

"A stomach that can grind glass balls to powder," commented Jules, "is certainly a first-rate mill."

"You shall hear something still more remarkable," returned his uncle. "Wait. 'As these balls,' continued the abbot, 'were polished and smooth, they could not create any kind of disturbance in the gizzard.' So he was curious to see what would happen if sharp and cutting bodies were introduced. 'We know,' he says, 'how easily little pieces of glass, broken up by pounding, tear the flesh. Well, having shattered a pane of glass, I selected some pieces about the size of a pea and wrapped them in a playing card so that they would not lacerate the gullet in their passage.

Thus prepared, I made a cock swallow them, well knowing that the covering of card would break on its entrance into the stomach and leave the glass free to act with all its points and sharp edges.' "

"With all those little pieces of glass in its stomach," said Jules, "the bird must surely have died."

"Not a bit of it. The bird would have come out all right if the experimenter had not sacrificed it to see the result. The cock was killed at the end of twenty hours. 'All the pieces of glass were in the gizzard,' the abbot tells us, 'but all their sharp edges and points had disappeared so completely that, having put these fragments on my palm, I could rub them hard with the other hand without inflicting the slightest wound.

" 'The reader,' he goes on, 'must be curious to learn the effect produced on the gizzard by these sharp-pointed bodies that rolled around there unceasingly until they lost their keen edges and sharp points. Opening the cock's gizzard, I examined minutely the inside skin after having well washed and cleaned it. I even separated it from the gizzard, which is done without difficulty, and thus it was easy to scrutinize it as closely as I wished. Well, after all my pains I found it perfectly intact, without a tear or cut, without even the slightest scratch. The skin appeared to me absolutely the same as that of the cocks that had not swallowed glass.' "

"So the bird that is made to swallow pieces of broken glass," said Jules, "grinds them up without injury and without even a scratch, while we could not so much as handle this dangerous stuff with the tips of our fingers without wounding ourselves. This power of the gizzard is really inconceivable."

"What follows is still more surprising," resumed Uncle Paul. "Spallanzani continues: 'The experiments with glass not having done the birds any harm, I performed two others that were much more dangerous. In a leaden ball I placed twelve large steel needles so that they stuck out of the ball more than half a centimeter, and I made a turkey swallow this ball, bristling with points and wrapped in a card; and it kept the ball in its stomach a day and a half. During this time the bird showed not the slightest discomfort, and in fact there could have been none, for on killing the bird I found that its stomach had not received the slightest wound from this barbarous device. All the needles were broken off and separated from the leaden ball, two of them being still in the gizzard, their points greatly blunted, while the other ten had disappeared, ejected with the excrement.

" 'Finally, I fixed in a leaden ball twelve little steel lancets, very sharp and cutting, and I made another turkey swallow the terrible pill. It remained sixteen hours in the gizzard, after which I opened the bird and found only the ball minus the lancets; these had all been broken, three of them, their points and edges entirely blunted, being found in the intestines, the nine others having been ejected. As for the gizzard, it showed no trace of a wound.'

"You see, my little friends, a bird's gizzard is the most wonderful organ of trituration in the world. What are the best-equipped jaws in comparison with this strong pouch which, without suffering so much as a scratch, reduces glass to powder and breaks and blunts steel needles and lancets? You can understand now with what ease the hardest seeds can be ground when the gizzard of the granivorous bird presses and rolls them pell-mell with small stones."

"Where glass and steel are broken up," said Emile, "grain ought to turn to flour as well as in a mill."

CHAPTER III

THE CHIEF KINDS OF POULTRY

"DIFFERENT KINDS of poultry, the originals of our domestic species, are living to this day in a wild state in the forests of Asia, notably in India, and in the Philippine Islands and Java. The most noteworthy is the Bankiva or red jungle fowl. In shape, plumage, and habits the male

RED JUNGLE FOWL

bird bears a striking resemblance to the common rooster of our poultry-yards; but in size it is smaller even than the partridge. It has a scalloped red comb, a tail of arched plumage, and a neck ornamented with a falling tippet of bright, golden-red feathers. This graceful little cock, irritable and full of fight, has the habits of ours. He struts proudly at the head of his flock of hens, over whose safety he watches with extreme care. If hunters range the forest, or if some dog prowls in the neighborhood, the vigilant bird, quick to perceive, suspects an enemy. He immediately flies to a high branch and thence gives forth a cry of alarm to warn the hens, which hastily conceal themselves under the leaves or crouch in the hollows of trees and wait motionless until the danger is past. To get within gun-shot of these birds is well-nigh impossible, and to capture them one must have recourse to the same snares one uses for catching larks."

"A fowl smaller than a partridge, and that they catch in the woods with snares for larks," remarked Jules, "ought to be a very pretty bird, but not of much use if raised in poultry-yards. Does our poultry come from such a small kind as that?"

"It certainly comes either from the Bankiva fowl or from other kinds just as small that live in a wild state in the forests of Asia; but when and how the hen and the cock became domesticated is wholly unknown. From the dawn of history man has been in possession of the barnyard fowl, at least in Asia, whence later the species came to us already domesticated. During long centuries, improved by our care, which assures it abundant food and comfortable shelter, the original small species has produced numerous varieties differing much in size and plumage. They are classed in three groups: the small, the medium, and the large.

"To the first group belongs the bantam or little English fowl, about the size of a partridge. It is a beautiful bird with short legs that let the tips of the wings drag on the ground, quick movements, gentle and tame habits. Its eggs, proportioned to the small size of the hen, weigh scarcely thirty grams apiece, while those of other hens weigh from sixty to ninety grams each. These pretty little pullets are raised rather as ornaments to the poultry-yard than for the sake of their diminutive eggs."

"These little fowl," observed Louis, "look from their size like the primitive kind."

"Yes, it was about like that they looked when man took it into his head to tame the wild fowl. In the poultry-yards of those times lived, not the large species of our day, but birds as small in body and as quick on the wing as the partridge. I leave you to imagine what care and vigilance were necessary in order not to frighten these timid little fowl and cause them to go back to the woods that they still remembered."

"It must have been as much trouble," said Louis, "as it would be for us to tame a covey of partridges. Such an undertaking would not be easy. We are a long way from those first attempts at domestication with our hens of to-day, so tame, so importunate even, that they come boldly and pick up crumbs under the very table."

"The common poultry, that which stocks the greater number

of farms, belongs to the medium-sized breeds. Its plumage is of all colors, from white to red and black. Its head is small and ornamented with a red comb, sometimes single, sometimes double, coquettishly thrown to one side. The cock, for its proud bearing and magnificent plumage, has no equal among the other species. The common fowl is the easiest to keep, for its activity permits it to seek and find for itself, by scratching in the ground, a great part of its food in the form of seeds and worms. It may be found fault with for its wandering proclivities, favored by a strong wing which it avails itself of to fly over hedges and fences, to go and devastate the neighboring gardens.

"Among the other medium-sized species which, associated with the common fowl, are found in poultry-yards as ornaments rather than as sources of profit, I will name the following:

"First, the Paduan fowl, recognizable by its rich plumage and particularly by the thick tuft of feathers that adorns its head. This beautiful headdress of fine plumage, so proudly spread out in fine weather, is, when once wet by rain, nothing but an ungraceful rag, heavy and tangled, which tires the bird and makes the rustic life of the poultry-yard impossible as far as it is concerned.

"The Houdan fowl wears a thickly tufted top-knot which is thrown back over the nape of the neck. Sometimes this head-dress covers the eyes so completely that the bird cannot see in front nor sidewise, but only on the ground, which makes it uneasy at the slightest noise. The plumage is speckled black and white, with glints of purple and green. The cheeks and the base of the beak are draped with little upturned feathers. Each foot has five toes instead of four, the usual number—not counting the cock's spur, which is simply a horn, a fighting weapon, and not a toe. Three of the toes point forward and two backward.

"The fowl of la Flèche, so renowned for the delicacy of its flesh and its aptness for fattening, has no crest and is long-legged, with black plumage of green and purple luster. The legs are blue and the comb rises in two little red horns.

"Similar but better developed horns, accompanied by a thick headdress of feathers, adorn the Crève-cœur species. The hen is a beautiful black; the cock wears, against body plumage of the same dark color, a rich gold or silver tippet.

"Finally, to the large species belongs the Cochin-China, an ungraceful bird, with very strong body and shapeless and disordered plumage, generally reddish white. Its eggs are brownish in color."

CHAPTER IV

THE EGG

"WHEN MOISTENING your slices of bread with egg, has it ever occurred to you to examine a little the structure of what furnishes your repast? I think not. To-day I am going to tell you something about this: I will show you in detail this wonder called an egg.

"First, let us examine the shell. In hens' eggs it is all white, as also in those of ducks and geese. Turkeys' eggs are speckled with a multitude of little pale red spots. But it is particularly the eggs of undomesticated birds that are remarkable for their coloring. There are sky-blue ones, such as those of certain blackbirds; rose color for certain warblers; and somber green with a tinge of bronze is found, for example, in the eggs of the nightingale. The coloring is sometimes uniform, sometimes enhanced by darker spots, or by a haphazard sprinkling of pigment, or by odd markings resembling some sort of illegible handwriting. Many rapacious birds, chiefly those of the sea, lay eggs with large fawn-colored spots that make them look like the pelt of a leopard. I will not dwell longer on this subject, interesting though it may be, as in telling you the story of the auxiliary birds I have already described the eggs of the principal kinds."

"I have taken care," interposed Jules, "to remember the curious variety of coloring that eggs have. I recall very distinctly the nightingale's, green like an olive; the goldfinch's, spotted with reddish brown, especially at the larger end; the crow's, bluish green with brown spots; and so many others that I hesitate to say which are my favorites, so nearly equal are they in beauty."

"Let us learn now about the nature of the shell," his uncle continued. "The substance of the shell is, in the hen's egg, as white as marble; its own color not being disguised by any foreign pigment. This pure white and its other characteristics, hardness and clean fracture, do they not tell you of what substance the shell is composed?"

"Either appearances deceive me greatly," answered Louis, "or the shell is simply made of stone."

"Yes, my friend, it is indeed of stone, but stone selected with exquisite care and refined as it were, in the bird's body.

"In its nature the eggshell does not differ from common building-stone; or rather, on account of its extreme purity, it does not differ from the chalk that you use on the blackboard, or from the magnificent white marble that the sculptor seeks for the masterpieces of his chisel. Building-stone, marble, and chalk are at bottom the same substance, which is called lime, limestone, or carbonate of lime. The differences, great as they may be, have to do with the state of purity and degree of consistency. That which building-stone contains in a state of impurity from other ingredients is contained also in white marble and chalk, but free from any admixture. Thus in its nature the eggshell is identical with chalk and marble, harder than the first, less hard than the second, being between the two in an intermediate state of pure lime. To clothe the egg, therefore, with a solid envelope, the hen and all birds without exception use the same material as the sculptor works with in his studio and the scholar uses on the blackboard.

"Now, no animal creates matter; none makes its body, with all that comes from it, out of nothing. The bird does not find within itself the material for the eggshell; it gets it from outside with its food. Amid the grain that is thrown to her the hen finds little bits of stone left there through imperfect cleaning; she swallows them without hesitation, knowing full well, however, that they are little stones and not kernels of wheat. That is not enough; you will see her all day long scratching and pecking here and there in the poultry-yard. Now and then she digs up some worm, her great delicacy, and from time to time some fragment of limestone, which she turns to account with as much satisfaction as if she had found a plump insect."

"I have often seen hens swallowing little stones like that," remarked Emile. "I thought it was all their own carelessness or gluttonous haste, but now I begin to suspect the truth. Would not those little stones be useful in making the eggshell?"

"You are right, my little friend. The particles of lime swallowed with the food are converted into a fine pap, dissolved by the digestive action of the stomach. By a rigorous sorting the pure lime is separated from the rest, and it is made into a sort of chalk soup which at the right moment oozes around the egg and hardens into a shell. By swallowing little particles of lime, the hen, as you see, lays by materials for her eggshell. If these materials were wanting, if the food given her did not include lime, if, imprisoned in a cage, she could not procure carbonate of lime for herself by pecking in the ground, she would lay eggs without any shell and simply covered with a flabby skin."

"Those soft eggs that hens sometimes lay come then from lack of lime?" asked Louis.

"They either come from the bird's not having had the necessary carbonate of lime in her food or in the earth she pecked, or else her bad state of health did not permit the transformation of the little stones into that chalky pap which molds itself around the egg and becomes the shell. In countries where carbonate of lime is scarce in the soil, or even totally lacking, it is the custom to break up the eggshells and mix the coarse powder in the fowl's food. It is a very judicious way of giving the hen in the most convenient form, the stony matter necessary for the perfect formation of the egg."

"Sometimes," observed Louis, "we find on the dunghill eggs of a queer shape and as soft as hens' eggs without the shell. Instead of a chicken, a snake comes out of them. They say they are laid by young cocks."

"You are repeating now one of the false notions prevalent in the country—a foolish notion springing from a basis of actual fact. It is perfectly true that eggs soft, rather long, almost cylindrical, and of the same size at both ends, may be turned up by the fork as it stirs the warm manure of a dunghill. It is also perfectly true that from these eggs snakes are hatched, to the great surprise of the innocent person who thinks he sees there the product of some witchcraft. What is false is the supposed origin of the egg. Never, never has the cock, be he young or old, the faculty reserved exclusively for the hen, the faculty of laying. Those eggs found in dunghills, and remarkable for their strange shape, do not come from fowl; they are simply the eggs of a serpent, of an inoffensive snake which, when opportunity offers, buries its laying in the warm mass of a dunghill to aid the hatching. It is quite natural, then, that from serpents' eggs serpents should hatch."

"The ridiculous marvel of the supposed cock's eggs," returned Louis, "thus becomes a very simple thing; but one must first know that serpents lay eggs."

"Henceforth you will know that not only serpents but all reptiles lay eggs just as birds do. Snakes' eggs are flabby, and for covering have only a sort of skin resembling wet parchment. Moreover, they are long in shape, which is far from being the usual form. But the eggs of some reptiles, notably of lizards, have the shell firm and of the fine oval shape peculiar to birds' eggs. If you ever encounter in holes in the wall, or in dry sand well exposed to the sun, little eggs, all white, with shell as fine as a little canary bird's, do not cry out at the strangeness of your discovery; you will simply have come across the eggs of a gray lizard, the usual inhabitant of old walls."

CHAPTER V

THE EGG
(Continued)

"LET US return to the hen. We know the calcareous nature of the shell; now let us look at the structure. Open your eyes wide and look attentively; you will see on the shell, chiefly at the large end, a multitude of tiny dents such as might be made by the point of a fine needle. Each of these dents corresponds to an invisible hole that pierces the shell through and through and establishes communication between the interior and the exterior. These holes, much too small to let out the liquid contents of the egg, nevertheless suffice both for the emission of humid vapors, which are dissipated outside the shell, and for the admission of air, which penetrates within and replaces the evaporated humidity.

"The presence of these innumerable openings is absolutely necessary for the awakening and keeping up of life in the future chicken. Every living thing breathes, and all life springs into being and continues through the action of air. The seed that germinates under ground must have air. Planted too deep, it perishes sooner or later without being able to rise, because the thick bed of earth prevents the air from reaching it. The egg must have air so that its substance, gently warmed by the brooding mother hen, may spring into life and become a little chicken; it must have it continually, shut up as it is in its shell. Thanks to the openings with which the shell is riddled, the air penetrates sufficiently to meet the needs of respiration; it quickens the substance of the egg and the little being slowly forming within."

"One might say," Emile here put in, "that these holes are so many little windows through which air reaches the bird in its narrow cell of the egg."

"These windows, as Emile calls them," his uncle went on, "deserve our attention from another point of view. Eggs are a precious alimentary provision; the difficulty is to keep them for any length of time. If they get too old they spoil and give out then an infectious, bad smell. Well, then, what causes the eggs to spoil and changes them to repulsive-smelling filth is again air—the same air so indispensable to the formation of the chicken. That which gives life to the egg under the heat of the brooding hen brings destruction just as quickly when the warmth is wanting. If, then, it is proposed to preserve in a state of freshness as long as possible eggs destined for food, it is necessary to prevent the access of air into their interior, which is done by closing the openings in the shell. Several means may be employed. Sometimes eggs are plunged for a moment into melted grease, from which they are drawn out covered with a coating that obstructs all the orifices; sometimes they are varnished. The simplest method is to keep them in water in which a little lime has been dissolved. This dissolved lime deposits itself on the shell and closes the openings. These precautions taken, the air can no longer find a passage to penetrate into the interior and the eggs are preserved in good condition much longer than they would be without this preparation. Nevertheless they always spoil in the long run."

"If I have properly understood what you have just told us about the need of air for the awakening of life," remarked Jules, "eggs thus coated with varnish or lime will not hatch when under the brooding hen?"

"Evidently not. Rendered impervious to air by the varnish, lime, grease, or what not, the eggs might remain indefinitely under the brooding hen without ever coming to life; for want of the quickening action of the air, life would no more awaken in them than in simple stones. You understand, then, that the method of preservation by means of a coating that closes the orifices of the shell must only be employed for eggs destined for food, and that care must be taken not to make use of it in those destined for hatching.

"But this is enough about the outside of the egg. Now let us break the shell. What do we find within? We find a delicate membrane, a supple skin which lines the whole of the shell and forms a kind of bag, without any opening, filled with the white and yolk. When by some accident the limy coating is lacking, this membrane constitutes the sole covering of the egg—a covering as soft as thin parchment soaked in water."

"Then soft eggs without any shell have this membrane all exposed?" queried Jules.

"Exactly. A new-laid egg has its shell completely filled; but it soon loses some of its humidity, which evaporates through the orifices in the shell. A void is then created in the interior, near the large end, where the evaporation is most rapid. At this end, therefore, the membrane detaches itself from the shell that it lined and draws further in with the contents of the egg shrunk by the evaporation. Thus is produced at the large end a cavity which the air from outside enters and which for this reason is called the *air-chamber*. This chamber, wanting at first, grows little by little according to the space left by the moisture's evaporation; consequently, the older the egg, the larger the space. If the egg is placed under the hen, the heat of the mother aids evaporation and causes the quick formation of the air-chamber. There gathers, as in a reservoir, the supply of air needed for the vitality of the egg and the respiration of the coming bird. So the empty space at the large end is a respiratory storehouse.

"When you eat an egg boiled in the shell, break it carefully at the large end. If the egg is very fresh the white will be seen immediately under the shell without any empty space; but if it is old you will find an unoccupied hollow of varying size. That is the air-chamber. According to its size you can judge of the egg's freshness. But it would be more desirable to be able to recognize, before using and breaking it, whether an egg is fresh or stale. I have seen the following means used, which would seem very strange if what I have just told you about the air-chamber did not furnish the explanation. The tip of the tongue is applied to the large end. If the egg is fresh a slight impression of coolness can be felt; if stale, the tongue remains warm. This little mystery is based on the different manner of behavior of liquids and gases when brought into contact with heat. Water and liquids in general take away rather quickly the heat of the bodies with which they come in contact; air and other gases, on the contrary, take it away very slowly. That is why water seems cold when we plunge our hand into it, while the air, lower in temperature, seems warm by comparison. In reality, if both be of the same temperature, air and water give us different sensations: water is cool to us because it draws our heat away; air warm because it does not take away that same heat. So if the egg is fresh, and consequently the shell completely filled, the tip of the tongue applied to the large end feels the same sensation as comes from contact with liquids; that is to say, a feeling of coolness. But if the egg is stale, an air-chamber has formed and the resulting sensation is that produced by contact with a gas; that is to say, a sensation of warmth, since the tongue loses none of its natural heat."

"That is certainly a curious test," said Jules, "and I shall make it a point to carry it out at the next opportunity."

"Let us go on with the egg. Now comes the *glair* or white, so called because heat hardens it to a pure white matter. For the same reason, science calls it *albumen*, from a Latin word, *albus*, meaning *white*. The glair is arranged in a number of layers, which at both ends of the egg twist round one another and form two large knotty cords called *chalazæ*. To see these cords you must break a raw egg carefully in a plate. Then you can distinguish, on each side of the yolk, a mass where the glair is thicker and rather knotty. There, somewhat injured by the breaking of the egg, are found the two cords in question. To give you a clear idea, take an orange, put it in your handkerchief, and twist the latter in opposite directions at both ends. The orange in its handkerchief covering will represent the spherical yolk surrounded by the glair; the two twisted ends of the handkerchief will be the two strings of white, the two chalazæ. By means of these two tethers the yolk, the most important and most delicate part of the egg, is suspended as in a hammock, in the center of the glair, without being exposed to disturbances that would be dangerous for the germ of life situated at a point on its surface. This glairy hammock, with its two suspending cords, has another rôle—a very delicate one. The first outlines of the coming chick will appear at a certain point of the yolk. As the little being forms and grows, it needs more space while still remaining tightly enveloped and held in position so as to avoid the slightest disturbance in the half fluid flesh just beginning to assume its proper shape. How are these conditions realized in the egg? To understand the matter thoroughly let us go back to the orange wrapped in a handkerchief twisted at both ends. Is it not true that if both ends untwist a little, the orange, supposing it to need by degrees more room, will always find the necessary space without for a moment ceasing to be enveloped and motionless? In the same manner the suspending cords of the white slacken and gradually untwist as the little bird grows, at the expense of the yolk, in its soft hammock of glair; the needed space is made, and at the same time the feeble little bird remains just as finely swaddled and suspended in the center of the egg, protected from contact with the hard shell."

"At the beginning," interposed Jules, "you called an egg a marvel. I see that there are, in fact, in the egg things very worthy of our admiration: the shell, with its numerous air-holes; the cavity at the large end; the air-chamber where provision is made for breathing; the soft little bed of glair with its suspending cords that untwist to make more room, and perhaps that is not all?"

"No, my friend, that is very far from being all. I limit myself here to the simplest things and those that are not beyond your grasp. How would it be if you could follow me in the unfolding of higher ideas? You would see how everything in the egg is arranged with infinite delicacy, with a foresight that we may call maternal, and then you would find my word *marvel* the right one. But, not to go beyond your small powers of comprehension, I abridge, much to my regret.

"The yolk or yelk (which means the yellow part) is round and bright yellow; hence its name. At a point on its surface, generally at the top, no matter what the position of the egg, is seen a circular spot, dull white, where the matter is a little more condensed than elsewhere. It is called the *cicatricle*, or little scar. That is the sacred spot where lies the spark of life which, animated by incubation, will quicken the substance of the egg and mold it into a living being; it is the point of departure, the origin, the germ of the bird. The yolk itself is the nutritive reservoir whence are drawn the materials for this work of creation. Quickened by the heat of the brooding hen and by the action of the air, it becomes covered with a network of fine veins. These swell with the substance of the yolk, which turns to blood; and this blood, carried hither and thither, becomes the flesh of the being in process of formation. The yolk, then, is the bird's first food, but food that no beak seizes and no stomach digests, none being in existence yet. It changes to blood and afterward to flesh without the preparatory work of ordinary digestion; it enters the veins directly, and thus nourishes the whole body.

"Animals with udders—the mammifers—also have nutriment for the very young in the form of milk, which is indispensable for the weak stomach of the nursling. Well, the yolk is to the bird in its shell what milk is to the lamb and kitten; it is its milk-food, as it can have no recourse to maternal udders. The popular saying has perfectly caught the strict resemblance: they call a drink prepared with the yolk of an egg, 'hen's milk.' "

"That is what Mother Ambroisine makes me take when I cough in the winter," said Emile.

"The delicious beverage that Mother Ambroisine gives you when you have a cold is very properly called 'hen's milk,' since it is made with the equivalent of milk; that is to say, the yolk of an egg."

CHAPTER VI

INCUBATION

"INCUBATION MEANS *lying upon.* The brooding bird does in fact crouch or lie upon her eggs, warming them with the heat of her body for a number of days with indefatigable patience. When a hen wishes to set,[1] she makes it known by her repeated cluckings, little cries of maternal anxiety, by her ruffled feathers, her restless movements, and particularly by the perseverance with which she stays on the nest, even when it has no eggs, where she has been in the habit of laying.

"Some hens with wandering dispositions go back to the instincts of their wild race. They leave the hen-house and seek a hedge or thicket, where they select a hiding-place to suit them, and there make a little hollow in the earth which they line as well as they can with a mattress of dry grass, leaves, and feathers. That is a nest in the rough, without art, a shapeless construction in comparison with the clever masterpiece of the chaffinch and goldfinch. It is, furthermore, worthy of remark that all the domestic birds, as if man's intervention had destroyed their skill by freeing them from want, fail to display in the construction of their nests the admirable resourcefulness shown by most wild birds. Here might be repeated the saying, as true for man as for beast, necessity is the mother of invention. Sure of finding, when the time comes for laying, the basket stuffed with hay by the hand of the housewife, the domestic fowl does not trouble herself to build a nest, an undertaking in which the tiniest bird of the fields shows itself a consummate architect. At the most, when her adventurous disposition makes her prefer the peril-

1   Uncle Paul and his nephews are here allowed to defy the purist, as they probably would in real life.—*Translator.*

24

ous shelter of the hedge to the safe retreat of the poultry-yard, the hen, gleaning with her beak a few straws and leaves, and plucking, if need be, some of her own feathers, succeeds in making, for her period of brooding, a disordered heap rather than a nest. There, every day, unknown to all, she goes and lays her egg. Then for three whole weeks she is not to be seen, or only at intervals. That is the time of incubation. At last, some fine day, she reappears, very proud, at the head of a family of young chickens, peeping and pecking around her."

"I should like," said Emile, "to have some hens that set like that in the fields and then come home again some day with their family of little chickens."

"I must admit it is a sight worthy of interest, that of a hen that has stolen her nest returning to the farmhouse at the head of her newly hatched young chickens. Her eyes shine with satisfaction; her clucking has something joyful about it. 'Look,' she seems to say to those who welcome her, 'see how fine, alert, and vigorous these young chickens are; they are all mine; I raised them there all alone in a corner of the hedge, and now I bring them to you. Am I not a fine hen?' Yes, my dear biddy, you are a fine hen, but also an imprudent one. In the fields prowl the weasel and the marten which, if you are absent a moment, will suck the blood of your little ones; in the fields the fox is watching to wring your neck; in the fields there are cold, rain, bad weather, grave peril for your shivering family. You would do better to remain at home.

"The greater number follow this prudent advice and do not leave the poultry-yard. In the semi-obscurity of a sheltered quiet corner is placed the egg-basket, lined with a bed of hay or of crumpled straw. In it are put from twelve to fifteen eggs, the largest and freshest being chosen, and preferably those not more than a week old. If they were two or three weeks old they would not be sure to hatch, as in many of them the germ would have become too old and would have lost the power to develop. These arrangements made, the eggs are left to the setting hen without being touched again.

"Whoever has not seen a setting hen has missed one of the

most touching sights in this world: the devotion of the mother-bird to her eggs, her self-forgetfulness even to the point of sacrificing her own life. Her eyes shine with fever, her skin burns. Eating and drinking are forgotten, and in order not to leave her eggs a moment a hen might even let herself die of hunger on the nest if some one did not come every day and gently take her off and make her eat. Others, less persevering, leave the basket of their own accord, snatch up a little food, and immediately go back to the nest."

"Do hens keep up that tiresome setting very long?" asked Emile.

"It takes twenty or twenty-one days for the young chickens to come out of the shell. During the whole of that time, night and day, the mother remains squatting on the eggs, except for the rare moments that she spares, as if grudgingly, for the necessities of nourishment. Her only distraction in this complete retirement is to turn the eggs over every twenty-four hours and change their place, moving those outside into the center, and *vice versa*, so that all may have an equal share of heat. That is a delicate operation, and it must be left to the hen's care to move the eggs with her beak. Let us be careful not to interfere with our clumsy hands, for the bird knows better than we how to manage it."

"If the hen is so careful to move the eggs every day and give them all the same amount of heat," said Jules, "it must be heat alone that makes them hatch?"

"Yes, my friend, simply the heat of the mother makes the eggs hatch. That is why the hen can be dispensed with and the eggs hatched by artificial heat, provided it be well regulated, gentle, and continued for a long time without interruption. The Egyptians, an ancient people of great skill, practised this method thousands of years ago. They put the eggs by hundreds of dozens into a sort of oven gently heated for three weeks, the period of natural incubation. At the end of that time the peepings of the countless brood did not fail to announce the success of the operation."

"What a big family that oven-hatched brood must have been!"

exclaimed Emile. "It would have taken a hundred hens to set on all the eggs, but in this way they were all hatched at once."

"A setting hen ceases to lay, and it was doubtless in order not to interrupt the beneficent daily production of eggs that the Egyptians invented artificial incubation in an oven.

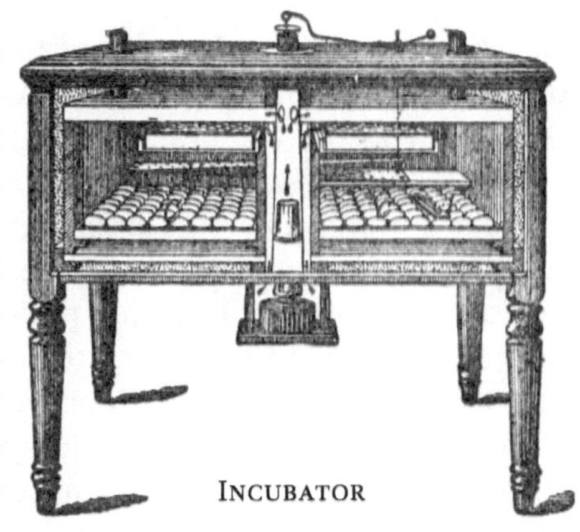

INCUBATOR

For the same reason sometimes with us recourse is had to this means, especially where the raising of poultry is made a business; only the incubation is no longer carried out in an oven but in ingeniously contrived incubators. In a drawer, on a bed of hay, the eggs are placed in a single layer. Above, and separated from the brooder by a sheet-iron partition, is a bed of water, which a lamp, kept always alight, warms and maintains at the temperature that the hen's body would give; that is to say, forty degrees centigrade. In twenty-one days under this warm ceiling the eggs hatch just as they would under the hen."

"Oh, Uncle," cried Emile, "I should really like to have an incubator like that in a corner of my room and watch the progress of the hatching every day by opening the drawer."

"What you would like to do, others, more skilful, have already done, not only opening the drawer but breaking an egg each day so as to see how things are going. I told you that the germ of the bird is a round spot of dull white, the cicatricle, which by its mobility is always on top at the surface of the yolk, no matter what the position of the egg. After five or six hours of incubation you can already distinguish in the center of the cicatricle a minute glairy swelling which will be the head, and a line which will be the backbone. Pretty soon there begins to beat, at regular intervals, the organ most necessary to life, the heart, which chases through a network of fine veins the blood formed, little by little, out of the substance of the yolk, and distributes it everywhere to furnish materials to the other organs just coming into being. It is toward the second day that these first heart-beats, destined to continue henceforth until death, become apparent. Thus irrigated with running flesh—for blood is nothing else—this organism thenceforward makes rapid progress. The eyes show themselves and form a large black spot on each side of the head; the quills of the large feathers form in their sheaths; the scales of the feet are outlined in a bluish tint; the bones, at first gelatinous, acquire firmness by becoming incrusted with a small quantity of stony matter. From the tenth day all the parts of the young chicken are well formed. The little being, softly suspended in its hammock by means of the two suspending cords that untwist little by little to give more room as it grows, is bent over on itself, the head folded against the breast and hidden under its wing. Note, my friends, that it is precisely this attitude of deep sleep inside the egg that the hen assumes when she wants to sleep. Crouched on her perch, she again folds her head on her breast and tucks it under her wing, just as she did when she was a little chicken in its shell.

"In the meantime the little bird keeps growing on the yellow and white matter; matter which soaks and penetrates it and, vivified by the air, becomes its blood and its flesh. One day it breaks the thin membrane under the shell, and there it is more at ease with the increase of space given it by the air-chamber. Now an attentive ear can distinguish feeble peepings inside the shell; it is the seventeenth or eighteenth day. A couple of days more, and the young chicken, summoning all its strength, will apply itself to the arduous work of deliverance. A pointed callosity, made expressly for the purpose, has formed on the upper part of the tip-end of the beak. Here is the tool, the pick, for opening its prison; a tool for that particular purpose and of very short duration, which will disappear as soon as the shell is pierced. With this provisional pick, the little chicken begins to hammer the shell; perseveringly it pushes, strikes, scratches, until the stone wall yields. For the most vigorous it takes several hours. Oh, joy! the shell is broken; there is the young chicken's little head, and all yellow velvety down, and still wet with the moisture of the egg. The mother comes to its aid and completes its deliverance; others, weaker or less skilful, take twenty-four hours of painful effort to free themselves. Some even exhaust themselves in the undertaking and perish miserably in the egg without succeeding in breaking the shell."

"Those are the very ones the mother ought to help," said Jules.

"She would be careful not to, for fear of a worse accident than a difficult birth. How could she direct her blows accurately enough not to wound the tender little chicken just inside the shell? The slightest false move would cause a wound, and at so tender an age any wound is death. We ourselves, with all the dexterity and care possible, could not, without danger, help the bird in distress; it can be tried as a last resort, but the chance of success is very small. The young chicken is the only one capable of carrying through this delicate deliverance if strength does not fail it. The hen knows this wonderfully well, and so does not interfere except to finish freeing the prisoner when half out of its shell. Let us hope that things will turn out as we wish, and that on the twenty-first day the whole family may be warmed under the mother's wings without mortal accident at the moment of hatching.

"From the instant of leaving the shell the young chickens already know how to peck food and how to run around the mother who, clucking, leads the way. They have besides a little fur of downy hair that clothes them warmly. This development is not found in all birds; far from it. Pigeons, for example, come naked from the egg and do not know how to eat; the father and mother have to feed them by disgorging a mouthful of food into their beaks. The young of the warbler, chaffinch, goldfinch, tomtit, lark, in fact of nearly all the field birds, are naked, very weak, at first blind, and completely incapable of feeding themselves, even with the food just under their beaks. The parents, with infinite tenderness, have for a number of days to bring it to them and put it into their beaks."

"That is a difference that has always struck me," commented Jules. "Little sparrows open their mouths wide to receive the food offered them, but for a long time they do not know how to take it even if it is put at the very end of their beak. On the contrary, little chickens easily pick up from the ground for themselves the seeds and worms that the mother digs up for them."

"I will tell you, if you do not already know," continued Uncle Paul, "that the young of the duck, turkey, goose, and, among wild birds, the partridge and quail, have the same precocity as those of the hen. They are clothed with down on coming out of the egg, and know how to eat. One of the causes of this difference in the way young birds act immediately after hatching comes from the size of the egg. The chick is formed wholly from the substances contained in the egg; the larger the egg in proportion to the size of the animal, the stronger and more developed the young. Therefore the kind with the largest eggs are clothed at the time of hatching; they can run and know how to eat, unaided. Where the eggs are relatively small the young are hatched weak, naked, blind, and for a long time, motionless in their nest, demand the mother's beakful of food.

"The largest egg known is that of an enormous bird that formerly lived in the island of Madagascar, and of which the species appears to-day to have been completely destroyed. This bird is called the epyornis. It was three or four meters tall and thus rivaled in stature a very long-legged horse or, better still, the animal called a giraffe. Such birds ought to lay monstrous eggs; such in fact they are; their length is three decimeters and a half and their capacity nearly nine liters."

"Nine liters!" exclaimed Emile. "Oh, what an egg! Our large vinegar jug only holds ten liters. Certainly the young that come from that ought to know how to run and to eat."

"To equal in bulk the egg of the epyornis it would take one hundred and forty-eight hen's eggs."

"I think they could make a famous omelet with only one of those eggs."

"A fine large one could be made, too, with an ostrich-egg, which in size represents nearly two dozen hen's eggs. It need not be added that young ostriches know how to run and to eat as soon as they come out of the shell.

"Those are the largest eggs; now let us consider the smallest ones. They are those of the humming-bird, a charming creature whose splendid plumage would outshine the most brilliant costly metals, precious stones, and jewels. There are some as small as our large wasps and that certain spiders catch in their webs just as the spiders of our country catch gnats. Their nest is a cup of cotton no bigger than half an apricot. Judge then the size of the eggs. It would take three hundred and forty to make one hen's egg, and fifty thousand to make one laid by the epyornis."

"I imagine the little humming-birds in their nest must be all naked at first and blind, taking their food from their mother's beak."

"From the smallness of the egg it could not be otherwise."

CHAPTER VII

THE YOUNG CHICKENS

"THE HATCHING of the eggs does not take place all at once; sometimes it is twenty-four hours before all the eggs are broken. A danger thus arises. Divided between her desire to continue setting and her wish to give her attention to the newly born, the mother may make some sudden movement and unintentionally trample on the tender creatures, or even leave the nest too soon, which would cause the loss of the backward eggs. What, then, is to be done? The first-born are taken as carefully as possible and placed in a basket stuffed with wool or cotton and put in a warm place near the fire. When the whole family is hatched it is restored to the mother.

"The first days are hard ones for the young chickens; they are so delicate, poor little things, so chilly under their light yellow down. Where will they be kept at first? Shall it be with the grown-up poultry, a turbulent crowd, quarrelsome, rough, and without any consideration for the weak? What would become of them, the little innocents, not yet well balanced on their legs, in the midst of the greedy hens which, in scratching for worms, might give them some brutal kick? How dangerous for them to be with the quarrelsome cocks that disdain to look out for the frightened little giddy-heads straying about under their very spurs! No, no, that is not the place for them.

"What they require is a place set apart, isolated from the rough grown-up poultry, heated to a mild temperature, and carpeted with fine straw. If this place is wanting, recourse is had to a coop, a sort of large cage, under which the mother is placed with some food. Sometimes the bars of this refuge are far enough apart to permit the young chickens to come in and go out at will, so as to enjoy their play; sometimes they are too close together for this, and then the coop is lifted a little at one side when it is desired to give liberty to the captives. But the mother always stays in the cage, whence she watches over the young chickens, calling them to her at the least appearance of danger. If the weather is fine, the coop is placed out of doors in an exposed spot, with a sheltering canopy of canvas, foliage, or straw, when the sun is too hot."

"There the young chickens are safe," said Emile, "out of danger of any accident amongst the boisterous population of the poultry-yard. If some danger arises, the hen gives her warning call, and those that are outside immediately scamper through the narrow passage and take refuge with their mother. Now about their food."

"Food is not forgotten: under the coop is a plate containing water, and another with pap. For very young chickens it is not yet time for strong food, hard grain which requires a vigorous stomach to digest; they must have something at once nutritious and easy to digest. Their pap is composed of finely crumbled bread, a few salad leaves well chopped up, hard-boiled eggs, and a pinch of fine millet to accustom them by degrees to a diet of grain. The whole is carefully mixed.

"On coming out of the shell, the young chickens, like other birds from a relatively large egg, are quick at taking food for themselves; nevertheless it is necessary, from their utter inexperience, for the mother to show them how to strike the beak into the pap. Let us witness this lesson of the first mouthful. The farmer's wife has just put the food under the coop. 'What is this?' perhaps the innocent little chickens ask, their stomachs beginning to cry hunger now that they have been nearly twenty-four hours out of the shell. 'What is this?' All flurried with joy, the mother calls them to the plate in accents resembling articulate speech. They approach, tottering on their little legs. The hen then gives a few pecks in the mess, but only pretends to eat, so as not to diminish the dainty food reserved for the little ones. One of the chickens, perhaps a little quicker of apprehension than the rest, seems to have understood; it seizes a crumb of bread in its beak but immediately lets it fall again. The mother begins again, urges, encourages with her voice and look, and this time swallows in plain sight of them all. The young chicken returns to its crumb and after two or three attempts succeeds in swallowing it, half closing its eyes with satisfaction. 'Ha! how good it is!' it seems to say; 'let us try again.' And another crumb goes down; then a little piece of yolk of egg follows. Henceforth it can manage for itself. The example spreads; one here, another there, tries its beak; the hen repeating her patient lesson for the less clever of the brood. Soon they have all understood and are vying with one another in their assaults on the pap. Then comes a lesson in drinking. How to plunge the beak fearlessly into the water, how to raise the head heavenward so as to let the mouthful of liquid go down the throat, is what the hen will show her pupils by repeated examples. In imitating her, some giddy one will perhaps put its foot into the water or even fall into the plate, a fearful possibility for the inexperienced drinker. But the hen will dry the unfortunate one under her wings and show it another time how to manage better. To be brief, in a single short session the whole brood has been taught the two chief needs of this world, eating and drinking."

"They are scholars quick to learn," said Jules. "It is true the prompting of the stomach, hunger, must have helped them."

"Hardly a week has passed before the young chickens are out of the coop and running around, though not to any great distance, for if one appears to want to go off the mother admonishes it and recalls it to more prudent ways. If she suspects the slightest danger she recalls them all to her retreat by a persuasive clucking. Immediately the little chickens scamper back, squeeze between the bars or crawl under the lifted end of the coop, and regain the refuge where no intruders can penetrate. When the time comes for these first sallies outside the coop, the hen can be set free and allowed to lead her family where she pleases.

"One of the most interesting sights of the farm is that of the hen at the head of her young chickens. With a slow step, measured by the feebleness of her brood, she goes hither and thither on the chance of finding something of value to her, always with vigilant eye and attentive ear. She clucks with a voice made hoarse by her maternal exertions; she scratches to dig up little seeds which the young ones come and take from under her beak. Here is a good place chanced upon in the sunshine for a rest from walking and for getting warm. The hen crouches down, ruffles up her plumage and slightly raises her wings, arching them in a sort of vault. All run and squat under the warm cover. Two or three put their heads out of the window, their pretty heads, all alert, framed in their mother's somber plumage. One, in its boldness, settles down on her back, and from this elevated position pecks the hen's neck; the others, the great majority, hide in her down and sleep or peep softly. The siesta finished, they resume their promenade, the mother scratching and clucking, the little ones trotting around her.

"But what is this? It is the shadow of a bird of prey, which for a moment has darkened the sunshine of the courtyard. The menacing apparition did not last more than the twinkling of an eye; nevertheless the hen saw it. Danger threatens, the rapacious bird is not far away. At the note of alarm the young chickens hasten to take refuge under the mother, who makes a rampart for them of her wings. And now the ravisher may come. This mother, so feeble, so timid, that a mere nothing would put her to flight on all other occasions, becomes imposingly audacious where her brood is concerned. Let the goshawk appear, and the hen, full of tenderness and intrepidity, will throw herself in front of the terrible talons. By the beating of her wings, her redoubled cries, her furious pecks with her beak, she will hold her own against the bird of prey, until at last it beats a retreat, repulsed by this indomitable resistance.

"The attachment of the hen to her young is shown in another very remarkable circumstance. As she is an excellent brooder, they sometimes give her ducks' eggs to hatch. The hen brings up her adopted family as she would her own; she exercises the same care over the little ducks as she would over chickens of her own. All goes well as long as the ducklings, covered with a velvety yellow down, conform to the ways of their nurse and run under her wing at the first summons. But a time comes when their aquatic instinct awakens. They smell the pond, the neighboring pond, where the frog croaks and the tadpole frisks. They go waddling along, one after another, the old hen following them in ignorance of their project. They reach the pond and dash into the water. Then it is that the hen, believing the very lives of her little ones in peril, gives vent to the most desperate outcry. In her mortal terror the poor mother races in distraction along the bank, her voice hoarse with emotion, her plumage bristling with fear. She calls, menaces, supplicates. An angry red mounts to her comb, the fire of despair illumines her eye. She even goes—miracle of mother love—she even goes so far as to risk one foot in the water, that perfidious element, the sight of which makes her almost faint with fear. But to all her supplications the little ducklings turn a deaf ear, happy in their pursuit of the silver-bellied tadpole among the cresses."

"Oh, the little rascals," exclaimed Emile, "not to listen to their nurse's warnings! However, as they are ducks they can't get along without water."

"They go there very often alone at first, in spite of the hen's remonstrances; then, reassured by the first attempts, she willingly leads them to the bath and from the bank watches their joyful gambols."

CHAPTER VIII

THE POULARD[2]

66 IN A month the young chickens are strong enough to do without the tender care of their early days. The pap, the dainty dish of hard-boiled eggs mixed with lettuce and bread crumbs, is no longer served to them, but their rations consist simply of grain and green stuff. This kind of weaning is not effected without some regret on their part at the remembrance of the pap; but the mother makes amends for it by teaching them to scratch the earth and seek insects and worms, a royal feast for them. She shows them how a fly should be snapped up when warming itself in the sun against the wall; how the worm is to be caught and drawn from the ground before it goes into its hole. She shows them in what manner to proceed in order to derive the largest profit from a tuft of grass where the ants have stored their eggs; with what nice attention they must search the under side of large leaves where various insects are in hiding. How to carry out little predatory excursions in the neighboring cultivated fields when opportunity offers, how to scratch up the newly made garden-plots and rummage in every nook and corner, pillaging here and pilfering there—this, too, is all comprised in the educational curriculum prepared by the careful mother. After a couple of weeks of such practice the pupils are past masters; they lose the name of chickens and take that of pullets and roosters. Then the family disbands, the hen returning to her laying of eggs, and the chickens, thenceforth expert in the difficult science of earning their living, being left to themselves.

2   The poulard (French *poularde*) bears the same relation to the pullet as the capon does to the young rooster.—*Translator.*

"Very diverse fates await them. Some, fortune's favorites, will grow peacefully to increase the poultry-yard; others, more numerous, as soon as they are large enough will be given over to the kitchen knife; some, chosen from those easiest to fatten, will undergo a diet that will make them peculiarly suitable for the table. Let me tell you to-day through what grievous trials the poor bird passes to become, by artificial aid, the plump, fat, succulent fowl that we call a poulard."

"Then a poulard is not a separate species of hen?" asked Jules.

"No, my friend. The poulard is only an ordinary hen artificially subjected to a kind of life that fattens it. All species do not lend themselves with equal success to this artificial fattening; the best known in this respect is that of la Flèche, which furnishes the celebrated poulard of Mans.

"I have already told you a few words about this species, which is distinguished from the others by its dashing appearance and long legs. The plumage is entirely black, touched with glints of violet and green. The cock carries proudly, for comb, two horns of brilliant red flesh; its wattles are pendent and very long. The hen has two similar but shorter horns; her wattles are small and rounded; finally, her legs have not the disproportionate length of the cock's tall stilts. Such are the patients preëminently destined for the cruel industry of fattening. Let us come now to the practice of it.

"The greatest care in this world is that of the family. You know with what continual and laborious solicitude the hen watches over her little ones, with what self-sacrifice the mother spends herself in order to keep her nest of eggs warm. If pains were not taken to remove her from the nest and make her eat, she would let herself starve to death, sacrificing her own life for the sake of her eggs. Is it possible for a bird to take on flesh with such ardent maternal love burning in her veins? Certainly not. The first condition for becoming large and fat is to consider one's self alone, a thing permitted only to the beast whose end is to become an excellent roast.

"Well, in order that the hen may consider solely herself, think of nothing but eating and digesting well, so as to take on fat and flesh abundantly, it is put out of her power to lay, which in turn takes from her all idea of brooding and of raising young chickens. Out of a mother, ready to devote herself unstintingly, is made a brute that, if only its crop be full, has no care of any kind; in fact, a veritable fat-factory. The operation is a cruel one. With the blade of a penknife a slight incision is made in the stomach, and the organ in which the eggs are formed is removed. With a little care the slight wound soon heals, and the mutilated bird is ready for the life of a poulard. Let loose in the poultry-yard, it has henceforth nothing to do but eat, digest, and sleep; sleep, digest, and eat. Leading such a life, the bird soon begins to grow fat. Things go all the better and quicker, however, if the bird cannot move freely, cannot come and go at will; for it is to be remarked that no more than love of offspring does love of liberty fatten those that feel its generous ardor. You will ponder that later, my children, when you are older. So they confine the poulards in coops."

"What sort of coops?" asked Emile.

"They are low cages divided into cells, with one poulard to a cell. Crouching in its narrow compartment, the fowl cannot move or even turn round. Solid partitions bar the view except in front near the feed-trough, and prevent its seeing its neighbors, its companions in confinement, so that nothing may distract it from its ceaseless work of digestion. The cage is placed in a room heated to a mild temperature, far from all noise and in a semi-obscurity which induces sleep, so favorable to the functions of the stomach. At punctually regulated hours, far enough apart for appetite to be aroused, but near enough together to prevent its becoming actual hunger, which would impair the well-being of the stomach and hinder the fattening of the bird, three meals a day are served in the feed-trough. Raw beets, cooked potatoes, crushed grain, curdled milk, barley, wheat, maize, buckwheat, compose the menu in turn, so as to excite by variety and choice of food an appetite that satiety daily makes more languishing. Thus fed to repletion, the poor creature, with nothing to distract it from the filling of its crop, eats to pass the time, falls asleep from sheer stupor, awakes, and begins to eat again, only to fall asleep once more. Toward the end of this treatment the poulard, gorged beyond measure, refuses to eat any more. To arouse the last feeble promptings of appetite recourse is had to more delicate food, calculated to keep alive a few days longer the desire for nourishment. For solid food a dough of fine flour is served, and for liquid refreshment, milk, pure milk, if you please. If the bird, already stuffed to bursting, positively refuses to eat any more, it is made to eat by force."

"By force?" said Emile, "when it is bursting and can eat no more?"

"Yes, my friend, by force. Willy, nilly, it must still swallow for some days longer, after which comes the end of its miseries. It is killed and appears on the table as a tender and juicy roast abounding in fat.

"This forced feeding is the essential feature in the method followed to obtain the renowned poulards of Mans.

"According to the masters of this art, the process is as follows: Without preliminary subjection to the mutilation I spoke of, the fowls are placed in narrow cages in a warm, dark room, the doors and windows of which have been made tight to prevent the free circulation of air. For food, a mixture of barley-flour, oats, and buckwheat is moistened with milk, and the dough is divided into little pieces or oblong balls shaped like an olive and of about the length of the little finger. At meal times, which must be very regular, the feeder takes three hens at a time, ties them together by the legs, puts them on his knees, and, by the light of a lamp, begins by making them swallow a spoonful of water or whey; then, taking them by turns, he introduces a bolus into the beak of each of the hens, and to facilitate the descent of the large pieces he presses lightly with his fingers, passing from the base of the beak down to the crop. While the bird that has been fed is recovering from its painful deglutition, the two others are treated in the same manner. To this first ball are added a second, a third, and so on up to a dozen or fifteen, all put into the beak and swallowed willingly or otherwise. Their crops sufficiently full, the three hens are replaced in their cages, where they have nothing to do but sleep and peacefully digest their copious meal. The others go through the same treatment, three by three, in a fixed order."

"And if the crop is stuffed too full with these twelve or fifteen lumps of dough," asked Jules, "may not the bird die, choked with food?"

"There is no great danger; all will go well. Remember the bird's astonishing powers of digestion and the experiments I related to you on this subject."

"It is true that a gizzard capable of getting rid of leaden balls stuck with needles or lancets ought easily to dispose of a few lumps of dough."

"Besides, heed is taken not to go beyond the fowl's digestive powers. A halt is called as soon as the crop appears to be full. It takes from six weeks to two months of this treatment to bring the poulard to perfection."

"I am too fond of the poulard served up as a choice roast to speak ill of what I have just heard; nevertheless I will admit, Uncle, that this barbarous fattening process is repulsive to me. I pity those poor things crouching there in the dark, in cells where they cannot move, and forcibly crammed with food until almost stuffed to death."

"This sympathy proceeds from a good disposition, and I approve of it; but, after all, what is to be done? Since we need the poulard, we must needs countenance the process by which the hen is turned into the poulard. Our life is sustained by animal life. Therefore all that our pity can do is to lessen as much as possible the unavoidable suffering and, above all, see to it that the victims of our needs do not become also the victims of a useless and stupid brutality."

CHAPTER IX

THE TURKEY

"OF OUR barnyard fowls, the turkey is the most remarkable except the peacock, which is raised only for the incomparable richness of its plumage. The turkey-gobbler has his head and neck covered with bare bluish skin, embellished behind with white nipples and in front with red ones, which swell and hang down in large pendants, resembling sealing wax in color. Over his beak falls a piece of flesh, short and wrinkled when the bird is in repose, hanging far down and of brilliant coloring when he wishes to display his charms. In the middle of his breast is fastened an unkempt sort of mane. To show off, he bridles up, inflates his red pendants, elongates the piece of flesh over his beak, throws his head back, spreads out his tail feathers in the shape of a wheel, and lets the tips of his half-opened wings trail on the ground. In this grotesquely proud posture he turns slowly to let himself be admired from all sides. From time to time a low sound, *puff-puff*, accompanied by a sort of convulsive stretching of the wings, is the sign of his supreme sat-

TURKEY

isfaction. If some noise, especially whistling, disturbs him, he hauls down his colors and, stretching his neck, hastily gives a *gloo-gloo-gloo* that seems to burst from the very depths of his stomach."

"By whistling to the turkeys feeding in the fields," said Emile, "I can make them repeat their cry as often as I want to. The turkey hens do not say *gloo-gloo*; they peep plaintively."

"This fowl is a recent acquisition of our poultry-yards," resumed Uncle Paul. "It came to us from North America in the sixteenth century. As America was called West Indies in contrast with the Asian or East Indies, the bird originating in the forests of the New World was called the Indian cock (*coq d'Inde*) and the Indian hen (*poule d'Inde*); from which have come the French terms *dindon* and *dinde*. For a long time the bird spread but little; it was raised merely as a curious rarity. The first that appeared on the table was, they say, at the wedding feast of Charles IX.

"The turkey lived, and still lives to-day, in a wild state, in the forests of the United States of North America. Its habits are described by a celebrated naturalist, Audubon,[3] who, with his gun on his shoulder, his notebook, pencil, and brushes in his game-bag, traversed the most secluded solitudes in order to observe, paint, and describe birds.

" 'The nest,' he tells us, 'which consists of a few withered leaves, is placed on the ground, in a hollow scooped out by the side of a log, or in the fallen top of a dry leafy tree, under a thicket of sumach or briars, or a few feet within the edge of a cane-brake, but always in a dry place... When depositing her eggs, the female always approaches the nest with extreme caution, scarcely ever taking the same course twice, and when about to leave them covers them carefully with leaves, so that it is very difficult for a person who may have seen the bird to discover the nest...

" 'The mother will not leave her eggs when near hatching, under any circumstances, while life remains. She will even

3   The quoted passages are from Audubon's "Ornithological Biography," vol. I, pp. 2–9, and are here reproduced *verbatim*, though very freely treated by the French author.—*Translator.*

allow an enclosure to be made around her, and thus suffer imprisonment, rather than abandon them. I once witnessed the hatching of a brood of turkeys, which I watched for the purpose of securing them together with the parent. I concealed myself on the ground within a very few feet,

TURKEY

and saw her raise herself half the length of her legs, look anxiously upon the eggs, cluck with a sound peculiar to the mother on such occasions, carefully remove each half-empty shell, and with her bill caress and dry the young birds, that already stood tottering and attempting to make their way out of the nest. Yes, I have seen this, and have left mother and young to better care than mine could have proved—to the care of their Creator and mine. I have seen them all emerge from the shell, and, in a few moments after, tumble, roll, and push each other forward, with astonishing and inscrutable instinct.' "

"That's the kind of hunter I like," declared Jules; "one who knows how to restrain himself at the touching sight of a nest of young birds. What did you say his name was?"

"Audubon."

"I shan't forget that name again."

"And that will be right, for few observers have discoursed on birds with so much sympathetic understanding as he.

"I continue to draw from his account. 'About the beginning of October,' says he, 'when scarcely any of the seeds and fruits have yet fallen from the trees, these birds assemble in flocks, and gradually move towards the rich bottom lands of the Ohio and Mississippi... When they come upon a river, they betake themselves to the highest eminences, and there often remain a whole day, or sometimes two, as if for the purpose of consultation. During this time, the males are heard *gobbling*, calling, and making much ado, and are seen strutting about, as if to raise their courage to a pitch befitting the emergency. Even the females and young assume something of the same pompous demeanor, spread out their tails, and run round each other, *purring* loudly, and performing extravagant leaps. At length, when the weather appears settled, and all around is quiet, the whole party mounts to the tops of the highest trees, whence, at a signal, consisting of a single *cluck*, given by a leader, the flock takes flight for the opposite shore. The old and fat birds easily get over, even should the river be a mile in breadth; but the younger and less robust frequently fall into the water—not to be drowned, however, as might be imagined. They bring their wings close to their body, spread out their tail as a support, stretch forward their neck, and striking out their legs with great vigor, proceed rapidly toward the shore; on approaching which, should they find it too steep for landing, they cease their exertions for a few moments, float down the stream until they come to an accessible part, and by a violent effort extricate themselves from the water. It is remarkable that, immediately after thus crossing a large stream, they ramble about for some time, as if bewildered. In this state, they fall an easy prey to the hunter.

" 'Of the numerous enemies of the wild turkey, the most formidable, excepting man, are the lynx, the snowy owl, and the Virginia owl... As turkeys usually roost in flocks, on naked branches of trees, they are easily discovered by their enemies, the owls, which, on silent wing, approach and hover around them for the purpose of reconnoitering. This, however, is rarely done without being discovered, and a single *cluck* from one of the turkeys announces to the whole party the approach of the murderer. They instantly start upon their legs, and watch the motions of the owl, which, selecting one as its victim, comes down upon it like an arrow, and would inevitably secure the turkey, did not the latter at that moment lower its head, stoop, and spread its tail in an inverted manner over its back, by which action the aggressor is met by a smooth inclined plane, along which it glances without hurting the turkey; immediately after which the latter drops to the ground, and thus escapes, merely with the loss of a few feathers.' "

"To make a breastplate of the tail spread out like a wheel is a very ingenious means of defense," remarked Emile. "The turkey is not so foolish as people think."

"It is so far from being foolish that we have not in the poultry-yard a more impassioned lover of liberty. In their native country turkeys wander through the great woods from morning to night in untiring search of insects and fat larvæ, fruit and seeds of all kinds, acorns and nuts especially, of which they are very fond. Thus the stay-at-home habits of the poultry-yard do not suit them at all. They must have the open air of the fields and the exercise of long walks. Moors, woods, hills abounding in grasshoppers, are their favorite haunts. Their timid nature makes them very docile. A child armed with a long switch is enough to lead the flock to the fields, however numerous it may be. Then, step by step, to-day in one direction, to-morrow in another, the flock explores the stubble and gleans the grain fallen from the ear, traverses the grassy meadows where the crickets leap, and penetrates the woods where is found abundant pasturage of chestnuts, beechnuts, and acorns.

"In spite of these rambles afield, which remind it a little of the wandering life it leads in the immense forests of its native country, the turkey never acquires in domesticity the plumpness of body and richness of plumage that belong to it in its free state. It is a curious fact that, contrary to all our experience with other animals, which have improved under human care and have increased in size, the turkey alone has degenerated in our hands, as if preyed upon by an ineradicable regret for its native forests, where bellows the buffalo, chased by the red-skinned Indian. The domestic turkey is not much more than half as large as the wild one. And then what a difference in the plumage! Our poultry-yard fowl is of a uniform black or of a dull red, sometimes white. The bird of the wooded solitudes of the New World is splendid in costume. Bronzed brown predominates, but the neck, throat, and back have, in the light, metallic reflections;

and as the plumage is clearly imbricated, the whole gives the appearance of scale armor in gold and steel. Furthermore, the large wing-feathers have a pure white spot on the tip."

"From that description," said Jules, "I see well enough that the bird has not gained by living with us."

"Nor has its flesh gained in nutritive quality, that of the wild turkey being considered incomparably superior."

"It is just the opposite with the common hen," observed Louis. "Originally as small as the partridge and with as little flesh, it has developed into the fat poulard."

"Such as it is," said Uncle Paul, "the domestic turkey is none the less, next to the common fowl, the most valuable acquisition of the poultry-yard. Let us now turn our attention to it.

"The laying of its eggs takes place in April, when about twenty to a nest are laid, of a dull white with reddish spots. These eggs are scarcely ever used as food; not that they are bad—far from it—but they are too precious and too few to be converted into omelets. As fast as the turkey-hen lays them they are gathered and kept in a basket lined with hay or old rags until the time for setting. The gathering of these eggs is not always easy. Faithful to her wild habits, the turkey-hen does not willingly accept the poultry-house nest. She steals away to lay her eggs in neighboring straw-ricks, underbrush, and hedges. One must watch her proceedings therefore, foil her ruses, and from time to time visit her favorite haunts.

"Incubation presents no difficulties, the female turkey being so good a brooder. Like the common hen, she devotes herself to her eggs with passionate love; like the hen, too, while setting she forgets her food, so that she must be taken off the nest every day and made to eat and drink, as otherwise she might let herself die of hunger. The little ones hatch at the end of thirty days. There is nothing more delicate than these new-born chicks; the least cold chills them, a shower of rain is fatal to them, even the dew imperils their lives, and a hot sun kills them in a trice. If there is delay in feeding, and the mother, of ponderous bulk, awkwardly plants her feet in the midst of her numerous offspring, then the greedy little things are liable to be trampled on and crushed to death. Another danger awaits them at the age of two or three months. Young turkeys hatch with the heads covered with down, with no sign of the red nipples that will ornament them later. Within two or three months these nipples, real collars, and pendants of coral begin to show; they say then that the red is starting. At this time there takes place in the bird a painful change which to many is mortal, especially in a damp season. To succor the sick ones, they are made to swallow a few mouthfuls of warm wine. All things considered, there are numberless chances of death for the turkey-hen's brood. Add to that the small number of eggs laid, and we can understand why, in spite of its great utility, the turkey is less common than the ordinary fowl.

"Audubon has told us that when, from his concealment in the bushes, he witnessed the mother turkey's anxious procedure, the young ones left the nest almost as soon as the shell was broken. For a moment the mother warms and dries them under her breast; then, trotting and tumbling, they abandon the bed of leaves, never to return. In domesticity it is much the same; no sooner are they hatched than the little turkeys leave the nest and thenceforth have no other shelter than the cover of their mother, who protects them under her wings exactly as the hen protects her brood. She also takes the same care of her family, exercises the same vigilance in foreseeing danger, shows the same audacity in coping with the bird of prey. For the first few days the refuge afforded by the wide and deep coop, so useful to the little chickens, is not less useful to the young turkeys. The hen-turkey is put there with choice provisions, and the little ones are free to come and go as they please. These provisions consist of a pap similar to that given to young chickens and composed of bread-crumbs, curds, chopped salad leaves and nettles, a little bran, and hard-boiled eggs. Later comes grain, oats in particular. When the weather is fine the coop is put out of doors in a sunny spot, on very dry ground, and the brood is allowed to play about for a couple of hours in the middle of the day. Great care must be taken to avoid rain, dew, and dampness; a wet turkey chick is in grave danger.

"The more delicate the bird at the beginning, the more robust it is when it has successfully passed the period called the red. It no longer needs the shelter of the poultry-house at night. However cold it may be, it sleeps in the open air, roosting on the branches of some dead tree or on a perch fixed to the wall. Vainly does the north wind whistle and the frost nip; the turkey rests peacefully in the manner of its fellows in the woods of America, and without fear lest a snow-owl come to disturb its slumbers and compel it to spread its tail quickly and make a breastplate against the marauder's talons.

"I will finish this story with a few words on a curious method of fattening used in certain countries, especially in Provence, Morvan, and Flanders. Over and above the usual food that fattening birds eat voluntarily, they force both the gobbler and the hen to swallow whole nuts."

"Whole, but without the shell?" queried Emile.

"No, my friend; with the shell too; in fact, nuts just as the tree bears them."

"A nut with the shell, no matter how small, must make a hard mouthful to swallow, and still harder to digest."

"I don't deny it; but finally, with the finger pushing the nut a little into the throat, and the hand gently pressing from the base of the beak to the crop, the voluminous mouthful ends by going down, not without some grimaces on the part of the bird."

"And reason enough for them!" exclaimed Emile.

"One nut would be nothing; but that is not all. The next day they force it to swallow two, the next three, and so on, augmenting the dose each day. In Provence they stop at forty nuts a day; elsewhere they go on to a hundred."

"And the turkey does not die, stuffed thus with nuts as large and hard as stones?" asked Jules.

"You would be pleased to see how the bird prospers and fattens on food that would choke any other creature."

"With a hundred nuts in its crop, or even only forty," was Louis's comment, "the turkey can't be very comfortable."

"They are not swallowed all at one time, but in portions during the day."

"No matter," persisted Jules; "if you hadn't already told us, according to that learned Italian—Wait a minute; what was his name?"

"The abbot Spallanzani."

"Yes, the abbot Spallanzani. If you hadn't told us about his experiments and the wonderful power of the gizzard, I should never be able to understand how a turkey could manage to digest nuts, shell and all, up to forty and even a hundred a day."

"Everything is reduced to a sort of soup in the gizzard—shells and kernels; all becomes as soft as butter; and the bird, fat as a pig, finally serves as the chief dish at the Christmas feast."

CHAPTER X

THE GUINEA-FOWL

"ONCE UPON a time—That begins, you see, like the stories of Cinderella and of the Ass's Skin. Are we going to spend our time in the recital of the wonders of some fairy godmother? Not at all. I am simply going to tell you the story of the guinea-fowl; and this story happens to be connected, in its first part, with a certain fable told thousands and thousands of years ago, in the evening by the fire-side, to little boys, just as to-day you are told the tragic adventures of Hop o' my Thumb with the Ogre. I start again then.

"In that corner of the world known as Greece, a corner so illustrious in ages long past, there was once upon a time a valiant young man, son of the king of the country, whose favorite occupation was hunting. I say occupation and not recreation, because in those hard times when industrial pursuits were just beginning, the country was overrun with wild animals from which one had constantly to defend oneself and one's flock, only recently herded together under the shepherd's crook. At the risk of their own lives brave men undertook this harsh duty. Many succumbed to it, some acquired renown great enough to survive the lapse of centuries and come down to our time. Surrounded by a heroic aureole, the names of these ancient slayers of monsters have reached us. Such is the name of Meleager, borne by the young man I just mentioned.

"The skin of a wild beast on his back for clothing, in his hand a stout stake sharpened to a point and hardened in the fire, on his shoulder a quiver full of arrows pointed with little sharp stones, in his belt a bludgeon of hard wood and a stone hatchet sharpened on the sandstone, the ardent hunter ranged over the country, tracking the formidable animals to their very lairs in dark forests and mountain caves overgrown with an impenetrable barrier of reeds."

"Why didn't those men," asked Emile, "if they had to fight such ferocious animals, use something better than sharpened sticks and stone-pointed arrows? Why didn't they take regular firearms?"

"For the very best of reasons: metals were unknown, and iron, one of the latest to be discovered, was not used by man until long after this time. Men armed themselves, therefore, as best they could, with the point of a bone or the sharp edge of a broken stone."

"I understand, then," said Louis, "how dangerous such hunts must have been, and how courageous the hunters. To-day one would cut a sorry figure attacking a wolf with only a sharpened stake for a weapon."

"And how would it be if one found oneself face to face with the wild boar of which Meleager rid the country? According to the old writers who handed down the affair to us, it was an animal such as had never been seen before and will never be seen again. Heaven, in its wrath, had sent it to ravage the fields. It surpassed in size, they say, the strongest bulls. From its blood-shot eyes lightning darted; from its horrible mouth exhaled a fiery breath that instantly withered the leaves of trees; with a few blows of its snout it uprooted oaks; with its tusks, more formidable than the elephant's, it ripped up the earth and sent great masses of rock flying like so much dust. What became of the poor people when this brute rushed at them in all its fury? They all fled, wild with terror, their hands upraised to heaven, their voices choked with fright."

"There must be some exaggeration there," interposed Louis. "A wild boar does not grow to such a size and such strength."

"Yes, certainly, there is exaggeration in this as in many other stories in which the real facts, coming down through long centuries, finally become greatly magnified and take on most marvelous additions. Let us bring things back to something like probability. An enormous wild boar sets the country in a panic. For a people unprovided with good weapons and having no refuge but fragile huts of reed, it must be a very dangerous situation.

"To exorcise the common peril, Meleager calls together the best men in the neighborhood and places himself at the head of the hunters, among whom are to be found two of his uncles, his mother's brothers, violent men and very jealous of the fame their nephew has already acquired by his valorous exploits. They go to meet the monster. The first to approach the beast pay for their temerity with their lives. Already several have been made to bite the dust, without any result, when Meleager, more fortunate and no doubt also more skilful, succeeds in stabbing the beast with his stake. Victory is his, and the boar should belong to him, or at least the head, as a trophy of his courage; but his uncles, furious at their nephew's acquisition of a new title to fame in addition to so many former ones, do not look at it in that light. The dispute becomes heated, and, as usual in those brutal times, the disputants pass quickly from argument to blows. Meleager, beside himself with wrath, kills his two uncles with the same stake that has drunk the blood of the beast."

"Oh, wretched man!" cried Jules.

"Evil overtook him. On hearing of the death of her two brothers, Meleager's mother loses her reason from grief. She draws from a cupboard, where she has kept it with the greatest care, a firebrand blackened at one end. With a hand trembling with anguish, she takes this firebrand, this precious firebrand for which hitherto she would have given her very eyes, life itself, and throws it into the fire, where it is straightway consumed. Ah, what has she done, the unhappy mother, what has she done! At that moment her son Meleager is dying, consumed by an inner fire; he is dying, he is dead, for the firebrand has just given its last flicker. In her despair the poor mother kills herself.

"The connection between this firebrand that was reduced to ashes and Meleager's end escapes you; I hasten to throw some light on this point. I will tell you then that at Meleager's birth a firebrand suddenly sprang from beneath the ground and began to burn in the middle of the room, while a voice from the depths, like an infernal rumbling, said: 'This child will live until the firebrand is consumed.' "

"Why, this is nothing but a fairy tale!" Jules exclaimed.

"Very true. History here gives place to fable. Now the firebrand was burning on the floor and threatened soon to be entirely consumed. They hastened to pick it up and extinguish it with water. From that time the mother preserved it with the greatest care, as the most precious thing she had, persuaded that her son would live to a great age, when, crazed with grief at the news of her brothers' death, she threw it into the fire. As the subterranean voice had said, the moment the firebrand was consumed Meleager succumbed, devoured by an inner fire."

"It's a good story," was Emile's comment, "but I don't at all see what it has to do with the guinea-fowl."

"You will see in a minute," his uncle reassured him. "Inconsolable at the death of their brother, Meleager's sisters unceasingly shed tears that rolled like pearls over their mourning garments; night and day they filled the house with their distressing sobs. Heaven had pity on them and changed them into birds until then unknown, into guinea-hens, whose plumage is still sprinkled with the tears of the unhappy girls, and whose unceasing cries are the continuation of their sobs. Such, according to the ancients, is the origin of guinea-fowls, called by them *Meleagridæ* in honor of the hero of the legend.

"The childish imagination of the ancients elaborated this story of the metamorphosis of Meleager's sisters out of the two most prominent traits of the guinea-fowl, its plumage and its cry. On a background of bluish gray, the color of mourning, are sprinkled innumerable round white spots. Those are the tears, running in pearly drops over the bird as they ran over the somber garments of the inconsolable sisters. The guinea-fowl's voice is a discordant, continuous, unendurable cry, in which the fable recognizes, unquestioningly, the painful sobs of Meleager's sisters."

"Those resemblances are ingenious," said Louis, "but they do not take the place of real knowledge of the guinea-fowl's origin. Not even in those old days could every one have believed in the singular tale you have just told us."

"Many were satisfied with it and sought no further information. And even in our day, my friend, in this so-called enlightened century, is it so unusual that the more absurd a thing is the more easily it takes root in our minds? Many were satisfied with the story,

GUINEA-FOWL

but the wise knew well that the bird came to us from Africa, and for that reason called it the African fowl.

"These old names are now out of use and are replaced by the word guinea-fowl, or *pintade*, which some, not without reason write *peintade* (painted). In fact, the white spots, spread over the bluish-gray ground of the plumage, are so round and so regularly distributed that one might say they were traced with a brush by a painter. The bird looks painted; hence its name.

"The guinea-fowl has rounded outlines. Its short wings, its drooping tail, and the general arrangement of the feathers on its back give it a deformed appearance, which is misleading, for when plucked the bird shows none of its former gibbosity. The neck is lank. Imitating in that respect its compatriot, the camel, the guinea-fowl straightens it up and stretches it out when it runs away, and then it looks like a rolling ball. The head is small and partly bald, like the turkey's. Two wattles, tinted red and blue, hang from the base of the beak. The top of the skull is protected by dry skin, which rises in the shape of a helmet and is perhaps not without use when in their quarrelsome moods the guinea-fowls have a trial of skill in splitting one another's head with blows of the beak.

"Many qualities recommend this bird to our notice. The eggs are excellent and numerous, a hundred and more annually. They are a little smaller than the hen's, with remarkably thick shells of a yellowish or dull reddish color. Its flesh is superior, veritable game, nearly equal to that of the pheasant and partridge; and yet the guinea-fowl is rare almost everywhere. Three great faults are the reason: its cry, its quarrelsome disposition, and its wandering habits.

"First, its cry. He who has not had, for hours and hours, his ear tortured by the satanic music of the bird is ignorant of one of the most irritating of minor torments. The rasping of a file upon the teeth of a saw in process of sharpening, the discordant screech of a strangling cat, the final roulade of a braying donkey, are trifles in comparison. And this charivari goes on from morning to night with a reënforcement of the orchestra when the weather is about to change or something unexpected happens to worry the performers. If one is not blessed with a special ear, if the head is not void of all preoccupation, one simply cannot stand this deafening racket. They say the guinea-hens have inherited the wailings of Meleager's sisters; but I like to think that the poor girls put a little more reserve into the heartbreaking expression of their grief. In short, never tell Uncle Paul to have guinea-hens under his window; he would flee to the farthest depths of the forest, never to return. There are others, and they are numerous, whose nerves are irritated just as much by the insufferable bird; that is why the guinea-fowl is rare in poultry-yards, and by reason of its music escapes the spit.

"Second, its love of fighting. The parchment helmet standing up on top of the head betrays at the first glance the quarrelsome mania of the bird. The guinea-fowl is the bully of the poultry-yard; it domineers over the others and for a mere nothing will pick a quarrel. Hens and chickens are tormented for the possession of a grain of oats; the cock must on all occasions have a trial of skill with the beak to make his and his family's rights respected; the turkey-gobbler himself, the burly gobbler, must reckon with it. The guinea-cock, quick at attack, delivers ten assaults and twenty blows of the beak before his big adversary can put himself on the defensive. When at last the gobbler parries and thrusts, the turbulent aggressor makes use of tactics that he seems to have learned from his compatriot, the Arab. He turns his back on the enemy, flees in haste, then abruptly returns to the charge and hurls himself suddenly on the gobbler at a moment when the latter is off his guard. The beak having dealt its blow, the flight recommences. Nearly always the gobbler is forced to capitulate. I leave you to imagine what sort of harmony must prevail in a poultry-yard harboring such disturbers of the peace.

"Third, its *wanderlust*. The narrow limits of the poultry-yard are irksome to guinea-fowls. They are glad enough to be on hand at feeding time, but, their crops once full, they must have a long walk across country. Off they go, always by themselves, without ever admitting the common poultry to their ranks. To the music of its harsh chatter the flock goes on from one hedge to another, one bush to the next, snapping up insects. The distraction of the hunt makes them forget distance, and soon they are beyond supervision. Let a dog appear, and these half-tamed game-birds are seized with a foolish panic. They fly in all directions, with a cry of alarm resembling the harsh note of a rattle. The disbanded flock will have much trouble in getting together again; perhaps when they do come together one or two will be missing. Another inconvenience no less grave: during these excursions the eggs are laid almost anywhere, in the wheat-field, on the broad meadow, amid the tangled underbrush. Except by attentive watching at the moment of laying, it would take a sharp eye to find the nest of the suspected bird.

"The guinea-hen broods in about the same manner as the common hen, but it is preferable to set the eggs under a common hen; she will perform the imposed task perfectly and make no distinction between her own eggs and those of a stranger. The hatching takes place about the twenty-eighth or thirtieth day. On coming out of the shell, the little guinea-chicks can walk and eat alone quite as well as the other chickens. They need warmth and assiduous care. The first week they are fed with a pap of bread-crumbs and hard-boiled eggs, to which are added ants' eggs or at least a little chopped meat. After that they have the same diet as ordinary chickens. Like young turkeys they pass through a critical period, the time when the red begins to show on the bald skin of the head. To pass through it well, the best way is to give them strengthening food and shelter them from all dampness."

CHAPTER XI

THE PALMIPEDES

"THE WORKMAN is known by his tools, and by the tools of the feathered creatures—that is to say, their beaks and claws—their way of life is not less easily recognized. If it were not already known to us, who could fail to infer the carnivorous disposition of the hawk from the shape of its beak—short, sharp, and hooked—and from the structure of its talons, armed as

HAWK

they are with pointed nails grooved underneath with a narrow channel after the manner of certain daggers, to facilitate the flow of blood from the wound? Does it call for any extraordinary perspicacity to recognize, in the heron's long legs, veritable stilts which enable it to traverse, step by step, without getting wet, the inundated flats, as does the hunter in his long, waterproof marsh boots? And then, that long beak, pointed like a nail, does it tell us nothing? Does it not say that the bird bores deep in the tufts of rushes and in the soft mud to pull out reptiles and worms?"

"It is the heron," put in Emile, "that the fable tells about when it says:

> "The long-necked, long-beaked heron went walking;
> On its stilt-like legs one day it went stalking."

"Yes," said Uncle Paul, "that is the bird. Everything about the heron is long—legs, beak, neck. The length of its legs enables the bird to explore the swamp at its ease all day long without wetting a feather; its length of neck is needed that it may reach the ground without stooping; and the long beak is indispensable for burrowing in the tall tufts of grass where the reptile

Heron

lurks, and for probing the mud where the worm buries itself."

"I begin to see now," said Jules, "how the character of a bird may be judged from its shape. The heron bears its trade stamped on its form."

"The duck, in its turn, makes an equally unmistakable announcement. Let us forget its habits, which are so familiar to us, and try to rediscover them in the shape of the legs and beak.

"The duck's beak is very wide and flat, and round at the end. Shall we compare it with the hen's beak, a slender pair of pincers that snaps up seeds and kernels one by one? Comparison is impossible. Do we see there a tool working in the manner of the heron's pointed probe? Still less. Shall we make it the equivalent of the bloody hooked beak of the bird of prey? No one would dream of such a thing, so great is the difference. But one sees at once in this wide, rounded beak a spoon shaped expressly for scooping up food from the water, just as our table-spoons enable us to take out pieces of bread or lumps of rice swimming in a thin soup. The duck dabbles, then it dips up water in large spoonfuls—that is to say, in beakfuls—and seeks its food therein. It is a soup of the thinnest sort and, in itself, of no nutritive value. Consequently the liquid that fills the bird's mandible must be rejected, but at the same time it must be drained out in such a manner as to leave behind what little alimentary matter it may contain. For this purpose the edges of the beak are fringed with a row of thin, short blades which let the liquid run out when the bird has once filled its mouth."

"That's an ingenious way to eat," remarked Jules. "In order to snap up what it takes a fancy to, perhaps a tadpole, or a little water shell, or a worm, the duck is obliged to fill its beak with water. To swallow the whole mouthful without sorting would simply stuff the crop with a useless liquid. What does the bird do? It closes the beak, and the water, driven back, runs out through the fringed edges as if through a grating. The tadpole alone remains behind the grating, and goes down into the stomach."

"You can see, any time," observed Louis, "the ducks on the pond dipping up water by the mouthful. It certainly isn't just for drinking that they work their beaks so."

"Certainly not," assented Uncle Paul, "they drain the water of the pond through the fringe of the beak to gather worms and other small aquatic prey.

"The spoon-shaped beak of the duck indicates the bird's dabbling habits; now let us see what the feet have to say. They are composed of three toes connected by an ample and supple membrane. Is that, I ask you, the footgear of a bird destined to long walks? With such a sole, so fine, so tender, and by its extent of surface exposing itself so much to the hardness of the stones, is the duck made for foot-racing? Note, on the contrary, the foot of the hen and the guinea-fowl, both untiring walkers. The toes are short, knotty, and sheathed with strong leather, without any connecting membrane. That is the true footgear of the pedestrian. But what will become of the duck on rough ground, with its wide sandals that a mere nothing can wound? You all know its pitiful walk. It waddles along, as ill at ease as a person afflicted with corns on the rough pavement of some of our streets. No, the duck is not made for walking.

"But in water those expanded feet will make vigorous swimming oars. If the bird throws them out behind, they spread wide open merely with the resistance of the water; and their fan-shape gives them purchase enough to send the duck forward. When the duck draws them in again under its breast, they are closed automatically by the resistance of the liquid acting in a contrary direction; the membrane refolds in the manner of a closed umbrella, thus doing away with all shock or recoil. The twofold essential of a perfect oar lies in its presenting to the water the greatest possible surface on the stroke, and the least possible surface on the recovery, so as to furnish adequate purchase against the water in the first movement and to offer only very feeble resistance in the second. If the oar moved alternately forward and backward while presenting the same extent of surface to the water and driven with the same vigor, the recoil would equal the advance and there would be no progress. Man, with all his skill, does not yet know how to ply his oar so that it shall offer this alternating maximum and minimum of surface. Therefore, in propelling a boat, he is obliged to bring the oars back to their first position through the air instead of through the water, which latter would be much more direct. The duck scorns this clumsy method: with its foot, which opens wide of itself in the backward thrust and closes again of its own accord in the return movement, it moves forward or puts about, without ever lifting the oars from the water.

"Thus the duck is an expert swimmer; the shape of its feet tells us as much, and a glance at any duck-pond demonstrates it. Who has not admired the aquatic evolutions of the bird, so awkward on land with its tender feet, so graceful when once on the water, its proper element? Sometimes they race with one another, whitening their breasts with a band of foam; sometimes, in order to

ALBATROSS

explore the depths with their beaks, they plunge half-way in and point their tails heavenward; sometimes, also, yielding to the current, they let themselves drift idly down-stream or hold their position by paddling a few strokes when necessary. Water is their chosen domain; there they take their recreation, seek their food, and enjoy their sleep.

"The membrane connecting the duck's toes is called a web, and the feet converted into oars by means of this membrane are spoken of as webbed. Similar feet are found in all good swimming birds such as the swan, teal, goose, and many others. Hence this group of birds, especially skilled in swimming, is designated by the term of *palmipede*, meaning web-footed."

"Then the duck is a palmipede?" asked Emile.

"It is a palmipede, as also the goose, swan, and teal. All four are equally endowed with a large spoon-bill shaped for dabbling in the water; that is to say, a wide, round beak; but there are palmipedes, notably among sea-birds, that live on prey, on fish, and consequently are equipped with the crooked mandible appropriate for a predatory life. Such, to take but a single example, is the albatross, of which I here show you the picture. By its ferociously hooked beak it can easily be recognized as a sea pirate, an insatiable devourer of fish."

"I certainly don't like its looks," declared Emile. "But tell me now what name they give the heron on its tall stilts."

"The heron belongs to the group of stilt-birds or wading-birds. That is what they call all birds mounted on long legs for traversing the marshes."

"A bird on stilts is a stilt-bird; it would be hard to improve on that. It is just the kind of name I like."

"Instead of allowing ourselves to be turned from our theme by the heron and its stilts, let us come back, my little friend, to the palmipedes, the swimming birds. Clothing made expressly for the purpose is required by the bird that passes the greater part of its time on the water. It is indispensable that this clothing should keep out both cold and wet. Well, the plumage of an aquatic bird, especially in very cold countries, is a marvel of delicate precautions. The outside feathers are strong, placed very accurately one on the other and glossed with an oily varnish that water cannot wet. Have you ever noticed ducks as they come out of the water? They may have prolonged their bath for hours, swimming, diving, playing; but they leave the stream without getting the least bit wet. If a drop of water has got between their feathers, they have only to shake themselves a moment, and they are perfectly dry. That, you must agree, is a precious privilege, to be able to go into the water and not get wet."

"A privilege that, for my part," rejoined Emile, "I have often envied without being able to explain—the secret of a duck's keeping dry when right in the water."

"I will explain the secret to you. Watch the ducks as they come out of their bath. In the sun, some lying at ease on their stomachs, others standing up, they proceed to make their toilet with minute care. With their large beak they smooth their feathers, one by one, coat them over with an oily fluid, the reservoir of which is situated on the bird's rump. There, just at the base of the tail, is found, hidden under the down, a kind of wart of grease, from which oil oozes constantly. From time to time the beak presses the wart, draws from the oily reservoir, and then distributes here and there, methodically, all over the plumage, the oil thus obtained."

"That greasy wart might be called a sort of pomatum pot," suggested Emile.

"It is a pomatum pot, if that comparison pleases you. Thus greased, thus anointed with pomatum, feather by feather, the duck furnishes no foothold for moisture, because, as you all know, water and oil do not mix, and from an oiled surface drops of water run off without wetting it. Such is the secret of the duck's keeping itself dry when immersed in water."

"That is one of the most curious things I ever heard of," declared Jules, "and one that I shouldn't have known anything about for a long time if it hadn't been for Uncle Paul. Should I ever have guessed that the duck presses a certain wart on its rump to get the grease for oiling its feathers?"

"The duck's secret is known to all birds without exception; all have this oil-sac on the rump, and obtain from it the oil for giving luster to their plumage and making it impervious to wet; but aquatic birds are more abundantly provided in this respect. And it is only right that those most exposed to dampness should have the largest reservoir of this oily coating."

"In all birds the fattest part is always the rump," said Louis. "Grease gathers there by preference, no doubt, to maintain the store of oil in the oil-sac?"

"Evidently. It is in this storehouse that the oil attains its perfect state and becomes the finished product that oozes from the sac. As to the making of it in the first place, nearly all parts of the body take part; and as the swimming bird uses a great deal of this pomatum, the result is that the palmipede tends to fatness and, as it were, sweats grease: witness the plump duck and goose, which carry under the breast a heavy, fat swelling. As a general rule, the web-footed fowl of our poultry-yards is analogous to the pig: it is a fat-factory. We divert to our own use the excess of fat accumulated primarily for the supply of the oil-sac on the rump and the maintenance of the luster that distinguishes the plumage.

"The palmipede, you see, is admirably protected against wet. Neither rain nor the finest drizzle can penetrate the first covering of feathers, always kept, as it is, well coated with the varnish laid on by the point of the beak. The bird can plunge into the deepest water, swim on its surface, or sleep there cradled by the waves, and the wet will not reach it. Neither will cold affect it, for under this outer covering is found a second, designed for resisting inclement weather and made of what is most efficacious for preserving the heat of the body. This under-clothing of aquatic birds is a down so delicate and soft that, unable to compare it with anything else, we have given it a special name, that of eiderdown. In its proper place I will come back to this down. For the present let us confine ourselves to a general survey of the palmipedes, and of the duck in particular."

CHAPTER XII

THE DUCK

"I WILL begin with the wild duck, parent stock of our domestic duck. It is a splendid bird, at least the male, for the costume of the female is less rich, as may be remarked in all the other species. The head and upper part of the neck are emerald green, with glints as of polished metal, while beneath is a white collar, its dull coloring contrasting with the brilliance of the adjacent tints. A brownish purple extends from the base of the neck down over the breast, where it gradually fades into gray on the sides and stomach. Changeable green, mixed with black, colors the region of the tail, whence rise four small feathers curling in the shape of a crook. In the middle of each wing a spot of magnificent azure is encircled, first, with velvety blue, then with white. The back, sides, and stomach are speckled with black spots on a gray ground. Finally, the beak is yellowish green, and the feet are orange. Such is the duck in its wild state, and such it often is under domestication, notwithstanding the numerous variations of plumage that captivity has caused it to undergo."

"The head superbly clothed in green," observed Emile, "the little curly tail-feathers, and the spot of blue in the middle of the wing—I have noticed all these lots of times in tame ducks."

"The wild duck is strong of wing and a pas-

WILD DUCK

sionate lover of travel. Consequently it is found nearly everywhere; but it does not stay long anywhere, unless it be in the most northerly regions, Lapland, Spitzbergen, and Siberia, where it delights in the solitude so favorable for nesting undisturbed and passing the summer. Twice a year it visits us: in the spring on its way to the North, and in the autumn on its return from the Pole, when it goes as far as Africa to take up its winter quarters in warmer countries. On a gray November day when it threatens snow you can see, passing from north to south, at a great height, migrating birds arranged one behind another in two files which meet in a point, like the two arms of a V. It is a flock of ducks emigrating. They are fleeing the approach of cold weather and seeking a milder climate, perhaps beyond the sea, where they may find assured nourishment in waters that do not freeze. The better to cleave the air and husband their strength on such a long journey, the flying squadron arranges itself in the form of a wedge, the point of which opens the way through the resisting air. The post at the tip is the hardest, since the leader of the file, being the first, has to overcome the resistance of the atmosphere. Each one takes it in turn for a certain time, and when it is tired falls back to the rear to rest while another takes its place."

"To come from countries near the Pole to this one, and still more to Africa," said Jules, "is a very long journey, at least a thousand miles. I can understand how, in order to accomplish it, the ducks must save their strength by arranging themselves in the form of a wedge, point foremost. But tell me, Uncle, what makes these birds prefer the countries of the extreme north, where they go to pass the summer and build their nests? Wouldn't they be better off with us than in those wild countries, so cold and covered with snow and ice a great part of the year?"

"Such is not the opinion of the duck, which prefers the gloomy solitudes of the most desolate islands to countries disturbed by the presence of man. In those peaceful spots it can raise its family in complete security; and, besides, provisions abound in the neighboring waters, which are thawed out for several weeks by the summer sun. Neither is it the opinion of the teal, goose, plover, lapwing, and many others, which all, as soon as spring comes, leave us and return to the North, journeying by long stages. Then it is that, from his ambush in a hut of foliage in the middle of a swampy field or in the dried bed of a wide torrent, the hunter imitates with a reed whistle the plaintive note of the plover, to call the migrating bird to his nets. The flock arrives, circles about a moment undecided, suspects danger, and flies off again into the distant blue, where it is soon lost to sight. Whither is it going? It is going where its instinct calls it, to the solitudes of the North. At the first thawing of the ice, when the ground, still wet from the melting snows, begins to be clothed with flowers, in fact in May or June, it will reach perhaps the Faroe Islands, perhaps the Orkneys or Iceland, or maybe Lapland. It is never without a lively interest that I watch the flight of one of these migrating flocks, better guided on its audacious journey than the navigator with the aid of the compass. I picture to myself the joys of arrival, the common delight when the long flight finally ends on the home island, the friendly land where, in a mossy hollow, the red-marbled eggs will presently be laid.

"For a great many birds, and among them the duck, the archipelagoes of the North are a promised land, an earthly paradise. The most varied species meet here from all parts of the world. What a lively scene, therefore, what a festival, when nesting time comes! Nowhere else is there such a reunion of birds. Let me tell you the strange scene that takes place then, according to travelers who have witnessed it.

"We are at Spitzbergen, facing some towering cliffs that overlook the sea and extend back in the form of receding shelves, one above another, like the rows of seats in a theater. These shelves are all covered with myriads of female birds sitting on their eggs, with heads turned seaward, as numerous and as crowded as the spectators in a theater at a first-night performance. They cackle to each other from neighbor to neighbor and seem to be engaged in an animated conversation, as a diversion from the tedium of prolonged incubation. All around the cliff, on the bosom of the waters, swimmers of all kinds dive and dabble, chasing, pecking, and beating one another. Others fill the air with their hoarse or shrill cries, going unceasingly from sea to nests and from nests to sea, calling to their mates, wheeling around above them, caressing their little ones, playing with their brothers, and showing in a noisy and innocent way their fears and wants, their joy and happiness. To describe the agitation, confusion, noise, cries, croakings, and whistlings of these countless birds of all shapes and colors and styles, is quite impossible. The hunter, dizzy and stunned, knows not where to fire in this living whirlpool; he is incapable of distinguishing and still more of following the bird he wishes to aim at. Wearied by vain effort, he directs his fire at the very midst of the cloud. The shot is sped. Immediately confusion is at its height; clouds of birds, perched on the rocks or swimming on the water, take flight in their turn and mingle with the others; a deafening discordant clamor rises to the skies. Far from dissipating, the cloud grows thicker and whirls about still more. Cormorants, at first motionless on the rocks betwixt wind and water, become noisily excited; sea-gulls fly in circles about the hunter's head and strike him in the face with their wings. All these different species, peacefully assembled on an isolated rock in the midst of the glacial ocean waves, seem to reproach man for coming to the very end of the world to trouble the joys of the brooding mother. The females, still motionless on their eggs in the midst of this disorder, content themselves with joining their protests to those of the indignant males."

"I have never heard anything like that before, Uncle," said Jules. "Under the roof-tiles we sometimes find a dozen nests of sparrows living as neighbors; but how far these little gatherings are from the Spitzbergen throngs! Those rocks on the borders of the sea are populous towns, with nests for houses and birds for inhabitants."

"Are there ducks on those rocks, too?" asked Louis.

"No, my friend," replied Uncle Paul; "there are only sea-birds. Wild ducks and geese flock by themselves and make their nests inland, far from the waters of the sea, which do not suit them. They prefer the borders of a lake or swamp. Their nests are built on the ground among tufts of grass. Sometimes they are so numerous one could not take a step without treading on eggs."

"Oh, what a fine harvest of eggs I should have if I were there!"

"You forget, my child, that Uncle Paul expressly forbids you to touch birds' nests. However, as once is not a habit, and as, moreover, the temptation would be irresistible, I would shut my eyes and would leave you to your own devices if we were on those famous bird-rocks of Spitzbergen, Greenland, or Lapland. Basket, hat, handkerchief, all would soon be full; you would simply be perplexed what to take and what to leave. All shapes are there together. There are some eggs as round as balls, some oval and like those of our own poultry, some equally pointed at both ends, and some very much enlarged at one end and small at the other, almost like pears. All these sea-birds' eggs are large, because the young, on leaving the shell, must be strong enough to follow their parents on the water and begin to earn their own living. And then, what variety of color and design! There are white eggs, yellowish eggs, and red eggs. Some are dark green, imitating the color of the waves that roar at the base of the rock; others seem to borrow their pale blue from the azure itself. These are diversified with areas of different colors, like the maps in your geography; those are painted with large spots and remind one of the leopard's skin."

"Oh, if I were only there!" sighed Emile.

"As we are not there, let us leave the beautiful rock-eggs to the birds and return to the duck.

"It is in order to get back to these northern countries, their paradise, that wild ducks pass over us at the end of winter. The journey is chiefly made at night, the day being reserved for rest among the rushes. While the flock sleeps, each bird's head under its wing, some members station themselves at favorable points and, vigilant scouts, watch over the common welfare. At the first appearance of danger the cry of alarm is sounded, a sort of hoarse clarion call. Immediately the flock takes wing or dives under the water. In descending from the upper air and alighting on a suitable spot, the cautious bird is equally prudent. The flock comes and goes several times, and circles about repeatedly to give the place a thorough examination. If nothing disquieting appears, it descends in an oblique flight, grazes the surface of the water with the tips of its wings, and then swims to the middle of the pond, far from the shore where the danger would be greatest. Nothing, then, is more difficult than to catch a flock of wild ducks off their guard. The hunter has recourse to a ruse and turns to his own account the friendly relations that always exist between the tame duck and its brother, the wild duck. Hidden on the edge of the pond in a reed hut, he releases two or three tame ducks, whose cries call the strangers and bring them within gunshot.

"Although the laying of eggs generally takes place in the northern regions, there are always a few pairs of ducks that linger and make their nests with us, either from being tired with too long a journey or because they have strayed away from the migrating flocks. For her nesting place, the mother chooses some cluster of reeds in the middle of the swamp. She beats down and flattens the central rushes; then, using her beak to intertwine the outer ones, she succeeds in weaving a kind of coarse basket, which she lines with warm down, plucked from her breast and stomach. More rarely she establishes herself in some large tree where she makes use of a nest abandoned by the magpie. The rude structure of dry sticks is restored, and especially is it well lined with fine feathers plucked from her own body. The eggs are laid in March and number about fifteen. Incubation takes thirty-one days. Whenever the need of food makes her leave the nest for a few minutes, the mother takes care to cover the eggs with a thick layer of down, so that they shall not become cold. When she comes back it is never in a straight line or uninterrupted flight. She alights at some distance from the nest, then cautiously approaches by tortuous windings, varied every time and calculated to baffle whoever may be watching her.

"The young ones are born clothed with a delicate fur of yellow down, which they keep for some time. As soon as hatched, the brood is led to the water and abandons the nest, never to return to it. If the pond is too far away for such young legs, or if the nest is at the top of some tall oak, the father and mother take the little ones tenderly by the nape of the neck and carry them one by one to the shore. The removal accomplished, the mother goes into the water, the boldest one of her brood follows her, and the others imitate its example. Their aquatic education immediately begins. In order to swim you must do so and so, are the parents' instructions; and to dive and tack about you must do like this. The tadpole, that dainty morsel, is caught in this manner, but if you don't catch it with the first snap of the beak, you get it by diving. The little shell-fish hides under the leaves, and that's where you must hunt if you want to find it. The larva frequents warm mud; seek, my children, near the shore and you will find it. The lively frog calls for nimble tactics: a quick snap of the beak will fetch him. All that is so soon and so well understood by the ducklings, that the mother does not have to look after their food; her part is simply to gather them under her wing to keep them warm when the family retires to the shore to rest or to pass the night.

"Apart from the love of traveling, which many centuries of domestication have caused to be forgotten, the habits of the tame duck do not differ from those of the wild. The female duck begins to lay in February or March, and lays from forty to fifty eggs a year, if one is careful to remove them as they are laid. These eggs are slightly larger than the hen's, smoother, rounder, sometimes dull white, sometimes a little greenish. The duck is impelled by instinct to lay them among the neighboring reeds and rushes, and it is therefore necessary to watch her if one does not wish to run the risk of losing the eggs.

"Domestication does not by any means always improve the qualities of animals subjected to our care. If there is gain in corpulence, in quantity of alimentary matter, there is frequently loss on the side of what might be called the moral qualities. So it is that the tame duck is not so good a brooder nor so devoted a mother as the wild one. The hen, on the contrary, has forgotten none of her maternal duties; she even carries them to excess in the hen-house, until she lets herself die of starvation on her nest, a thing she would not do in her wild state. Hence, it is to the hen, a better mother than the duck, that the latter's eggs are usually entrusted.

"The period of incubation is thirty-one days, the same as with the wild duck. If the brood is hatched at a time of year when the weather is still cold, it would be dangerous for the ducklings to go immediately into the water, whither their instinct calls them, and whither the mother duck that had brooded them would not fail to lead them. Hence the little ones and their mother, hen or duck, are put under a coop in a place apart, where there is no danger of trampling or other rough treatment from the rest of the poultry. During this sequestration the food consists of a mixture of barley flour, boiled potatoes, bran, and chopped nettles, all made into a mush with greasy dish-water. Ducklings have a strong stomach and active digestion; they need from six to eight meals a day, so quickly does their food pass. Let us not forget to put a large plate of water under the coop. It will serve them as a swimming basin in which their wide beaks will practise dabbling and their webbed feet will learn their destined use. Daily sport on this little sheet of water will help them to have patience until the great day when larger evolutions on the broad pond will be allowed.

"A week, two weeks, pass in this way. At last the longed-for moment arrives. The mother duck leads her family to the neighboring pond, or the ducklings find their way thither unaided if they have a hen for a nurse. I have told you of the fright of that adoptive mother when she sees her little ones throw themselves joyously into the water, deaf to her supplications. If the pond is not too deep, the hen wades in till the water reaches half-way up her legs, and runs along the edge, calling her dear brood. In vain her courageous devotion, to no purpose her anxiety and grief: the ducklings gain the deep water whither she cannot follow them, and, heedless of the mother admonishing them from the shore, they wag their little pointed tails with joy.

"Like the pig, the duck will eat anything and everything. In still waters, in which it delights, it snaps up tadpoles and little frogs, worms of all kinds and soft shell-fish, water insects and little minnows. In the field it eats the tender herbage and makes prey of the slimy slug and even the snail, no whit abashed by the latter's shell. In the poultry-yard offer it the kitchen leavings, parings of all kinds, garden refuse, dish-water, and garbage, and the glutton will feast royally.

"Thus because of its voracity the duck is easy to fatten; provided it has abundant food and a chance to play in the water, you may be sure it will take on fat without any other care. Nevertheless, in order to obtain certain results it is necessary to go beyond the bird's natural gluttony and have recourse to forcible feeding. For a couple of weeks ducks are shut up in a dark place. Morning and evening, a servant takes them on her knees, crosses their wings, and opens their beak with one hand while with the other she stuffs their crop with boiled maize. Thus gorged to excess with food, the miserable ducks pass their captivity resting on their stomachs, always panting, almost breathless, half stifled. Some die of surfeit. Finally the rump, distended with fat, spreads the tail-feathers out fan-wise so that they cannot be closed again. This is a sign that the fattening process has reached its extreme limit. Haste is then made to behead the poor creature, which otherwise would soon die of suffocation."

"And why, if you please," asked Jules, "these horrible tortures if the duck fattens so easily by itself?"

"Alas, my friend, the satisfaction of the stomach makes us cruelly ingenious. In the state of continual suffocation that overtakes the bird when it is gorged with boiled maize, a mortal disease sets in, the disease of the glutton, among men as among ducks. The liver becomes tremendously enlarged and changes to a soft, shapeless mass, oozing grease. Well, this liver, decomposed by disease, furnishes to the palate of connoisseurs an incomparable delicacy. I take their word for it, not being able to speak from experience, as I have none; for, between you and me, my friend, I own that such delicacies would be repugnant to your Uncle Paul. In my humble opinion, it is paying too much for a greasy mouthful to subject the duck to those frightful tortures. I will add that the pasties of Amiens and the celebrated ragouts of Nérac and Toulouse are made of these livers.

"To bring this subject to a close, a few words on a second kind of duck, less common in our poultry-yards than the first.

It is the Barbary duck, called also the musk duck on account of its odor of musk, and likewise known as the silent duck, because it utters no cry. It is much larger than the common duck, its plumage is darker, of a variegated black and green, and the head of the male is adorned with scales and with fleshy growths of a bright red color."

CHAPTER XIII

THE WILD GOOSE

"WHEN WE say of some one, 'He is as silly as a goose,' we think we have applied the strongest term indicative of foolishness that our language furnishes. Is the goose then so silly? That is what I am about to discuss with you, my friends.

"I agree at the outset that its appearance is not such as to give a high idea of its intellectual faculties. Its head is too small for its body, its diminutive and expressionless eyes, its enormous beak hiding its whole face, its waddling walk made still more awkward by the fatty protuberance that hangs down under its stomach and strikes its feet, its neck sometimes awkwardly outstretched, sometimes sharply bent as if broken, its cry surpassing in hoarseness the note of the hoarsest clarion, its angry or frightened whistle resembling the hiss of the snake when surprised—all that, I hasten to acknowledge, does not prepossess one in favor of the bird. But how often, under a rude exterior, is hidden a refined nature! Let us not judge the goose by its appearance, but let us go deeper before forming a fixed opinion."

"I see what you are up to, Uncle," interrupted Jules; "you are taking up your favorite refrain, the praise of the slandered. A while ago you extolled the two ugliest of creatures, the bat and the toad; now you are going to undertake the

GOOSE

defense of the goose and clear it of the slander it suffers in being called silly."

"Why should I deny it, my child? Yes, my favorite occupation is pleading the cause of the weak, the miserable, the traduced, the outlawed. The strong and the powerful are not wanting in admirers, so I can pass them over very quickly; but I should reproach myself all my life were I to forget the forsaken and not bring to light their good qualities, unrecognized and, indeed, too often shamefully misrepresented as they are. As to its treatment, the goose needs no pleading of mine: it is too valuable to us not to be taken care of as it deserves. The only reproach I have to bring has to do with the reputation for stupidity it has been made to bear. I am well aware that the goose, as a sensible creature, is superbly indifferent to this calumny, and I offer it my congratulations; but, after all, this false repute is an instance of error, and wherever I find error I give it battle.

"First, I will show you the goose as an adept in geography. In spite of our books, maps, and atlases, how the reputedly silly bird would surpass all of us and many others! Know that in its wild state the goose is an impassioned traveler, even more so than its companion, the duck. Influenced by considerations of convenience, the latter often nests in our latitudes; the goose is more given to mistrust and passes us by. For the laying of its eggs it must seek regions as near the Pole as possible, regions of never-melting ice. The desolate wastes of Greenland and Spitzbergen, and, still farther north, the islands lost in the fogs of the polar ocean, are the regions whither they feel bound to return every summer. The point of departure, where the bird has passed the winter in the midst of plenty when its native country was plunged in continual night and buried under fathomless depths of snow and ice—the point of departure is far south, in central Africa perhaps, so that the distance to be covered measures almost a quarter-circumference of the earth. Now, my friends, let us put ourselves in the place of the wild goose just about to take its flight for the long expedition, and see which of the two parties will be the more perplexed, the more stupid. I leave out of the account means of transportation: however good a mount we might have, we should cut a pitiable figure beside the goose, which with powerful wing soars above the clouds and conquers space. I pass by the means of transportation and ask only what direction is to be taken. I appeal to your knowledge of geography."

"Since it is only necessary to go north," answered Jules, "I should first make sure of the points of the compass. I should turn toward the sun, and if it is rising, the north would be on the left; if setting, the north would be on the right. This direction fixed, I should set out accordingly."

"In the supposed case that method is inapplicable. As an experienced traveler husbanding its strength and hence making the most of the cooler hours, the goose travels only at night."

"Then I would turn toward the constellation of the Bear, toward the polar star. The north is in that direction."

"Very good: you would find the north in that way if the night were clear; but if the night were dark and you could not see the stars, what would you do?"

"I should use a compass, the needle of which always points nearly northward."

"But if you did not have that precious instrument, the traveler's guide in the midst of the waste solitudes of land and sea—if you had no compass, how would you find your way, my friend?"

"In that case, Uncle, I should be very much perplexed. Perplexed is not the word; on the contrary, I should see very clearly that there was no possibility of my finding my way. I should not budge from the spot, for I might as well try to guide myself blindfolded."

"Here, my dear child, the bird reputed to be so stupid, so foolish, towers above us all by a thousand cubits. Without consulting the rising or setting sun, paying no heed to the constellations, for which it has no use, availing itself of no compass but its instinct, which says, 'This is the way'—in darkness as well as in light, the goose plunges into space and flies northward.

"But that is only the beginning of the problem. A simple northern direction leads, according to the point of departure, to very different regions, sometimes to Siberia, sometimes to

Spitzbergen and Lapland, sometimes to the northern islands of Iceland, Greenland, and what others shall I say? But no such vague destination will do for the goose. The bird must return to its native country, of which it retains an ineffaceable remembrance, just as a man, through all the shifts and changes of his stirring life, preserves the cherished memory of his own village. The goose, then, must again find the sea whose murmur it listened to in youth. In that sea is a certain islet, on that islet a certain moor, and on that moor a certain hidden retreat covered with rushes and sheltered from the wind by a rock. That is its birthplace; it must find its way.

"Propose such an undertaking to a navigator provided with first-rate charts and versed in all the special lore of his calling, and he would finally succeed, it is true, but would encounter difficulties due to the inhospitable seas of those parts. Propose it to one of us, who have none of the requisite nautical knowledge, and it would put our geography to the test without any chance of ultimate success. But this task which man, with all his reasoning powers, would in the great majority of instances be incapable of performing, the goose accomplishes without the slightest hesitation. As though the desired spot were right before its eyes, it goes straight forward. The featureless expanse of ocean and the confusing details of the landscape, the halts on the margins of lakes, the damp and obscurity of clouds that have to be traversed, the emotions of terror excited when the ambushed hunter discharges his leaden hail—none of these things diverts it from its course. If detours must be made in order to avoid danger or find food, it makes them, however long they may be, and then resumes the right direction without a moment's hesitation. It calculates its speed and regulates its halts so as to arrive neither too early nor too late; for it knows perfectly the order of the seasons, when the snow melts and when the grass turns green. At last, on a fine day when the first little flowers are just peeping through their snowy shrouds, it reaches its ocean inlet, its little island, its native heath, its cherished nesting-place.

"I have finished. Now, my friends, which one of you would

like to engage in a geography match—not with a veteran goose experienced in such voyages; you would be too hopelessly outclassed—but with the youngest gosling, the merest novice of them all?"

"On that subject," Jules made answer, "I admit that the youngest gosling knows more than I."

"And than I," chimed in Louis, and Emile added: "If the goose knew that I can't even find my bearings yet on the map, how it would make fun of poor Emile! You will tell us so much about its cleverness, Uncle, that after this I shan't be able to meet a goose without blushing."

"It is very praiseworthy to blush at one's ignorance," his uncle assured him, "especially on a subject as necessary as geography; for it is a sign that in future one will do one's best; but none may expect to rival the goose. We acquire our knowledge by reflection, study, observation, experience; an animal does not acquire knowledge, it possesses knowledge from its birth. Without ever having learned it, without ever having seen it done, it does everything belonging to its manner of living, and does it admirably well. A feeling not reasoned, a secret impulse proper to its nature, guides it in its acts; it is instinct, the marvels of which I have often related to you. If, to accomplish its astonishing journeys, the goose had to learn geography as we do, it would never see its beloved native land again; but it has as guide the infallible inspiration of instinct, and with this inner compass it wings its unerring way straight toward its natal islet, however hidden by polar fogs that islet may be.

"Its manner of traveling is not less remarkable. I have already told you something about the duck; I come back to the subject in order to emphasize the high degree of mechanical science possessed by the goose. A bird on the wing is held up by the air which its wings strike; it is also impeded in its progress by the air, the resistance of which it must conquer. To overcome this obstacle with the least possible fatigue what does the bird do, especially the crane, heron, stork, and other wading birds encumbered with long legs and a long neck? They bring the neck back on the breast, point their sharp beak forward, and, holding their outstretched legs close together, trail them behind. With form thus trimmed to extreme slimness, and with beak acting as the point of a spear-head, they cleave the air as a ship plows the wave with its sharp prow. No bird is wanting in this elementary principle of mechanics: to gather the members together and taper the body in the direction of motion, so as to encounter the least resistance. By undertaking these very long flights in large flocks the duck and the goose improve upon this general method.

"Before going further let us draw a comparison. I will suppose that you are a company of playmates running across lots, and you come to a tract all covered with thick brushwood that has to be parted with feet and hands before you can get through. If each one goes about it in his own way, one here and another there just as it happens, is it not true that the sum total of fatigue for the whole company will be the greatest possible, since each one will have spent his strength in opening a way for himself through the thicket? But now let us suppose, on the other hand, that one of you, the most vigorous of the company, walks at the head, parting the underbrush, and that the others follow him, step by step, taking advantage of the path opened by the leader of the file. Is it not true that under these conditions the sum total of fatigue will be the least possible?"

"All that is obvious," Emile replied. "They could even, if it were a long way through the brushwood, take turns in going ahead, and then no one would be really tired out."

"This device of Emile's has, as you already know, been put in practice from time immemorial by ducks on their long flights. Nor is the goose less happily inspired. If the flock is a small one, the birds composing it range themselves in a continuous single file, each following bird touching with its beak the tail of the preceding one, in order that the way opened through the air may not have time to close again. If the flock is numerous, two files of equal length are formed, and they join each other at an acute angle, advancing point first. This angular arrangement, which we find imitated in the ship's prow, in the farmer's plowshare, in the thin edge of a wedge, and in any number of utensils fashioned for penetrating a dense mass by overcoming resistance, is the one best suited for cleaving the air with the least possible fatigue. If, to arrange its flying squadron, the goose had taken counsel of the most consummate science of our engineers, it could not have done better. But the goose has no need of others; advised by its instinct, it knew long before us, who call it stupid, one of the great secrets of mechanics, the principle of the wedge.

"Moreover, to divide among all the members of the flock the excess of fatigue felt by the leader of the file in being the first to cleave with a stroke of his wing the resisting atmosphere, each one in its turn occupies the post of honor, the forward end of the single file, or the apex of the two joining files. It is a repetition of Emile's expedient for penetrating a considerable extent of brushwood. After its turn of service at the front the leading goose retires for rest to the rear of one or other of the branches of the angle, while a new leader takes its place. By this means of equitable rotation excessive fatigue on the part of any one of the migrating flock is avoided, and no stragglers are left behind."

"And no goose has to be urged to take what you call the post of honor, the arduous post at the front?" queried Emile.

"None has to be urged. It is their duty, and they all fulfil it with a zeal that in many instances man might take as a model. To the recusant slacker the smallest gosling would give a lesson in what is owing to the common welfare. As soon as the leader feels its strength weakening, the next one in order takes its place without having to be told."

"Decidedly," interposed Jules, "those geese, with their cleverness in geography and their skill in the art of flying in flocks and in devising means for mutual assistance, are not so silly as they are said to be."

"The flight of a flock of geese is generally very high; they do not come near the ground except in foggy weather. If on such an occasion some farm chances to be near, it occasionally happens that resounding clarion calls answer each other from sky to earth and earth to sky. That is the interchange of greetings between wild and tame geese. The wild ones invite the captives to come and join them in their pilgrimage to the promised land of the North. The proposal puts the poultry-yard all in a turmoil, so compelling is the call of instinct. The farm geese become excited, scream, beat their sides with their large wings; but the plumpness of captivity prevents their flight. One less impeded takes wing, rises in the air, and is gone."

"To Spitzbergen?" asked Emile.

"Yes, to Spitzbergen, if strength does not fail it, but it is very doubtful whether it will be able to follow its wild companions to the end.

"The goose feeds chiefly on herbage. With its wide beak furnished at the edges with little scales resembling sharp teeth, it browses the turf very much as does the sheep. A field of green wheat particularly delights it. If a rather large flock alights there the harvest is seriously injured. During the devastation sentries keep a look-out, some here, others there, motionless, neck out-stretched, eye and ear on the alert. Let danger approach, and immediately the trumpet sounds. At the warning the flock ceases grazing, runs with wings open to get a start, then takes flight and mounts obliquely to heights above the reach of a shot. The same precautions are taken in the hours of repose; furthermore, actuated by an excess of prudence, they refuse to trust entirely to the sentinels, but each sleeps with one eye open, as we say. Thus are the ruses of the hunter nearly always baffled when he tries to get near them.

"I will stop here for to-day. I hope that, without going into other details that would carry us too far, I have reinstated the slandered bird in your esteem. The goose is not silly; on the contrary, it possesses to a high degree the wiles, the talents, in fact everything necessary for the admirable fulfilment of its mission as a goose."

CHAPTER XIV

THE DOMESTIC GOOSE

"BEFORE AMERICA had given us the turkey, the goose was sought for its flesh, which does not lack merit, although inferior to that of the bird from the New World. Roast goose was the dish of honor at family feasts. Now that the turkey has supplanted it in the solemnities of the table, it is raised chiefly for its fat, which is very fine and savory, rivaling butter in its uses. As to its flesh, relegated to secondary rank and regarded as a mere accessory, it is salted and preserved like pork. The region of which Toulouse is the center is the most renowned for this branch of agricultural industry. Large flocks are raised there of a species of goose called the Toulouse goose, remarkable for its large size and its tendency to corpulence. Its pouch of fat hanging down under its stomach reaches even to the ground, and grows so heavy as to interfere with the bird's walk. The plumage is dark gray, with brown or black spots; the beak is orange, and the legs flesh color.

"When it is desired to fatten the goose to the utmost limit, the process calls for the fundamental conditions expounded in the chapter on the poulard; that is to say, as much food as the stomach can bear, immobility, complete repose, and almost continual sleep. These principles recalled to mind, let us consider the Toulouse method. The geese are shut up in a dark place, cool without being damp, where they cannot hear the noises of the poultry-yard. The trumpet-calls of their free companions would awaken in them vexatious regrets and would interfere with their digestion. Three times a day the woman employed to fatten them seats herself on a low chair and takes them one by one between her knees so as to control their movements.

She opens the beak by force and thrusts far down the throat the tube of a tin funnel."

"That funnel is for feeding them?" asked Emile.

"Precisely."

"Then they are compelled to swallow even if they don't want to."

"What does the fattener care? All that concerns her is not to wound the bird during the operation. Furthermore, to make the utensil slip into its place better she takes care to oil the end of it a little. The poor creature struggles and protests as best it can against the violence to which it is subjected. But all in vain: the woman keeps at it. Now she pours a handful of maize into the funnel, and as the grains would not descend of themselves, the bird contracting that part of its throat not reached by the tube, she pushes them down with little blows on the crop with a wooden rammer; she crams (that is the word) the patient's stomach with maize. From time to time a little cold water is given to aid this painful deglutition. When the crop is full, which is ascertained by the touch of the hand, the bird is set free; another takes its place and, willy nilly, receives the funnel in its throat. During the thirty-five days that this feeding lasts, a goose consumes forty liters of corn; that is to say, more than a liter a day."

"After such a cramming with quantities of corn rammed down by main force," remarked Jules, "the goose must get discouraged and pine away."

"Get discouraged! You don't realize a goose's appetite. The miserable creature becomes accustomed to this diet, even takes a liking to it, and toward the end of the operation comes of its own accord and opens its beak to receive the funnel which ere long proves fatal to it. Soon we see the pouch of fat under the stomach dragging on the ground, the orange color of the beak turning pale, the breathing rendered difficult, and every sign pointing to a near end—suffocation by excess of corpulence. But the knife forestalls this. The bird is cut into quarters and salted; its melted grease is put into pots or bottles, where it can be kept for two years with its beautiful white color and fine flavor unimpaired.

"In other countries the fattening process includes the application, in its utmost rigor, of the principle of immobility. Under an earthen pot, the bottom of which has been broken, the goose is put in such a way that only its head is left free, projecting through the opening. Thus immured in its earthenware coffin, which barely permits it to turn round, the goose has only one distraction, eating. With food served in abundance, it eats just for the pleasure of it, and consumes so much that at the end of two weeks it becomes a ball of fat. To get it out of its cell the pot must be broken.

"Elsewhere, especially in Alsace, the goose is shut up in a little pine box so narrow that the bird cannot turn round in it. The floor of the cell is made of slats far enough apart for the dung to fall through; the front wall is pierced with an opening for the passage of the head, and beneath this opening is a trough always full of water, in which are placed a few pieces of charcoal as a disinfectant. Charcoal, in fact, possesses the property of absorbing infectious gases, and thus prevents the corruption that might develop in the bird's drink. The captive in its narrow cage is kept in the cellar or at least in a dark place. Morning and night it is forcibly stuffed with corn softened by several hours' soaking in water; the rest of the time it thrusts its head through its dormer-window and drinks, dabbling as much as it pleases in the trough just below. With twenty-five liters of corn—for the northern species is smaller than that of Toulouse—the goose, at the end of a month, is fattened sufficiently.

"The presence of a ball of grease under each wing, together with difficulty in breathing, announces that the time has arrived for cutting the prisoner's throat; if deferred, it would die from suffocation.

"The lack of exercise that attends the fattening process in captivity, whether in a pot with broken bottom or in a pine box, makes its effects felt principally in the structure of the liver, which grows to an enormous size and becomes charged with fat, as I have already told you in speaking of the duck. With the method used in Alsace the liver attains the weight of half a kilogram and sometimes double that. Moreover, in the process of cooking, a goose yields from three to five pounds of fat admirably suited for use with vegetables through the rest of the year. Goose livers serve the same purposes as ducks' livers: they go to the making of the ragouts of Nérac and Toulouse, and they form the chief ingredient in the celebrated Strasburg *pâtés de foie gras.*

EIDER-DUCK

"We have not yet exhausted the uses of the goose. Before the invention of steel pens, in general use to-day, large goose quills were employed for writing. Their preparation consisted in passing them through hot ashes and then scraping them a little to remove their greasy coating, which would prevent the ink's flowing. Of very convenient size for the fingers, their combined firmness and elastic flexibility made them also admirably adapted for writing; but they had to be recut from time to time, and the handling of a penknife was not without its difficulties, its dangers even, in inexperienced hands like yours. So steel pens have almost entirely supplanted them.

"Another product of the goose's plumage consists in the small feathers and down used for bedding. I have told you how aquatic birds, especially those of cold countries, have under their outside coat of feathers, which is impregnated with oil to resist wet and storm, an inner coat composed of the finest down and very fit for protecting the bird from the cold. This down we called eiderdown. I revert to it now on account of its importance.

"The best eiderdown is furnished by a kind of duck called the eider-duck, intermediate in size between the goose and the tame duck. This duck lives in a wild state in the frozen regions of the North. It is whitish in color with a black head as well as black stomach and tail. The female, which is rather smaller than the male, is gray except for some brown spots under the body. Its food is composed of fish, which its untiring wing enables it to catch at long distances from the coast and well out to sea. On the water all day searching for fish, the eider-duck returns at night to some icy islet, a warm enough resting place for its purpose, well muffled as it is in eiderdown.

"In some hollow of the sharp rocks of the shore it builds its nest, composed on the outside of mosses and dry seaweed, and on the inside of a thick eiderdown lining which the mother plucks from her stomach and breast. On this soft little bed rest five or six dull green eggs."

"We have already seen the wild duck plucking its stomach to cover its eggs with down," put in Jules.

"The eider-duck does the same, but with a greater expenditure of down. When the mother leaves her nest for a moment, she shelters her eggs under an abundant covering of her finest down. After the departure of the brood, those who hunt for eiderdown, especially the Icelanders, visit the abandoned nests and collect the down, but not without danger, since the nests are generally situated in inaccessible places on the ledges of high cliffs. They can reach them only by being lowered with ropes along the face of the precipitous rocks.

"The quilts that we call eiderdown are large coverlets filled with these very fine feathers. Their flocky mass, very light in spite of its size, is the best covering for retaining heat. Those most in demand are made of the down of the eider-duck, and are so elastic and light that one can press and hold in two hands the quantity of down necessary for a large bed-coverlet. But as this down is rare and very high-priced, the coarser kind, from the poultry-yard duck and goose, is commonly used.

"Every year the sheep yields its fleece to the shearer, and in the same way, four times a year, the goose is robbed of a part of its fine feathers and down. The operation is especially easy at molting time, for then the feathers come out with the least effort. The goose is plucked, but not entirely, you understand, beneath the stomach, on the neck, and on the under side of the wings; it is only when dead that it is plucked completely. This harvest of feathers is put into a bag without being pressed, and must next be subjected for some time to the heat of an oven from which bread has just been taken out. This removes its disagreeable odor and the parasites that often infest it. If, however, other parasites appear later, notably moths, greedy, as you know, for anything of animal origin, such as cloth, hair, down, or wool, the feathers must be fumigated with burning sulphur.

"The eggs of the goose are white and remarkably large, as one would expect from the size of the bird. When one sees, generally in February, a goose dragging with its beak some bits of straw and carrying them to its nesting place, it is a sign that laying time is approaching. The goose is then kept at home instead of being sent out into the fields. A laying numbers fifteen eggs at the most; but if care is taken to visit the nest and remove the eggs as fast as they are laid, the number increases and may go, it is said, as high as forty. The goose has the same fault as the duck: she is not a very assiduous brooder. Hence it is thought best to have the turkey do the setting. As for the hen, she is, despite her motherly qualities, out of the question, however small the setting may be: goose eggs are so large that she could not cover more than half a dozen at the most.

"Incubation lasts a month. As the eggs do not all hatch at the same time and as the brooder, goose or turkey, might be tempted to abandon the backward eggs in order to take care of the first-born goslings, it is advisable to take the little ones from the nest as fast as they hatch and to put them in a wool-lined basket. When the hatching is all finished, the family is given back to the mother. Warmth and a special diet are necessary the first few days. The goslings are fed with a mixture of bread-crumbs, corn-meal, milk, lettuce, and chopped nettles. At the end of eight or ten days this careful treatment may cease, and if the weather is fine the mother goose can be allowed to lead the brood whither she pleases, even to the neighboring pond, providing the water is warm. The male, the gander, as it is called, generally accompanies the family, protects it, and proves his courage in time of danger. Woe betide the thoughtless person who, even with no evil intention, approaches the goslings. The gander runs at him, neck outstretched, with loud and hissing cry, and gives him battle with wing and beak. When I was young I knew a little scamp who threw a stone at the goslings and was straightway knocked down by a blow of the gander's wing and then well thrashed. Timely aid was rendered, else the imprudent assailant would have been disfigured by the bird."

"You caught it that time, stone-thrower!" cried Emile. "For my part, I never pick a quarrel with geese; but one day they chased me and caught me by the blouse. Oh, how frightened I was!"

"If you are not strong enough to defend yourselves, children, do not go near the goose when she has her little ones with her. She is very distrustful then and might do you harm."

CHAPTER XV

THE PIGEON

"THE STRONG resemblance that the tame pigeon often bears to the wild one known as the rock-pigeon makes us suspect this latter to be the ancestor of the bird that inhabits our dove-cotes. The rock-pigeon has ashy-blue plumage with black-spotted wings and pure-white tail. The neck and breast are changeable in color according to the light in which they are seen, and shine with a metallic luster, in which sometimes purple and sometimes golden green dominates."

"That is exactly the ordinary plumage of our pigeons," said Emile. "When they come and peck the bread that I crumble for them in the sun, I like to see their magnificent breasts shining first with one color and then with another, every time the bird moves."

"Fond of traveling and endowed with a power of flight in accord with this predilection, the rock-pigeon is scattered over the greater part of the world. Nevertheless it is rare in France, where a few wretched pairs, always in dread of the talons of the bird of prey or the hunter's shot, make their nests in the most sparsely settled cantons, on the shelves of high rocks. The rocky and mountainous regions of the Mediterranean islands are their chosen haunts in Europe."

"But it is no uncommon thing," Louis remarked, "to hear of wild pigeons being shot in this country."

"You confound the rock-pigeon, my friend, with another kind of wild pigeon, the wood-pigeon. This, as its name indicates, perches on the branches of tall trees, which the rock-pigeon never does."

"Yes, that's so," Jules interjected. "I have never seen pigeons that are descended from the rock-pigeon alighting on trees. They alight on rocks, on roofs, or on the ground."

"In its free state the rock-pigeon builds its nest in the hollows of rocks; the wood-pigeon, on the contrary, builds in trees, in the depths of dense forests, where it finds in abundance the acorn and beech-nut, its principal food. These habits are not the only difference between the two birds. The wood-pigeon is much larger; its breast has the color of lees of wine; its neck, gleaming with variegated metallic glints like that of its brother, is further adorned on each side with a white spot in the shape of a cross. Its flight is sustained and rapid, its cooing sonorous, its sight piercing. It feeds on all sorts of seeds, especially acorns, which it swallows whole.

"Wood-pigeons like to perch on dead branches at the tops of trees. During the cold winter mornings they stay there motionless, waiting for a little warmth to come with the rising sun and arouse them from their torpor. In summer they frequent full-grown forest-trees, and their cooing may be heard in the very midst of the dense foliage. Their nesting place is by preference at the junction of several forking branches. The male goes forth and gathers from neighboring trees, never from the ground, the building material of dry twigs. If he sees a dead twig attached to the branch on which he is perching, he seizes it with his claws, sometimes with the beak, and tries to break it either by leaning on it with all his weight or by pulling it toward him. Possessed of his prize, he returns at once to his mate, who contents herself with putting the materials into place without taking part in getting them. In building the nest, therefore, the male is the worker and the female the architect; but an architect without talent, we must admit, for the structure is nothing but a mass of intertwined sticks without lining of feathers and flock, and, worse still, without firmness. Hence it is not unusual for this nest to fall to pieces before the brood has taken its flight; fortunately the strong branches on which it rests save the young ones from a disastrous fall.

"Wild and mistrustful, the wood-pigeon has never been willing to accept the calculated hospitality of the pigeon-house; it

DOMESTIC PIGEON

prefers the perilous life of the woods to the full-fed existence of servitude. This is the wild pigeon that frequently falls before the hunter's fire. In certain defiles of the Pyrenees it is caught with large nets, hundreds at a time. The rock-pigeon, on the contrary, has from time immemorial been dependent on man; and in return for the shelter of the pigeon-house which protects it from birds of prey it has been willing to forget so completely the rocks where it first nested that to-day one seldom finds, at least in our country, any wild pairs.

"Not all our pigeons, however, show the same degree of tameness; far from it. Some, voluntary captives rather than real prisoners, are faithful to the pigeon-house only as long as they find suitable food in the neighboring fields, whither they go in flocks. If the house is not to their liking, or if food is lacking, they seek another abode, the more adventurous sometimes even returning to the wild life. The others, thoroughly enslaved, have completely lost their desire for independence. Seldom do they leave their roof, and some are such stay-at-homes that the most pressing hunger could not make them go out and try to find a little food for themselves in the neighboring furrows. Food must always be given them, for they are incapable of procuring it themselves.

"Those first mentioned, the pigeons that venture afield and find food for themselves, are called rock-pigeons, after the wild pigeon whose ways, and frequently whose plumage, they have retained in part. They are also known as flighty pigeons (*fuyards*), either on account of their occasional distant expeditions, or because they sometimes take flight from the pigeon-house and never return. They are the least costly to raise, but they are small and not very productive, as they lay only two or three times a year. The second kind, those that scarcely ever leave the pigeon-cote and cannot do without our care, are called cotepigeons. Their maintenance costs more because they must be fed all the year round; but in compensation they do not ravage the neighboring harvests, which cannot be said of the rock-pigeons;

POUTER PIGEON

and beside they are much more productive, their periods of laying numbering as many as ten a year. Modified from the earliest times by man's intervention, the cote-pigeon includes a number of varieties in which the traits of the primitive species are often no longer recognizable. Let us mention some of these.

"First of all are the pigeons with feathered legs and feet, looking as if they wore gaiters. This growth of feathers reaches to the very tips of the claws, forming a cumbersome and unsightly sort of footgear which is found to be due to captivity, the wild bird never having anything of the kind. Then come the pouter pigeons, which have the faculty of swallowing air and inflating the crop in a large ball, so that the base of the neck seems to be affected with the deformity known as goiter. That is their way of showing off: the larger the ball, the prouder they are of their figure."

"What a queer idea," Emile exclaimed, "to think it improves one's looks to have a frightful goiter or to wear those feathered leggings that trail in the mud and interfere with walking!"

JACOBINS

"A life of idleness, my friend, engenders many caprices: examples abound in man even more than in pigeons. But let us get on; these things do not concern us.

"Now, here are some pigeons that have their heads adorned with a crown of feathers, are shod like the preceding, and imitate in their cooing the roll of a drum."

"Then they ought to be called, from the roll of the drum, drummer-pigeons," declared Emile.

"You have hit it exactly: that is precisely their name. Here are others with trailing wings, tail erect and expanded like a fan, and the body in an almost continual state of trembling. You would say they had a fever. The spread tail gives them the name of fan-tails, while from their ceaseless shaking they are sometimes called shakers. Ruffled pigeons have the neck encircled with a ruff of disordered feathers. Jacobins wear a sort of hood resembling a monk's cowl. The turbit carries on the nape of its neck a tuft of feathers thrown back and hollowed out like a shell. Tumblers are remarkable for their strange evolutions in the air: in mid-flight they will suddenly let themselves fall and turn a somersault as if shot in the wing. This recreation is their favorite pastime."

"The pleasure of a vertical fall," remarked Jules, "accompanied by a somersault, must carry some fear with it. Perhaps that is what gives zest to this exercise."

"But the pigeon pulls up in time?" queried Emile.

"Whenever it wishes to," his uncle replied, "it brings to an end its downward hurtling from these airy heights, ordinary flying is resumed, and presently the tumbles begin again finer than ever. Here let us pause, without exhausting the list of varieties, amounting to twenty-four, counting only the principal ones. These few examples show you sufficiently what diversity pigeon-house life has stamped on the form, habits, and plumage of the primitive bird.

"All pigeons, wild as well as tame, lay never more than two eggs to a hatching, from which generally spring brother and sister. The cares of brooding are shared by the father and mother alike, a practice found in no other tame bird. In the morning, when hunger makes itself felt, the female calls the male by a peculiar cooing and invites him to come and take her place on the eggs, which he does with alacrity. About three or four o'clock in the afternoon the rôles change. If the pigeon which until then has remained on the nest does not see its mate coming, there follows an anxious search, with admonitory cooings and, in case of need, admonitory peckings; and the laggard is brought back to the serious business of brooding. But as a rule the mother is irreproachably punctual; she returns to the nest at the hour agreed upon and does not leave it again until the next morning. Incubation takes seventeen or eighteen days.

"The little ones are born naked, blind, ungraceful. The father and mother, sometimes one, sometimes the other, feed them from the beak. This beak-feeding method of the pigeons is exceptional and deserves special consideration. I need not tell you how other birds feed their brood; any one that has ever raised a sparrow will know that."

"The little sparrow," Jules hastened to explain, "opens its beak as wide as it can and the parents put into it the food they have brought, just as I put a grasshopper into it, or a piece of a cherry, or a soaked bread-crumb."

"Jules forgets," said Emile, "that it is well to tap the little bird on the tail to excite its appetite and make it open its beak."

"Emile's improvement is not indispensable," Uncle Paul replied. "If it is hungry the bird will open its beak without being asked. Into this beak that gapes so wide the parents put the point of theirs and drop whatever prize they have found; but if the little bird is very young the father and mother begin by half-digesting in their own stomach the food destined for the little one. Then they put their beak into the little one's and disgorge the nutritious pap that they have prepared.

"Well, pigeons do exactly the reverse: it is the father and mother that gape, and the little ones that plunge their beak deep down into the throat of the parent bird. The latter is then seized with a convulsion of the stomach accompanied by a rapid trembling of the wings and body. Little plaintive cries denote that the operation is perhaps not quite painless. From the crop thus done violence to, the half-digested nutritive matter comes up in a jet that passes into the half-open beak of the nursling. Twice a day the little pigeons receive their food in this way; twice a day, but no more, so painful to the nurses seems this mode of feeding from beak to beak."

"I should think," said Jules, "that the parents would feel rather uncomfortable when the young pigeon tickles their throat, deep down, with its beak. If we can judge by what would happen to us, the stomach would rebel and would throw up its contents painfully."

"That is apparently the way of it. The disgorged food is a pap of seeds all ground up fine in the crop; but for the first three or four days after hatching a special food is given, fine and strengthening, suited to the weakness of the little one. It is a white substance, almost liquid, having the appearance of real milk. It does not come entirely from digested food; for the most part it consists of a sort of milk-food that is distilled by the stomach on this occasion only. So for the first days of the brood's rearing the pigeons have, deep down in the throat, a sort of milk factory, or what one might call the equivalent of an udder."

"That reminds me," Jules interposed, "of a joke common enough among us fellows. When we want to gull some poor innocent, we tell him that pigeons suck. This jest comes nearer the truth than is commonly thought. Pigeons do not suck the breast, it is true, but it might well enough be said that they are suckled, since what they are fed on has so much resemblance to milk."

"Little pigeons stay in the nest a long time," resumed Uncle

Paul. "Entirely covered with feathers and almost as large as their parents, they still continue to receive parental care. To induce them to shift for themselves and give up their place when the time for a new laying approaches, some cuffs have to be given to these spoiled children that are so reluctant to leave home. But at last they consent, though not without returning from time to time to torment the mother with their lamentations and to beg her for something to eat. The father, less weak on the side of his affections, thenceforth receives these importunate lazy-bodies with a peck of the beak.

"Let us consider certain other details of the pigeon's habits. I will not tell you, these things being pretty well known to you, of the cooings of the pigeon when it puffs out its throat, of its ceremonious salutations, its bowing to the very ground, its pirouettes when it shows off before its mate. I shall interest you more by acquainting you with its gregarious instinct, which impels it to assemble in immense flocks when it travels, in its wild state, to find food."

CHAPTER XVI

A STORY FROM AUDUBON[4]

" **H**ERE IS what we are told on this subject by the celebrated ornithologist, Audubon, whom I have already quoted in describing to you the habits of the turkey as it is found in its free state in the great forests of its native land.

" 'The passenger pigeon, or, as it is usually named in America, the wild pigeon, moves with extreme rapidity, propelling itself by quickly repeated flaps of the wing, which it brings more or less near the body, according to the degree of velocity which is required...

" 'This great power of flight is seconded by as great a power of vision, which enables them, as they travel at that swift rate, to inspect the country below, discover their food with facility, and thus obtain the object for which their journey has been undertaken. This I have also proved to be the case, by having observed them, when passing over a sterile part of the country, or one scantily furnished with food suited to them, keep high in the air, flying with an extended front, so as to enable them to survey hundreds of acres at once. On the contrary, when the land is richly covered with food, or the trees abundantly hung with mast, they fly low, in order to discover the part most plentifully supplied...

" 'The multitudes of wild pigeons in our woods are astonishing. Indeed, after having viewed them so often, and under so many circumstances, I even now feel inclined to pause, and assure myself that what I am going to relate is fact. Yet I have

4   Audubon's narrative ("Ornithological Biography," vol. I, pp. 319–324) is here reproduced with greater accuracy than the French writer chose to observe. The omissions indicated occur in the French, but are not there indicated.—*Translator.*

seen it all, and that too in the company of persons who, like myself, were struck with amazement.

" 'In the autumn of 1813, I left my house at Henderson, on the banks of the Ohio, on my way to Louisville. In passing over the Barrens a few miles beyond Hardensburgh, I observed the pigeons flying from northeast to southwest, in greater number than I thought I had ever seen them before, and feeling an inclination to count the flocks that might pass within the reach of my eye in one hour, I dismounted, seated myself on an eminence, and began to mark with my pencil, making a dot for every flock that passed. In a short time finding the task which I had undertaken impracticable, as the birds poured in in countless multitudes, I rose, and counting the dots then put down, found that one hundred and sixty-three had been made in twenty-one minutes. I traveled on, and still met more the farther I proceeded. The air was literally filled with pigeons; the light of noonday was obscured as by an eclipse; the dung fell in spots, not unlike melting flakes of snow; and the continued buzz of wings had a tendency to lull my senses to repose.

" 'Whilst waiting for dinner at Young's inn, at the confluence of Salt River with the Ohio, I saw, at my leisure, immense legions still going by, with a front reaching from beyond the Ohio on the west, and the beech-wood forests directly on the east of me. Not a single bird alighted, for not a nut or acorn was that year to be seen in the neighborhood. They consequently flew so high, that different trials to reach them with a capital rifle proved ineffectual; nor did the reports disturb them in the least. I cannot describe to you the extreme beauty of their aërial evolutions, when a hawk chanced to press upon the rear of a flock. At once, like a torrent, and with a noise like thunder, they rushed into a compact mass, pressing upon each other toward the center. In these almost solid masses, they darted forward in undulating and angular lines, descended and swept close over the earth with inconceivable velocity, mounted perpendicularly so as to resemble a vast column, and, when high, were seen wheeling and twisting within their continued lines, which then resembled the coils of a gigantic serpent.

" 'Before sunset I reached Louisville, distant from Hardensburgh fifty-five miles. The pigeons were still passing in undiminished numbers, and continued to do so for three days in succession. The people were all in arms. The banks of the Ohio were crowded with men and boys, incessantly shooting at the pilgrims, which there flew lower as they passed the river. Multitudes were thus destroyed. For a week or more, the population fed on no other flesh than that of pigeons, and talked of nothing but pigeons. The atmosphere, during this time, was strongly impregnated with the peculiar odor which emanates from the species...

" 'It may not, perhaps, be out of place to attempt an estimate of the number of pigeons contained in one of those mighty flocks, and of the quantity of food daily consumed by its members... Let us take a column of one mile in breadth, which is far below the average size, and suppose it passing over us without interruption for three hours, at the rate mentioned above of one mile in the minute. This will give us a parallelogram of 180 miles by 1, covering 180 square miles. Allowing two pigeons to the square yard, we have 1,115,136,000 pigeons in one flock. As every pigeon daily consumes fully half a pint of food, the quantity necessary for supplying this vast multitude must be 8,712,000 bushels per day.

" 'As soon as the pigeons discover a sufficiency of food to entice them to alight, they fly round in circles, reviewing the country below. During their evolutions, on such occasions, the dense mass which they form exhibits a beautiful appearance, as it changes its direction, now displaying a glistening sheet of azure, when the backs of the birds come simultaneously into view, and anon suddenly presenting a mass of rich deep purple. They then pass lower, over the woods, and for a moment are lost among the foliage, but again emerge, and are seen gliding aloft. They now alight, but the next moment, as if suddenly alarmed, they take to wing, producing by the flappings of their wings a noise like the roar of distant thunder, and sweep through the forests to see if danger is near. Hunger, however, soon brings them to the ground. When alighted, they are seen industriously throwing up the withered leaves in quest of the fallen mast. The rear ranks are continually rising, passing over the main body, and alighting in front, in such rapid succession, that the whole flock seems still on wing. The quantity of ground thus swept is astonishing, and so completely has it been cleared that the gleaner who might follow in their rear would find his labor completely lost. While feeding, their avidity is at times so great that in attempting to swallow a large acorn or nut, they are seen gasping for a long while, as if in the agonies of suffocation.

" 'On such occasions, when the woods are filled with these pigeons, they are killed in immense numbers, although no apparent diminution ensues... As the sun begins to sink beneath the horizon, they depart *en masse* for the roosting-place...

" 'Let us now inspect their place of nightly rendezvous. One of these curious roosting-places, on the banks of the Green River in Kentucky, I repeatedly visited. It was, as is always the case, in a portion of the forest where the trees were of great magnitude, and where there was little underwood... My first view of it was about a fortnight subsequent to the period when they had made choice of it, and I arrived there nearly two hours before sunset. Few pigeons were then to be seen, but a great number of persons, with horses and wagons, guns and ammunition, had already established themselves on the borders. Two farmers from the vicinity of Russelsville, distant more than a hundred miles, had driven upwards of three hundred hogs to be fattened on the pigeons which were to be slaughtered. Here and there the people employed in plucking and salting what had already been procured, were seen sitting in the midst of large piles of these birds. The dung lay several inches deep, covering the whole extent of the roosting-place, like a bed of snow. Many trees two feet in diameter, I observed, were broken off at no great distance from the ground, and the branches of many of the largest and tallest had given way, as if the forest had been swept by a tornado. Everything proved to me that the number of birds resorting to this part of the forest must be immense beyond conception. As the period of their arrival approached, their foes anxiously prepared to receive them. Some were furnished with iron pots containing sulphur, others with torches of pine knots, many with poles, and the rest with guns. The sun was lost to our view, yet not a pigeon had arrived. Everything was ready, and all eyes were gazing on the clear sky, which appeared in glimpses amidst the tall trees. Suddenly there burst forth a general cry of "Here they come!" The noise which they made, though yet distant, reminded me of a hard gale at sea, passing through the rigging of a close-reefed vessel. As the birds arrived and passed over me, I felt a current of air that surprised me. Thousands were soon knocked down by the pole-men. The birds continue to pour in. The fires were lighted, and a magnificent, as well as wonderful and almost terrifying sight, presented itself. The pigeons, arriving by thousands, alighted everywhere, one above another, until solid masses as large as hogsheads were formed on the branches all round. Here and there the perches gave way under the weight with a crash, and falling to the ground, destroyed hundreds of the birds beneath, forcing down the dense groups with which every stick was loaded. It was a scene of uproar and confusion. I found it quite useless to speak, or even to shout to those persons who were nearest to me. Even the reports of the guns were seldom heard, and I was made aware of the firing only by seeing the shooters reloading.

" 'No one dared venture within the line of devastation. The hogs had been penned up in due time, the picking up of the dead and wounded being left for the next morning's employment. The pigeons were constantly coming, and it was past midnight before I perceived a decrease in the number of those that arrived. The uproar continued the whole night... Toward the approach of day, the noise in some measure subsided, long before objects were distinguishable, the pigeons began to move off in a direction quite different from that in which they had arrived the evening before, and at sunrise all that were able to fly had disappeared. The howlings of the wolves now reached our ears, and the foxes, lynxes, cougars, bears, racoons, opossums, and polecats were seen sneaking off, whilst eagles and hawks of different species, accompanied by a crowd of vultures, came to supplant them, and enjoy their share of the spoil.

" 'It was then that the authors of all this devastation began their entry amongst the dead, the dying, and the mangled. The pigeons were picked up and piled in heaps, until each had as many as he could possibly dispose of, when the hogs were let loose to feed on the remainder.'

"Here ends Audubon's story. What do you think of it, my friends?"

"I think," Jules replied, "that those flocks of pigeons darkening the sky and taking several days to pass over are the most astonishing thing I have ever heard of about birds."

"And I," said Emile, "am still thinking of that shower of dung that falls from the sky, as thick as flakes of snow in winter, when the pigeons are flying over. Everywhere they fly the ground is whitened with this singular shower."

"And those trees breaking under the pigeons' weight," Louis exclaimed; "those three hundred pigs let loose to surfeit on what the hunters have left—all that would seem incredible to me if Uncle Paul had not assured us it was so."

"It's a great pity," sighed Emile, "that we have no such flocks of pigeons here. If they are knocked down with nothing but a pole, as we knock down apples and nuts, I would undertake to bag a fine lot myself."

"Would you also," his uncle asked him, "undertake to find food for the pigeons, when for a single day's supply for one of their flocks it takes from eight to nine million bushels of seeds? You see well enough that such multitudes would be calamitous: the entire harvest of a province would scarcely be enough to fill the crops of these ravenous birds. Such flocks require vast tracts of woodland not exploited by man, such as America had sixty years ago, in Audubon's time. But to-day, in that country, as civilization extends its boundaries the primeval forests disappear and give place to cultivated fields. Food becoming scarce, pigeons also become scarce; and it is doubtful whether one could ever again witness such prodigious scenes as formerly."

CHAPTER XVII

A SUPPOSITION

"LET US suppose ourselves, my friends, in the heart of a desert country, left to shift for ourselves, without any of the resources that come with civilization. To defend life and procure food are our constant great care. Around us extend endless dark woods where roar, howl, bellow a thousand ferocious animals that would tear us to pieces with their claws or quarter us with their horns if they took us by surprise. To shelter ourselves from their attack, we have to choose between the refuge of a grotto, the mouth of which we close with fragments of rock rolled painfully into place, and the hollow trunk of an old tree, or, better, its large branches, if we can manage to climb up to them."

"It is the story of Robinson Crusoe on his Island," Emile interrupted.

"Not quite. I am supposing our state much worse than his. Robinson Crusoe had at his disposal a quantity of things saved from the shipwreck—tools of all kinds, formidable weapons, guns, powder, and shot. We have nothing, absolutely nothing but our ten fingers."

"Not even a knife to cut a stick with?" asked Emile.

"Not even a knife."

"Rather an unpleasant situation," remarked Louis; "and all the more so as we couldn't stay shut up all the time. We should have to leave our grotto to procure food, and then beware of the wolves and all the dangerous creatures in the wood."

"Nothing imparts courage like the terrible need of food. We should start out, then, armed with some stones and with a stick clumsily broken off with our hands. If the wild beast runs at us we shall do our best to knock it down."

"But what if we don't succeed?" was Emile's query.

"In that case we are done for: we shall become its prey."

"To tell the truth, Uncle, in spite of the pleasure the reading of Robinson Crusoe on his Island gave me, I prefer this trip through the woods to be simply a supposition on your part rather than a reality."

"Emile is not the only one of that opinion," declared Jules. "When I have nothing to defend myself with I don't like those woods where there are wolves and still worse things."

"I continue my supposition. Hunger drives us and we start. I assume that heaven favors us and that no serious danger comes to disturb us in our hunt for something to keep us from starving. If we are on the seashore we shall catch shell-fish; if inland, we shall gather berries from the brambles and sloes from the thicket. If we hunt long enough we may perhaps find a handful or two of hazel-nuts. That will be our dinner, which will beguile our hunger for a while without satisfying it."

"I should think so," exclaimed Emile. "Berries and sloes, and nothing else—a sorry feast! I'd rather have a crust of bread, no matter how hard."

"So had I. But the crust of bread means cultivated fields, the husbandman, the harvester, the miller, and the baker; it presupposes an advanced civilization, whereas we are in a wilderness. We must do without the crust of bread. If, however, you find something better than berries and sloes, I will gladly give up the detestable fruit."

"Since the woods where you suppose us to be," said Jules, "are full of all sorts of animals, there ought to be game in abundance."

"Yes, indeed, game is there in plenty."

"Well, then; let us hunt it, and then we will light a fire and I will see to roasting what we have got. That will be much better than horrid sloes, sour enough to set your teeth on edge."

"That is a good idea, but I see two great difficulties: first, we must catch the game; secondly, we must make a fire."

"Making a fire is the easiest thing in the world," Emile

declared. "All we need is a match, as long as there is plenty of wood."

"You forget, my friend, that there are no matches. We have nothing, absolutely nothing."

"That is true. What shall we do, then? If I remember right, Robinson Crusoe too had no end of trouble in making a fire. He finally found a tree that had been set on fire by lightning."

"Would you wait for a thunderstorm to come and set fire to a corner of the forest? Long before that we should have time to starve, for it is very seldom that lightning starts a fire."

"Must we, then, give up the roast that I was proposing?" Jules asked.

"Before giving it up we might try the means employed by certain savage tribes for obtaining fire. The operator takes his seat on the ground and holds between his feet a piece of soft and very dry wood in which a small cavity has been hollowed; then he twirls rapidly between his hands a stick of hard wood with its point in the cavity. As a result of this energetic friction the soft wood becomes heated at the bottom of the hollow, and ends by catching fire. Success necessitates, it is true, a rapidity of friction and a skill that certainly we should not be able to acquire without a long apprenticeship; but I pass over that difficulty and assume that we have a fire.

"Now for the game. A hare will be a great plenty for us. This animal abounds, and we should be very unskilful if we did not soon find one curling its mustaches with its velvety paw under a tuft of broom. But the hare has quick ears and sharp eyes. Long before we can get within striking distance it hears and sees us, and decamps. Run after it now if you think you can catch it."

"For my part," said Jules, "I won't undertake it."

"With the weapons we possess," Louis admitted, "with only our sticks and stones, the chase seems to me out of the question: all game of whatever sort would foil our attempts by its vigilance and rapid flight."

"Are you all thoroughly convinced of it?" asked Uncle Paul.

"I certainly am," replied Jules. "Not being able to match the game in fleetness of foot, we shall always come back from the hunt empty-handed."

"That's plain enough," Emile assented.

"Then let us be content with sloes, and if hunger presses too hard we must tighten our belts. Since, too, at any moment, some furious wild beast might pounce upon us and devour us, let us lose no time in getting back to reflect on our sad plight.

"Our wretched state is indeed lamentable. Incessant hunger torments us, despite the extreme abundance of game, which would be an invaluable resource for us, but which unfortunately we cannot turn to account. If, to stay our hunger, we go in search of wild fruit, a thousand dangers await us. We may fall into clutches that no stone will intimidate and no sticks cause to relax. We are without provisions, defenseless. A terrible alternative awaits us: to die of hunger or be devoured by those that are stronger than we."

"Such a Robinson Crusoe life I should not care for," declared Emile.

"Now let us suppose one thing more: Heaven takes pity on our distress and, to extricate us from our difficulty, offers us the aid of one of our domestic animals, whichever one we choose to name. Which will you ask for, children?"

"My stomach is so tired of sloes," Emile replied, "and my teeth are so set on edge with this sour fruit that I think I should choose a sheep. Some cutlets broiled over live coals would make up to me for my dinners on wild berries."

"But the sheep will soon be eaten up," objected Jules, "and then back you go once more to the sloes. I should prefer a goat. Every evening it would come back to the grotto with its big udders swollen with milk. In this way I should be sure of food with some variety, because I could make butter and cheese out of the milk."

"Your goat will perhaps not last so long as Emile's sheep. It must go out to get pasturage, and who can say that it will not be devoured by wolves in the woods the first time it ventures forth?"

"I will keep careful watch over it."

"But who will watch over you, my friend? Who will protect you?"

"That's so. Let us give up the goat and choose a cow. She is strong enough to defend herself with her horns."

"If one wolf is not enough, they will bring to the attack two, three, ten, and the cow will be overcome."

"The horse, mule, or donkey, in our supposed circumstances, cannot be very useful to us. I leave them out. With a hen I should at least have an egg a day."

"A poor dependence if one hen's egg has to be divided between four. Besides, what grain have you for feeding your hen? And how about the fox—will he leave her in peace?"

"The pig is still left," was Jules's final suggestion. "But there we have the same difficulty as with Emile's sheep: once the animal is eaten, hunger overtakes us again. I leave the choice to some one cleverer than I."

"My choice," said Louis, "would be the dog, without a moment's hesitation."

"What a queer choice!" cried Emile. "The dog will lick our hands in sign of friendship, he will bark in front of the grotto, and he will gnaw the bone we throw to him. But as there are no bones in our dinners of sloes, the poor beast will die of hunger without being of any use to us whatever."

"I can find use for him," replied Louis, "and it is a great one. With the dog, game, even the nimblest hare, will be caught in the chase, with such ambuscade as we can contrive on our part, and food will be assured for all—flesh for us, bones for the dog. Accompanied by him, we can go wherever we please, without the continual fear of being attacked any moment. If a wolf appears, our vigorous companion will cope with it, seize it by the nape of the neck, and give us a chance to lay on with the cudgel."

"Louis is right," declared Jules; "I vote for the dog."

"The reasons Louis gives," Emile chimed in, "are too clear to admit of any but a unanimous vote in the dog's favor."

"Yes, my friend," his uncle rejoined, "unanimous, even to the vote of your Uncle Paul, who for some moments has been making you live Robinson Crusoe's life in imagination for the express purpose of leading you to decide for yourselves in favor of the dog.

"In the early days, centuries and centuries ago, man lived mostly by the chase, as to-day the last surviving savage tribes still live. The raising of herds, the tilling of the soil, the manufacture of goods, all were unknown. Wild animals, hunted in the forests with stone weapons and pointed sticks, furnished almost the only resource. Their flesh gave food, their skins provided clothing. To catch the game, a fleet-footed auxiliary in the chase was necessary; to keep these dangerous animals in a proper state of awe, a courageous defender was needed by man. This auxiliary, this defender, and, best of all, this friend, devoted even to death, was the dog; a gift from Heaven to help man in his pitiful beginnings. With the aid of the dog, life was rendered less perilous, food more assured. Leisure followed, and from being a hunter man became a herdsman. The herd was formed, at first very indocile and at the slightest lack of watchfulness taking again to the wild life of old. Its keeping was confided to the dog, which, posted on some rising ground of the pasture, its scent to the wind and ear on the watch, followed the herd with vigilant eye and rushed to bring back the runaways or to drive off some evil-intentioned beast. Thanks to the dog, the herd gave abundance—milk and its products, flesh for food, and warm wool for clothing. Then, relieved from the terrible anxiety concerning daily provision, man took it into his head to dig in the earth and make it produce grain. Agriculture sprang into being, and with it, little by little, civilization. By the very force of circumstances, therefore, man in all countries is at first a hunter, later he becomes a herdsman, and ends by being an agriculturist. The dog is absolutely necessary to him, first for hunting, then for watching and defending the herd. Of all our domestic animals, accordingly, the dog is the earliest on record and the one that has rendered us the greatest service."

CHAPTER XVIII

A FRAGMENT OF HISTORY

"I UNDERSTAND," began Jules, "the usefulness of the dog to a man left to his own resources in a desert country in the midst of woods. With the help of this courageous friend he procures food and defends himself against animals that endanger his life. But in our countries around here, it seems to me, that wretched sort of existence can never have been known."

"In our countries things took their course just as everywhere else," his uncle replied. "Even in places now enjoying the most advanced civilization, man began with an era of misery of which it will be not unprofitable to give you some idea; then you will see better from what depths of barbarism the dog's services have helped to raise us.

"In the earliest times of which history has preserved some vague record, what was one day to be the beautiful country of France was a wild country covered with immense forests, where, living by the chase, there wandered some few tribes of Gaels; for thus the first inhabitants of our country were called. They were men of low stature, broad shoulders, white skin, long blond hair, and blue or green eyes. For weapons they had stone axes and knives, arrows tipped with fish-bones or a sharp piece of flint. Fastened to the left arm, they carried for defense a long and narrow wooden shield; with the right hand they brandished, as an offensive weapon, sometimes a stake hardened in the fire, sometimes a heavy bludgeon or club. For the perilous passage of rivers and of ocean inlets they had fragile little boats made of wicker, plaited as in our baskets, but covered on the outside with the hide of a wild ox to exclude the water."

AUROCHS

"But those are the weapons and boats of savages!" interposed Emile.

"Without doubt, my friend; and, equally without doubt, the first Gaels, ancestors of ours though they were, were veritable savages, differing hardly at all from those of our own day. They lived mainly by the chase, herds and agriculture being for ages unknown to them. In their gloomy forests, damp and cold, using only their poor weapons of stone and pointed sticks, they attacked a terrible wild ox, the aurochs or urus, which is now almost extinct. This ox, nearly as large as the elephant, had enormous horns, a mane of curly wool on its head and neck, beard under its throat, a deep, hoarse bellow, and a ferocious look. Its extraordinary strength and indomitable fury made it the terror of the forests."

"And weren't they afraid," asked Louis, "to attack this fearful creature with their stone hatchets?"

"They fell upon the furious animal without other weapons than pointed stakes and stone hatchets; but they had the help of powerful dogs that seized the beast by the ears and got the mastery of it. The urus held the place of honor among game. The valiant huntsman who killed it had for a cup, at the banqueting board, one of the animal's monstrous horns."

"What did they drink from those horns?" Emile inquired.

"At first clear water from the fountains; then, after the race had made some little progress, an intoxicating drink called cervisia, made from fermented barley. That was the forerunner of our beer."

"Can it be," asked Louis, "that our peaceful ox came from that intractable beast, the urus, as you call it?"

"Not at all. The domestic ox is a different kind altogether, originating in Asia and not in the ancient forests of Europe. In our day there is hardly a urus left. Hunted century after century by growing civilization, the formidable ox with a mane has long since deserted these regions to take refuge in the solitudes of the North. But these solitudes in turn have been taken possession of by man, and the aurochs has found its last retreat in the swampy forests of Lithuania in Poland. There a few pairs still live in perfect security, for it is expressly forbidden to kill them."

"And why do they keep those ugly oxen?" was Emile's next question.

"They are not numerous enough to do any harm, and it would really be a pity to exterminate the last one of these animals that afforded our ancestors such joy in the hunt.

"The Gaels hunted the elk also, a kind of large stag the size of a horse or even larger. The elk has under its throat a kind of goiter or fleshy pendant; its fur is short, stiff, and ash-colored; its horns, called antlers, are wide-spreading and flattened, and they extend in a vast triangular expanse with a deeply indented outline; the weight of each antler may amount to as much as thirty kilograms. That must, as you see, be a fine specimen of game: an animal that bears on its forehead, without effort, an ornament weighing a hundred weight and more."

"A stag as large as a horse must really be a noble prize for a hunter," said Louis.

"Without his companion, the dog," Jules put in, "man certainly could not have caught such an animal in the chase."

"The elk," resumed Uncle Paul, "though common at that period in our forests, is found to-day only in the wooded marshes of Russia and Sweden. It also inhabits, and in greater numbers, the northern part of America.

"You will notice that these two animals, the aurochs and the elk, which were formerly spread over our own regions, are now settled in climates much colder than ours. The few aurochs that have survived the general destruction of their species graze in the woods of Lithuania; the elk inhabits the extreme north of Europe and America. Transported to our warmer climate, they would soon perish, being unable to endure a temperature too high for them. Since they flourished here in ancient times, the climate of our regions must at that distant epoch have been colder, more severe, than it is to-day. Immense forests, always damp and full of shade, were doubtless one of the causes of this more rigorous climate. When these woods, impenetrable to the rays of the sun, were felled by the ax of nascent civilization, the soil warmed up freely and the temperature rose. But then the aurochs and elk, harassed besides by man, who explored all their retreats, fled a country too warm for them and took refuge in the cold fogs of the North.

"Despite this change of climate some animals have remained with us the same as in the old time of the Gaels. In our day the same wolf still howls with hunger in the woods, the same bears haunt the mountain caves, the same wild boar, beset by a pack of hounds in some bushy thicket, pokes its bristly snout out of the brake, sharpens its tusks, and gnashes its teeth as formerly when a band of tattooed hunters flung their stone hatchets at its head."

"Those first inhabitants of France were tattooed like island savages?" asked Jules.

"Yes, my friend. They decorated their bodies with designs in blue, a pigment extracted from a plant called woad; and to make the decoration ineffaceable they forced the coloring matter into the skin by pricking themselves till the blood flowed.

"This practice, called tattooing, is still found in our day in many countries, among tribes unacquainted with the benefits of civilization. At the other end of the world, at our antipodes, the natives of New Zealand are most expert in this kind of decoration. With a sharp awl, impregnated with divers colors, they prick themselves with little stabs and trace, point by point, fanciful designs which turn their skin into veritable living embroidery. Red and blue spirals turn in inverse directions from both sides of the forehead and continue in rose-work on the cheeks. Little palm-leaves spread over the nostrils; a sun darts its rays all around the chin; two or three little stars give a blue tinge to the lower lip. The rest of the body is ornamented in the same lavish manner: fantastic animals cover the middle of the back; a tortoise pokes out its head and four feet in the hollow of the breast; the hands and feet, pricked in fine tracery patterns, look as if covered with open-work gloves and stockings. Our ancestors of the stone-hatchet age decorated themselves very much like this."

"Those poor New Zealanders," remarked Emile, "must hurt themselves dreadfully, disfiguring themselves like that."

"The operation is indeed most painful, and yet they bear it without a murmur. A single needle-prick makes us recoil; those rude savages remain unmoved while the tattoo artist punctures their bodies with his awl."

"Why do they submit to such a torture?"

"Chiefly that they may cut a more dashing figure, present a more formidable aspect, before the enemy. In certain archipelagoes of Polynesia we should find still stranger customs. One tribe, for example, gashes the face by removing narrow strips of skin so that the cicatrized wounds form various patterns in hideous little red weals. Others pass a small pointed stick through the cartilage of the nostrils; others make a large hole in the lower lip and set a shell in it.

"Had the ancient Gaels similar customs? It is quite possible; at least it is certain that they tattooed themselves with woad. Certain customs are sometimes so tenacious that after many centuries in the midst of the most flourishing civilization tattooing has not entirely disappeared even with us. On the strong arms of some of our laborers are seen, any day, tattooed in blue, trade emblems and other devices. They are, without doubt, the survivals of primitive customs.

"The Gaels had long, silky hair, like flaxen tow, and they gave it a tinge of bright red by frequent washing in lime lye. Sometimes they smeared it with rancid grease and let it hang down over their shoulders in all its length; sometimes they gathered it above the forehead in a high tuft or mane, to make themselves look taller and to give themselves a more terrifying aspect."

"In a book of travels," said Jules, "I saw pictures of some

North American Indians with a tuft of hair like that on top of the head. The Gaels, then, had the same custom?"

"Yes, my child. Thousands of years apart, in the forests of the Old World and those of the New, the Gael and the Indian adopt the same head-dress, a coil of hair over the forehead. When he dresses for the combat, the Indian fastens to his top-knot of hair divers ornaments, such as the wing of a hawk, the claw of a leopard, the teeth of a bear. Thus doubtless the Gael likewise adorned his person when he made himself fine for the urus-hunt or for battle with some neighboring tribe.

"The Indian's top-knot is an audacious defiance, a horrible bravado. When the enemy is thrown to the ground, beaten down by a blow of the club, the conqueror seizes him by his top-knot, cuts the skin all round the head with the point of a sharp flint, then with a jerk pulls off the bleeding scalp all in one piece."

"Oh, how horrible!" cried Jules.

"This scalp is a trophy which he will dry in the smoke of his hut and will wear hanging from his waist as token of his exploit. His position in the tribe, his weight in the council, are proportioned to the number of scalps taken from the enemy. Now you understand the fierce bravado of the Indian with his top-knot of hair all gathered up and ready for the horrible operation. Let any one offer to touch it, and he will soon feel the weight of the wearer's club."

"I hope the Gaels did not have that abominable custom."

"They had one that was worse: they carried not only the scalp, but the whole head, which they dried in the sun, after nailing it by the ears to the entrance of the hut in the midst of hunting trophies, boars' heads and wolves' heads. Those were their titles of nobility."

"And we are descended from those frightful savages?"

"The tattooed Gaels with red hair, nailing the enemy's head to their door, are, as far back as history can show, the first inhabitants of our country; we count them as among our earliest ancestors. Some of their barbarous customs have come down to us, greatly modified, it is true. I have just given you an example, in tattooing; I give you another in the matter of trophies of the chase. After the manner of the ancient Gaels, it is still the custom in the country to nail to the big barn-doors wolves' and foxes' heads and the dead bodies of hawks and owls."

"Those who do that," said Louis, "little suspect to what horrible custom their practice is related."

"Your tattooed hunters interest me very much," Emile declared. "Their houses, dress, furniture—how about all those things?"

"In those wretched times a shelter under rocks, a natural excavation, a grotto, were the first dwelling-places. But there came a day when those wild retreats were found insufficient, and human ingenuity made its first attempts in the art of building. To provide oneself with a shelter was not enough; it was necessary above all to maintain an unremitting state of defense. The forests were overrun with formidable animals, and there was perpetual warfare between neighboring tribes. As a safeguard against surprise, wherever there were lakes, the houses were built on piling in the middle of the water.

"It must have taken a prodigious expenditure of energy for man, as yet so poorly provided with tools, to build these lake villages, or lacustrine villages, as they are called. With a stone ax the tree that was to be felled was laboriously girdled at the base, and then the application of fire completed the process. Whole days and perhaps the united efforts of a number of workers were necessary to obtain one joist such as a wood-cutter would now turn out with a few strokes of his steel ax. But with their tools of flint, hardly hitting the wood and falling to pieces with the slightest maladroit blow, it was an enormous undertaking for them. They were in about the same plight that our carpenters would be in if the latter were obliged to cut down and trim an oak with nothing but an old rusty knife. I leave you to imagine, then, the labor and patience expended in obtaining the thousands of joists needed in this piling. Apparently each head of a family furnished one as his share, which gave him the right to erect his hut on the common building-lot. At a later period, perhaps, in order to extend the area of the straggling village as the population increased, the furnishing of a new pile was required of each adult male inhabitant. It was the extraordinary contribution, the sacred debt, that he was obliged to pay once in his lifetime.

"The piles, pointed and hardened in the fire at one end, were dragged to the edge of the lake, where canoes of plaited wicker towed them to the chosen spot. There they were stood on end and driven into the soft mud until the tops were on a level with the water. Finally the spaces between the multitude of piles were filled with stones. The whole formed an artificial islet of great solidity, or rather a shoal submerged and covered with several feet of water. On the tops of the piles, just above the general level, cross-beams were laid, then boughs of trees, and on top of these beaten earth. Finally, on this artificial soil, beneath which circulated the waters of the lake, dwellings were erected.

"They were round or oval huts, made of a framework of interlacing branches and a layer of rich earth. A single opening, very low, through which one had to crawl, gave access to an interior, not unlike our baker's oven.

"The furnishing corresponded with the rudeness of the dwelling. Big tun-bellied pots of black clay variegated with grains of white sand held the provisions, which consisted of aurochs-flesh dried in the sun, beech-nuts, and hazel-nuts. These pots were rudely made by hand without any potter's wheel to give them a regular outline. Thick, misshapen, unsteady, they had an uneven surface and bore the finger-marks of those who had molded them. Some attempts at ornamentation appeared on the best jars, and took the form of a row of imprints made with the end of the thumb on the still soft clay, or a line of angular marks engraved with a thorn. The rest of the work was not less simple. To give our pottery, however slight its value, more consistency and hardness, we bake it in a very hot oven; we also coat it with a glaze to make it impermeable. The inhabitants of the lake villages were content to expose their pieces of wet clay to the rays of the sun until dry, without baking or glazing. Hence it was a sorry kind of pottery, good for the keeping of provisions, but incapable of holding water or of being used over the fire."

"How did they manage, then," asked Jules, "to get hot water and cook their food?"

"When one is unprovided with the invaluable saucepan, when one is without even those homely utensils that we think so little of, despite the inestimable service they render us, one imitates the Eskimos of Greenland, who cook their viands in a little skin bag."

"But that queer kind of pot would burn on the fire," asserted Emile.

"They are very careful not to put it on the fire. Stones are heated red-hot in the fire, and after they are thus heated they are popped into the little bag containing water and food to be cooked. After cooling off they are taken out to be reheated and dropped once more into the water, which finally boils. The result of such cooking is a mixture of soot, mud, ashes, and half-raw flesh; but with their hearty appetites the Eskimos are not over-particular. Besides, if they entertain a guest of distinction they begin by licking off with the tongue all the dirt on the pieces destined for him. Whoever should refuse to accept what was offered him after this extraordinary act of courtesy in cleaning it, would be regarded as an impolite, ill-bred person."

"Bah! the dirty things!" cried Emile. "I will take good care never to be one of their guests."

"And the tattooed hunters cooked in that way?" Jules inquired.

"For want of proper utensils they apparently employed similar means. But let us finish our inspection of the inside of the aquatic hut.

"The highest point in the roof is pierced for the passage of smoke from the fireplace situated in the center of the hut, between two stones on a bed of beaten earth, which prevents the floor, made of branches, from catching fire. On the walls are hung the hardwood tomahawk, flint hatchets, bone arrows, and the net of bark thongs, still damp from fishing in the lake and ornamented on the edges with round pierced stones. On the branching antlers of a stag the clothes are hung, consisting of leopards' and wolves' skins with the hair on. In the most sheltered corner rush mats and furs carpet the floor for the night's rest. Finally, in front of the door the little wicker boat bobs up and down. Into this boat its owners can step right from their threshold.

"The straggling village, in fact, instead of being built on a continuous artificial soil, is cut up into numerous passages of open water; the village streets are canals. To pass from one quarter to another, or merely to visit one's neighbor, one must go by water. So all day long there is a continual coming and going of boats from one group of huts to another. There is no less movement between the village and the shores of the lake, whither the men go a-hunting and whence they return with their boats laden with venison, when the aurochs or elk has succumbed to the combined exertions of men and dogs.

"Thus, in prehistoric times, were settlements established on the various lakes of France, and, still more, of Switzerland—lakes large enough to hold these villages by the hundred. To-day the fisherman whose line ripples their limpid waters sees in the blue depths, amid a great mass of stones, the tops of piles carbonized by the centuries, and large, bulging pieces of earthenware, which he breaks with his oar without suspecting their venerable origin. That is what is left us of the ancient lake villages."

CHAPTER XIX

THE JACKAL

"WHAT YOU have just told us, Uncle Paul," Jules remarked, "is not unlike what navigators tell us of the life of savages."

"Nevertheless," rejoined his uncle, "it is our own history, my friend; it is really a chapter of French history."

"I never read anything like it in my history-book."

"Your schoolbooks generally begin with the Frankish chief, Pharamond, at an epoch when civilization had already made considerable progress, and when agriculture and grazing had been known for a long time. My story goes back to a much earlier period, one almost lost in the darkness of the past, and shows us man in his painful beginnings, unskilled and almost wholly dependent on hunting for his food and clothing.

"In that state of extreme destitution in which the day's supply of food depended, above all, on fleetness of foot and quickness of scent, the dog was the most precious of acquisitions. With its aid, first the game fell more abundantly under the stone hatchet and flint-head arrow; then came the possibility of the herd, which, furnishing a reserve of food, freed man from the alternation of famine and abundance, and gave him leisure to devise means for the improvement of his condition. Then the ox was tamed, the horse mastered, the sheep domesticated, and finally came agriculture, preëminent source of our well-being. That is how the tattooed hunters of our country lost the barbarism of their habits and advanced from one stage of progress to another, until they became the cultivated race from which we are descended. First in Asia, then throughout all Europe, a similar development took place: everywhere the dog was the first and most valuable of man's conquests, and everywhere the dog has represented the first element of progress. Without the dog, there would be no such thing as human society, says an old book of the East, whence this most serviceable animal came. And the old book is a thousand times right, for without the dog the chase in old times would have been too little productive to satisfy the devouring hunger of a very thinly scattered population; without the dog, no herds or flocks, no assured food, and consequently no leisure, for the inexorable necessity of providing food would have occupied the whole time. Without leisure, no attempt at culture, no observations leading to the birth of science, no reflections bearing fruit in manufactures and commerce. The primitive mode of life was a hand-to-mouth existence, with a slice of broiled urus or elk to stay the cravings of hunger. A surfeit one day was followed by fasting the next; it all depended on the chances of the hunt. Hatchets continued to be fashioned out of stone, the tattooing of the body in blue went on, and at the entrance to the hut the enemy's head was still nailed as a horrible trophy of war."

"I see," said Louis, "how immensely useful the dog has been and still is to us; so I should like to know at what time and by whom this valuable animal was trained for our service."

"No one could give a satisfactory answer to that question. The taming of the dog goes back to the earliest times and all remembrance of it is lost. There is the same deep obscurity as to its origin and the wild species from which it is descended. Nowhere has the dog been seen by travelers in its primitive state, in a state of complete independence. If some dogs are found leading a wild life, they are runaways; that is to say, dogs that have fled from domestic life to live as they please in desert regions. Such are those that burrow and hunt for themselves in the vast plains of South America. They are certainly descended from domestic dogs carried thither by Europeans; for at the time of its discovery, nearly four centuries ago, the New World had no dogs. All that can be affirmed is that the dog came to us from Asia already trained for man's use. Apparently Asia made a gift to Europe of the oldest known domestic animals, such as the ox, the ass, and the hen.

Jackal

"On account of the almost infinite variety in respect to its coat, its shape, and its size, it is suspected that the dog is not derived from a single source but comes from various species that have been improved by man and profoundly modified in their characteristics by cross-breeding. Among these wild species to which is given the honor of being regarded as ancestors of the domestic dog, I will mention the jackal, which abounds in Africa as well as Asia.

"The jackal looks a little like the wolf, but is smaller and is harmless to man. Its coat is red, varied with white under the stomach and black on the back. It has a pointed muzzle and erect ears. Its timidity causes it to feed on the remnants left over by animals bolder and stronger than itself. When the gorged lion abandons its half-devoured prey, the jackals, crouching in the neighborhood and waiting until his lordship has finished, hasten up in companies to the disdained carcass and clean it to the bone. For the same reason the jackal frequents in troops the outskirts of villages and encampments in the hope of finding garbage and carrion. In the daytime it stays quietly in its den among the rocks, but at nightfall it issues forth in quest of food with a sort of sharp howling that continues all night. There is nothing so disagreeable as the nocturnal concert of a band of jackals prowling around dwellings. One of them begins with a cry something like *argee* in a very piercing and prolonged tone. Scarcely has it finished when a second takes up the refrain and improves upon it; then a third and a fourth, until the whole band has joined in, producing a veritable charivari composed of a mixed chorus of discordant howls. After this musical feat, solos are in order again, interspersed with choral productions;

and so it goes on until daybreak. Such is the infernal music that awaits the sleeper every night."

"Oh, what disagreeable neighbors!" exclaimed Jules. "If the dog had kept any of those detestable habits it would be a very troublesome animal, useful though it is."

"The dog shows not seldom, it must be admitted, a mania for making the night hideous; but it cannot be reproached with anything comparable to the jackal's concert. The dog has two cries, without counting those that are secondary. One of the two is natural, the howl; the other artificial, the bark. Is it necessary to point out to you the difference between the two?"

"I know what you mean, Uncle," Jules was quick to reply. "The dog howls when it gives a long, wild cry, so mournful and terrifying in the night; it barks when it gives those short, jerky yelps. It howls from fright, sadness, ennui; it barks with joy and pleasure."

"Yes, that is it. I told you, then, that howling is the dog's natural voice. In it can be found, but with a very different action of the throat and a less sharp tone, something of the jackal's cry. As for the bark, it is an artificial utterance; that is to say, it has been acquired. Dogs that have gone back to the wild state, as for example those of South America, can no longer bark. Deserters from civilization, they have lost the language and are reduced to their primitive howling, which they share with the jackal and the wolf."

"And how does a dog learn to bark when it is with us?"

"It learns by hearing its fellows, the other dogs, bark. If it were brought up far from its own kind, it would never know how to bark, any more than we could speak our language if we had never heard it spoken. Well, the jackal also can acquire the habit of barking by education. Placed in company with the dog, which by its example initiates it into a new language, it barks at first badly, then a little better, then well, and in a short time the scholar almost equals the master.

"The primitive species, if it really is the jackal, must have, as you see, undergone profound changes affecting even its most inveterate habits, to become the domestic dog. It must have lost its habit of nocturnal prowling, forgotten its predilection for concerts of ear-piercing cries, learned to bark, and, what is far more difficult, exchanged its timidity for boldness. Another improvement was indispensable. The jackal gives forth from all over its body a strong fishy smell. To become the companion of man and to live in his home, the animal had to be rid of this infection. That is what the progress of time has done almost completely: to-day the dog has scarcely any odor except when warm from rapid hunting; but it is likely, in view of its presumed origin, that in the beginning the dog was not precisely a bouquet of roses beside its master. Doubtless it was denied access to the hut, which it would have infected with its odor, and was relegated to a distant spot outside in the open air.

"Those are not all the jackal's defects. It is true the animal is easily tamed, but without acquiring the docility and attachment of the dog. When pressed by hunger, it is gentle and caressing toward the master who gives it something to eat; when satiated, it shows its teeth and tries to bite if any one reaches out to take hold of it. Children, whom dogs so love to play with, do not gain its confidence any more than grown people. Whoever should try to pull its tail in play would certainly get bitten."

"Our Medor has a much better disposition," said Emile; "the more pranks I play with him, the better he likes it. I'd a good deal rather play with him than with a stinking jackal."

"Medor owes his excellent qualities, particularly his honest, dogged patience, to the extraordinary pains taken during long centuries to improve his breed; but certainly the primitive dog must have been a pretty rough playmate for little boys. He did not allow any one to pull his mustache, did not give the paw, did not play dead with four legs in the air, did not wait for the command to jump and snap the crust of bread placed on the tip of his nose. The jackal, docile only when hungry, shows you what could be expected from Medor's surly ancestors."

"Then even with much care the tame jackal never acquires the dog's gentleness?" queried Louis.

"Never. Some, more tractable than others, grow a little more gentle, but without ever becoming entirely submissive. They always retain something of their primitive wildness and cannot be left wholly free without committing misdeeds or even running away from home."

"If thorough taming is impossible, I don't see how the dog can come from the jackal."

"Complete domestication does not take place so quickly as you think, my dear friend. A long succession of individuals is necessary, transmitting from one to another the desired aptitudes, and increasing them by turning to account such gain as may be noted in the best examples of each new generation. Let us assume that in ancient times man had taken into his keeping the half-tamed jackal, such as we could to-day possess ourselves of. However surly it may remain, the animal will be better after several years' education than it was at the beginning. With continued care the good qualities acquired, though weak, will, as we say of the snowball, increase by rolling. In fact it is a rule, as well with beasts as with us, that the son inherits the father's qualities, good or bad. Thus the jackal's little ones, brought up with man, will from their birth be half-tamed, as were their parents. As character is far from being the same in a whole family, some will be wilder, others more submissive. The first are rejected, the second kept, as soon as it is possible to recognize this diversity of disposition. Here, then, the sons, with continued training, become superior to the fathers. The same care, the same selection, in the third generation, will insure increased progress in the grandchildren. The acquired improvement will be transmitted by inheritance to the great-grandchildren, these will still further add to it, and it will be inherited by their descendants, or, if not by all, at least by some. These latter will be raised in preference to the others. However slight the progress from one generation to the next, it will continually be added to by the intervention of man who always selects for breeding purposes the most promising offspring, until, little by little, in course of time the beast that was intractable in the beginning at last becomes docile.

"This onward march, which is kept up by accumulating in

the animal, through inheritance, the qualities desired, by always picking out the individual possessing these qualities in the highest degree, is called selection, meaning choice or sorting. The method of selection, which to-day still renders the greatest service to the perfecting of species, has doubtless played an important part in the domestication of the dog; but that alone is not what has made the dog such as we now have him. The astonishing variety of dogs can only be explained by the multiplex origin of the animal and the crossing of the various breeds. I have just told you of one species, the common jackal, which is suspected to be one of the dog's ancestors. To finish what I have to say on this exceedingly obscure question, I will add a few words concerning a second species.

"There is found in the mountains of Abyssinia a jackal with very slender body, an arched abdomen, long and narrow head, long, upward-curling tail—in short, a veritable greyhound in every respect except that it has erect instead of drooping ears. Everything induces belief that this jackal is the progenitor of our greyhound.

"I will end with this conclusion of one of our most learned masters on the origin of domestic animals: 'Existing in great numbers in Asia, where, history tells us, the dog was first domesticated, jackals commonly live within reach of human habitations, to which they sometimes make their way of their own accord. They are eminently sociable, are easily tamed, and become attached to their masters. They associate freely with the dog. Finally, and this trait dispels my last lingering doubt as to their kinship, they resemble in the highest degree, both in shape and in color, and even in voice where they have learned to bark, the least modified of the canine species. In several countries the resemblance between jackals and dogs is so striking that it has led all travelers who have had an opportunity to compare these animals on the spot to the same conclusion: the jackal and the dog represent respectively the parent stock and the scion, and are to be found reunited again in various parts of Asia and Africa.' "

CHAPTER XX

THE CHIEF BREEDS OF DOGS

"LET US not dwell further on the dog's origin—a very obscure question, concerning which all that one can say is nothing but supposition, although more or less plausible. Let us turn to the study of the animal as found in a state of domestication.

"It would be hard to discover two dogs exactly alike. Were they of the same breed, the same shape and size, they would differ in coat, at least in some details. Three colors, red, white, and black, belong to the dog's coat; sometimes one alone for the whole body, sometimes all mixed, sometimes the three distributed in spots or in great splashes. If the coloring is varied, the spots are hardly ever arranged in order, but scattered by chance. There is want of symmetry in their distribution; or, in other words, on the two halves of the body, the right and left, the spots do not correspond. You might say the same of most domestic animals: you would nearly always note differences between two oxen, two horses, two goats, two cats; and would find that in the same animal both sides of the body are not exactly alike in the arrangement of the colors.

"It is just the reverse with wild animals: there is close resemblance between individuals of the same species, and symmetry of coloring on the two halves of the body. As one is, so are all, with very slight exceptions; as is the right side, so is the left. Whoever has seen one wolf has seen all wolves; whoever has seen from one side an animal with variegated coat has seen both sides. One of the most constant effects, therefore, of domestication is the replacing of this primitive regularity in color by irregularity, this similarity in individuals by dissimilarity.

"The dog's coat goes contrary to every rule except in one

most curious respect: if the animal is spotted with white, one of these white spots is always on the end of the tail. Examine a black dog, for example: if you see so much as one white speck on it, no matter where, on the flank, or on the shoulder, you will be sure to see one where I told you. Look at the end of the tail and you will find at least a touch of white there."

"So it is enough to see some white on any part of a dog to be sure that it will have some also on the tip of its tail?" This from Jules.

"Certainly," replied his uncle, "unless, of course, the animal has had its tail cut, in which case I will not answer for it."

"That is plain enough: with the tip of the tail missing the white touch is missing too."

"I will add that if the dog has only one white spot, that spot will always be on the tip of the tail."

"That singularity must have a reason?" queried Louis.

"Doubtless it has a reason, for nothing is left to chance in this world, not even the tuft of hair at the tip of an animal's tail. I will tell you, then, that the various wild species akin to the dog, jackals in particular, have, most of them, a white spot on the tip of the tail. It is a sort of family trait which the dog, their ally, perhaps their descendant, is sure to imitate every time it admits any white into its coat. Strange development! If the dog comes, as is supposed, from the jackal, it has lost its primitive savagery, its bad odor, its nocturnal cries, and has faithfully retained from its ancestry only the plume at the end of its tail. I will not undertake to explain why, in a fundamental change of habits, one insignificant detail, a mere nothing, shows greater tenacity and remains.

"To the differences in color are added differences in the quantity and quality of the hair. Most dogs have short, smooth hair; some have fine, curly hair, and look as if clothed in wool. Such is the barbet, also called sheep-dog, because its fur reminds one of the curly fleece of a sheep. Others, like the spaniel, have long and wavy hair, especially on the ears and tail. Finally, there are some wretched, unsightly dogs with the body entirely naked. One would think that some skin disease had bereft them of their last hair. They are called Turkish dogs.

"The size is not less variable. The Newfoundland dog is a majestic animal, as large as a calf; and then you will see a curly lap-dog, good for sleeping on drawing-room cushions, so tiny a creature that it could go into its master's pocket. Between these two extremes there are all degrees.

"If we enter on the details of shape, what diversity, again, do we find! Here the ear is small and stands up in a point; there it is large and covers the whole of the temple, and hangs down low enough to dip into the porringer out of which the animal eats. One, active in the chase, carries its slender body on long legs; another, apt at insinuating itself into the fox's narrow hole or the rabbit's burrow, trots on stubby members and almost touches the ground with its stomach. In this one the muzzle is gracefully tapered, made for caresses; in that, it is shortened into a brutal snout, adapted to warfare. Then there are some whose knotty and twisted legs seem crippled from birth; and there are others whose nose, black as coal, has the two nostrils separated by a deep trench."

"Those dogs look as if they had a double nose," Louis remarked. "They are said to have a keener scent than the others."

"I don't know how far the split nose may indicate keenness of scent. Let us go on and take a rapid glance at the principal breeds of dogs.

"Let us first mention the mastiff, vigilant guardian of the farm-house and courageous protector of the flock. It is a robust, bold animal, tolerably large, with short hair on the back, longer under the belly and on the tail. It has a long head, flat forehead, ears erect at the base and drooping at the tip, strong legs, and vigorous jaws. White, black, gray, brown are the colors of its coat. The mastiff has rustic manners, scent far from keen, intelligence little developed. It is found fault with for not being very docile and not lavishing its caresses. Is the charge well founded? When one leads a rude life in mountain pastures, often at close quarters with wolves, can one possess the pretty, endearing ways of the dog reared in idleness? Is not a severe manner the necessary condition of the grave duties to be performed? The mastiff has the qualities of its lot in life, and it has them to such a degree that it is not always of the same opinion as its master, knowing better than he what must be done to protect the flock. Let a wolf appear, and without considering whether it is the stronger or weaker, the brave dog will throw itself on the beast and seize it by the nape of the neck, even at the risk of perishing in the battle. The mastiff does not weigh the danger; it leaps to the call of duty—a noble quality, and one that has given rise to the likening of an energetic and resolute person to a good mastiff."

"This wolf-strangler," said Emile, "has my highest esteem, although he is not clever at offering the paw and playing dead."

"You will have no less esteem for the shepherd dog. It is of medium size, generally black, with long hair all over the body except on the muzzle. It has short, erect ears, tail horizontal or drooping. You know with what a swagger most dogs carry their tail over their back, curved like a trumpet. With them that is a sign of high satisfaction. If they are anxious, fear some misadventure, they lower it and carry it between their legs. The shepherd dog disdains this manner of erecting and curving the tail; he carries his modestly on a line with the body and keeps it more or less inclined according to the ideas with which he is preoccupied. That is the behavior of those wild animals most akin to the dog, such as the wolf and nearly all kinds of jackal: none of them curves the tail like a plume, but all carry it drooping. How does it happen that the smallest pug twists its tail into a corkscrew and bears it aloft with a pride bordering on insolence, while the shepherd dog holds his in the humble position adopted by the jackal and the wolf? This too, apparently, is a survival of old customs. Less changed in primitive characteristics than other species, the shepherd dog has retained from its wild ancestors the drooping carriage of the tail and the erect bearing of the ears.

"The mastiff is the protector of the flock, the shepherd dog its conductor. The former is endowed with brute strength, vigorous body, and powerful jaws, but is not distinguished for intellectual gifts. Notice in passing, my friends, that strength of body and strength of mind seldom go together. A herculean athlete, exhibiting his talents in public on fairday, will break a stone with his fist, lift an anvil and hold it out at arm's length, but would be incapable of putting two ideas together in his small brain. It is about the same with the mastiff: he boldly chases the wolves, but has none of the qualities of mind necessary for guiding the flock.

"This delicate function, calling for a high degree of intelligence, falls to the shepherd dog. While the master rests in the shade or amuses himself playing on his box-tree flute, the dog, posted on a neighboring rise, keeps the flock under his eye and watches that none wander beyond the limits of the pasture. He knows that on this side grows a field of clover where browsing is expressly forbidden. If some sheep goes near, he runs up and with harmless snappings turns the animal back to the allotted place. He knows that the rural guard would prosecute with all the rigors of the law if the flock should stray to the other side, newly planted with young oats. They must not attempt it; if they do, he comes threatening and insists upon a hasty retreat. Are the scattered sheep to be gathered together? On a sign from his master he is off. He makes the circuit of the flock, barking here, worrying there, and drives before him, from the circumference to the center, the straying throng, which in a few moments becomes a compact group. His mission ended, he returns to the shepherd for fresh orders—a word, a gesture, a simple look.

"I should like above all things to have you see him on duty when the flock is on the road, going to market or changing pastures. He walks behind, absorbed in his grave duties. Dogs from the neighboring farms come to meet him, and they pay him the polite attentions customary at the meeting of comrades. 'Go away,' he seems to say to them; 'you see that I have no time to exchange civilities with you.' And without glancing at them he continues his watchful following of the flock. It is wise of him, for already some sheep have stopped to crop the grass at the side of the road. To make them rejoin the flock takes but a minute. At this spot the hedge is open, and through the gap a part of the flock reaches a field of green wheat. To follow these undisciplined ones by the same breach would betray a lack of skill; the sheep, driven from behind, would only stray still farther into the forbidden field. But the wily keeper will not commit this fault; he makes a rapid detour, jumps over the hedge as best he can, and presents himself suddenly in front of the flock, which hastily retreats by the way it came, not without leaving some tufts of wool on the bushes.

"Now the flock meets another. A mixing up, a confusion of mine and thine, must be prevented. The dog thoroughly understands the gravity of the situation. Along the flanks of the two bleating flocks he maneuvers busily, running from one end to the other, back and forth, to check at the outset any attempt at desertion from one to the other flock."

"Then," said Emile, "he knows his sheep, every single one of them, to be able thus to distinguish which belong to him and which do not."

"One would almost say so, such discernment does he show.

"Scarcely is this difficulty overcome when another presents itself. Here, right and left, the road has no fences; access to the fields is free on both sides. The temptation to the flock is great, for here and there most inviting greensward appears. The dog redoubles its activity. Let us go to the left. Well and good; everything is in proper train. Now to the right. Ha, you down there! Will you please go on without stopping to crop the young grass? That is well. Now to the rear. What is that loiterer doing there? Back to the flock, quick, dawdler! Perhaps something new has happened on the left; let us go and see. And without a moment's relaxation the indefatigable dog goes first to one side, then to the other, then to the rear of the flock to hurry up the laggards and keep the intractable ones in the right path. If some, more headstrong, turn a deaf ear to his advice and scatter, he is after them in a moment, bringing them back by buffeting their shins with his muzzle."

"And by giving them a taste of his teeth too?" asked Jules.

"No, my friend; a well-trained shepherd dog does not use his teeth, which would wound the animal; a threat must suffice to bring his sheep to order. To teach him this moderation, it is necessary to take him quite young and exercise a great deal of perseverance, with caresses, dainties, and, if need be, punishment; above all, he must be brought up in the company of a comrade already very expert in the business, since example is the best of teachers. The first time he is sent after the sheep he is closely watched, and if he shows a disposition to bite he is severely corrected. The best shepherd dogs come to us from Brie, a part of old Champagne. From this country is taken the name generally used for the guardian of the flock. Other dogs are called Medor, Sultan, Azor; he is called Labrie."

"I understand," Emile nodded. "Labrie; that is to say, the dog of la Brie."

CHAPTER XXI

THE CHIEF BREEDS OF DOGS
(Continued)

"Let us continue our survey of the principal canine breeds. In size and strength the Dane approaches the mastiff, but is easily distinguished from it by its coat, which is generally white, with numerous round black spots. It is a magnificent dog, not very common, the guardian of fine houses, the friend of horses, and especially fond of running and barking before its master's carriage."

"Is that all it knows how to do?" Emile inquired.

"Pretty nearly."

"Then I'd rather have Labrie."

"I too. With its modest appearance and ill-kempt coat the shepherd dog has an intelligence and usefulness incomparably superior to the Dane's, lordly creature though the latter is with its royally bespangled coat like that of the tiger and panther. Never judge either people or dogs by their appearance.

"The harrier is endowed with a more tapering head, a longer muzzle, than any other breed. Its ears are half-drooping and point backward, its chest narrow, abdomen arched as if emaciated, legs long and slender, tail also long and slender, and its entire form distinguished by the same slenderness. It is the fleetest of all dogs. It routs out the hare in hunting; hence its name."

"Hare and harrier are indeed rather similar in spelling," observed Jules.

"Its color, less mixed than in the other breeds, is generally uniform, sometimes tawny, sometimes black, sometimes gray or even white. Some harriers have short hair, others long; in fact, there are some that are quite hairless like the Turkish dog. This dog is not very intelligent and shows no peculiar attachment to its master, but will fawn upon anybody. Its scent is imperfect, though its eyesight is excellent, and that is what guides it in the chase, while other dogs are guided by the scent.

"The spaniel owes the name it bears to its Spanish origin. This beautiful dog is characterized by its slender, moderately long head; by its long, wavy hair, which is particularly abundant on the ears, which are drooping and silky, and on the tail, which forms a tuft or plume. No dog has a more amiable and gentle aspect. Intelligence and attachment to its master can be read in its eyes. Of all dogs it is the one your Uncle Paul would choose by preference as a friend. To this worth in respect to moral qualities add this other virtue, that the spaniel is an expert hunter. In this breed are found dogs with the split or double nose; but this peculiarity does not seem to add to their keenness of scent.

"The barbet, otherwise water spaniel or sheep dog, is another of your Uncle Paul's favorites on account of its exceptional intelligence, its gentle disposition, and its unequaled faithfulness. Who among you does not know the barbet with its big round head, full of good will, its large drooping ears, short legs, squat body, long, fine and curly hair, almost like wool, which has given it the name of sheep dog? When half-shorn, as it is in the summer, it is still more comely. The hind quarters are naked and show the rosy skin; the fore part of the body is covered with a thick mane as white as cotton wool. A coquettish tuft finishes off the tail, elegant ruffles adorn the legs, the muzzle bears a mustache and small beard, which latter perhaps accounts for its name of barbet.

"Sheep—let us call it thus, as it is generally called—Sheep is a past master in accomplishments. He plays dead, offers the paw, jumps over an extended cane, stands up with a piece of sugar on his nose, and goes through his drill with a gun and with a paper cap set swaggeringly over one ear. But those are the least of his talents. Sheep is the clever one of the family. With careful education it is possible to cram this dog's excellent noddle with the most astonishing things. I have known some, my children, that could tell the time by their master's watch without a mistake."

"They could tell the time!" cried Jules incredulously. "You are jesting, Uncle."

"No, my friend, I am not jesting. The watch was shown to the dog, who looked at it attentively, seemed to make a calculation in his mind, then barked just as many times as the hand marked hours."

"That is capital, I declare!"

"But there is still better coming. I know of a barbet that plays dominos with its master, and the master does not always win, either. As such talents are exercised by bread-winning barbets for those who show them off, I am inclined to believe that the dog's intelligence is aided in the game by some signs from the master that pass unperceived by the spectators. No matter: there is enough to confound our poor reasoning powers in the calculating faculty of the animal as it counts its points, makes out those of its adversary, and as a result pushes the proper domino with the end of its nose.

"To his intellectual faculties Sheep adds, in a high degree, the faculties of the heart, which are still more to be desired. Sheep is the blind man's dog and guides him patiently, avoiding every obstacle, through the crowd by means of a string attached to the animal's collar. When the master stands on the street-corner, begging pity with his shrill clarinet, Sheep, seated in a suppliant posture, holds the wooden bowl in his teeth and offers it to the passers-by. If the master dies, the dear master who shared the crust of bread with him like a brother, Sheep follows the coffin, lonely, sad, pitiful to see. He crouches on the mound that covers his master, pines there for a few days, and finally falls asleep there in the sleep of death. By what name should such a devoted creature be called? The blind call him Fido (the faithful one), and this name is in itself the finest of elegies."

"The barbet is a noble dog," declared Jules.

"In addition to all this it is a good hunting dog. As it willingly jumps into the water, is a skilful swimmer, and retrieves with indomitable zeal, it is much in demand for hunting water-fowl.

When the master's shot has brought down a wild duck, Sheep goes and fetches it from the middle of the pond. Sometimes a bitter wind is blowing and the water is frozen. Sheep does not care for that: he swims bravely through the broken ice, brings back the game, shakes his wet coat, and waits, shivering with cold, for the report of another shot before starting off again."

"He will certainly have earned the duck's bones when the game comes on to the table," said Emile. "To jump into the icy water like that! Poor fellow! Brrr! it makes the shivers run down one's back only to think of it."

"Because of his exploits in duck-hunting this dog is known also as the water spaniel. But now let us pass on to another breed.

"The hound is preëminently the dog of the chase. It has an extremely keen scent, which enables it to trace the route followed by the game simply from the odor of the emanations left by the passage of the animal. Guided by a faint odor that would be imperceptible to any other nose, it goes as straight to the hare as if it had had it constantly in sight. There is a wonderful sensitiveness in its nostrils which our sense of smell only distantly approaches. It is a sense superior in delicacy to sight, which distance and want of light place at a disadvantage, whereas distance and obscurity do not in the least impair the infallibility of the dog's nose. Let the hare, warmed by the chase, merely graze with its back a tuft of bushes; that is enough and more than enough to put the hound on the track. To witness the unerring assurance of the pursuit, one might imagine that the hunted animal had traced in the air a trail visible to the dog."

"That sort of thing," Emile interrupted, "may be seen any day without going into the woods with the hunter. The master, unknown to the dog, hides his handkerchief in a place hard to find; then he says to the animal, 'Seek!' The dog sniffs the air a moment to get a clue, and then runs to the handkerchief and brings it back in high glee. If I had such a nose nobody would play hide-and-seek with me: I should find my playmates too easily."

"Most dogs, some more, some less, have an astonishingly keen scent; but the hound is the best endowed in this respect, especially in all that concerns the chase, and so it is the hunter's favorite. It has rather a large muzzle, strong head, vigorous and long body, tail uplifted, very short hair, generally white varied with large black or brown spots, and ears drooping and remarkably large."

"One could use them like a handkerchief to wipe the animal's nose and eyes," Emile interposed.

"The beagle stands very low on its legs. Moreover, its legs, especially the fore legs, are contorted, crippled in appearance. One would say that the dog had undergone some violent strain from which it had not entirely recovered. Its head, its large and drooping ears, its short hair, are almost the same as the hound's. The beagle is also an ardent hunter, the willing companion of him who, gun on shoulder, tramps over the rocky hills beloved by rabbits. With its short and twisted legs it trots rather than runs; but its slowness is more deadly to its victim than speed, for it allows the game to play and loiter in seeming security before it. Without suspecting the approach of the insidious enemy Jack Rabbit gambols and curls his mustache, and already the beagle is face to face with him, transfixing him with sudden terror. The shot is fired: all is over with Jack, who leaps into the air and falls back inert on the wild thyme."

"Poor Jack, so treacherously surprised! Now the hound does at least announce itself and let the rabbit scamper away as quick as it can. It is a contest of speed between the two. But the dumpy beagle creeps through the bushes and pops out all of a sudden."

"The beagle has not its equal for routing out the fox from its hole. Its gait, which is almost a crawl, enables it to penetrate the farthest corners of the fox's abode. If it finds the malodorous animal there, it gives voice and holds the place with tooth and nail while allowing the hunters time to break into the fox-hole and capture the chicken-stealer.

"The wolf-dog is the teamster's favorite. A thousand times you have seen it, petulant and wrathful, running back and forth on the top of a loaded wagon and barking from the top of this fortress at the children teasing it below. It is superb in its anger, with its little leonine mane, its plumy tail tightly rolled in a cork-screw, and its pretty red collar with bells and fox-hair fringe. It has erect, pointed ears like the shepherd dog's, slender muzzle, hair short on the head and paws, long and silky on the rest of the body. No dog knows better how to curl its tail and hold it proudly."

"Is that all it knows how to do?" asked Louis.

"The wolf-dog is too intelligent not to have other merit than its pretty ways. Loubet (that is commonly its name) knows, if need be, how to turn the spit by means of a revolving drum in which it jumps continually, as does the squirrel in its rotary cage. If it has the companionship of a good shepherd dog, it easily learns the latter's calling and becomes a pretty good flock-tender."

"That is better than raging on the top of a wagon and barking at the passers-by," was Louis's comment.

"I do not know," resumed Uncle Paul, "a more repulsive, brutal physiognomy than that of the bulldog. Look at its head, massive and short, with thick muzzle and flat nose, sometimes split; its heavy upper lip hanging down on each side and dripping with saliva, while the front teeth are exposed to view; its small eyes, with their hard expression; its ears torn by bites or made uglier by cropping;—think of all these marks of a brutal nature and tell me for what sort of occupation the bulldog is properly fitted."

"Its occupation," answered Jules, "is read in its gross physiognomy: the bulldog is made for fighting."

"Yes, my friend; for fighting and nothing else. Let no one ask it to watch over a flock, accompany the hunter, retrieve the fallen game, or even turn the spit; its dull intelligence does not go so far as that. Its one gift is the gift of the jaw that snaps and does not let go; its one passion, the frenzy of combat. When its teeth have once fastened themselves in an adversary's flesh, do not expect them to loosen their hold: a vice is not more tenacious in its grip. Calls, threats, blows, nothing avails to separate two bulldogs fighting each other; it is necessary to seize them and bite them hard on the end of the tail. The sharp pain of the bite can alone recall them from the fury of combat."

"I wouldn't undertake the operation; the animal might turn against the one trying to make it let go."

"For the master there is no danger, as the bulldog is strongly attached to him. Boldness, strength, and indomitable tenacity in battle make this dog an efficient protector such as it is well to have at one's side in a rough encounter. To leave the enemy as little hold as possible, it is the custom to crop the dog's tail and ears; furthermore, the neck is protected with a collar studded with iron points.

"This pugnacious breed is especially in favor in England, and it is from the English word *dog* that we French take our word *dogue*, in the sense of *bulldog*."

"Then *dogue* means *dog*?" asked Emile.

"Nothing else. From the same word comes the diminutive *doguin* (pug-dog), by which we designate that little growling, scatter-brained poltroon, glutton and good-for-nothing, better known to you under the name of *carlin* (pug). Like the bulldog, it has a round head, short and flat-nosed muzzle, and hanging lip; and up to a certain point it has also the bulldog character, which it shows by a noisy rage, not having the size or strength necessary for anything further."

"That's the funny little dog that barks at me in the doorway and immediately runs in if I pretend to go after it."

"The Turkish dog is another useless animal. Its size is that of the pug. It is remarkable for its almost naked skin, oily-looking, black, or dark flesh-color, and spotted with brown in large splashes. It has little intelligence and no attachment to its master. Its singular nakedness, which in our climate makes it shiver with cold a good part of the year, is its only merit, if it be a merit. I should rather call it a very disagreeable infirmity. Those who take pleasure in raising these poor animals clothe them in winter with a cloth coat."

"A dog that needed a tailor to furnish it with a winter costume would never do for me," declared Emile. "I'd much rather have Medor, the spaniel, and Sheep, the barbet. They don't shiver when it snows, and they are good friends, too."

CHAPTER XXII

THE VARIOUS USES OF DOGS

"To guard the flock, drive away the wolf, discover game—those are the dog's great functions; but an intelligent dog can learn to do a thousand other things. I have just shown you Sheep leading the blind and Loubet turning the spit. Traits abound in which the most varied aptitudes are revealed. For example, who has not seen or at least heard of the errand dog faithfully performing its appointed tasks? It receives a basket containing a purse and a slip of paper on which are written the articles desired. It may be it is to fetch tobacco for the master or get the day's provisions from the butcher. The order understood, the animal sets out, basket between its teeth. It reaches the butcher's door quickly, scratches for it to be opened, puts down the basket, takes out the purse, presents it, and waits until served. Sometimes the return is attended with difficulties. Comrades are met with; attracted by the smell, they desire to investigate the basket's contents. 'If you would only consent to it,' they say, 'what a splendid opportunity! We would divide together.' But, without slowing up, the errand dog raises its lips a little, shows its teeth, and growls: 'Don't bother me, you good-for-nothings! You see plainly enough this is for my master.' And it gravely continues on its way, fully prepared to make things lively for the miscreant that should presume to poke its nose into the basket. Thanks to its haughty bearing, the provisions reach home without further adventure."

"The dog must be very well drilled in its duty," commented Louis, "not only to resist temptation like that, but also to refuse to listen to the evil counsels of its comrades."

"And it never occurs to it to stop and have a feast with its friends when it is carrying a pound of tender cutlets?" queried Jules.

"Never, for these delicate commissions are confided only to dogs whose temperance has been proved."

"The fable," Jules remarked, "says somewhere:

> "Strange thing, indeed: to dogs is temperance taught,
> Which man, the teacher, ever fails to learn."

"Ah, yes, my friend; this beautiful virtue of temperance is hard enough for men to acquire. I know a little boy, now, that was sent one day to a friend's house with a basket of figs or pears, and he couldn't help tasting the fruit on the way, under the pretense of seeing whether it was perfectly ripe."

Here Emile lowered his head with a confused air and scratched his nose, apparently recalling some past misdeed of this sort on his part. But his uncle appeared not to notice him and continued thus:

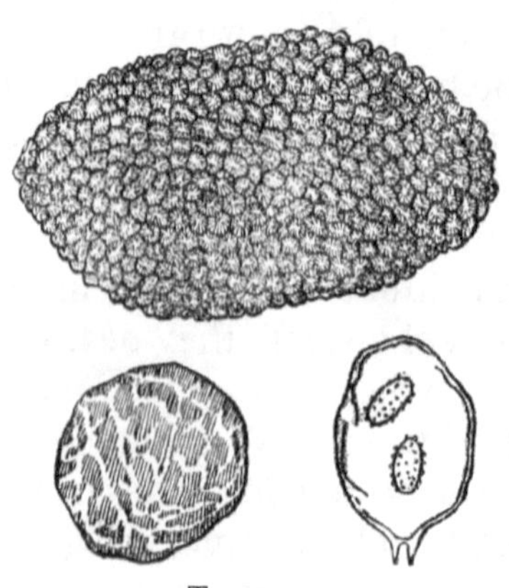

TRUFFLE

"Now let us talk about the truffle-hunting dog. To any of you that may not know it already, I will first say that the truffle is a sort of mushroom always growing beneath the soil, more or less deep, never in the open air. In shape it is quite different from ordinary mushrooms. It is round and plump, varying in size from that of a walnut to that of a man's fist, has a wrinkled surface, and its flesh is black, marbled with white. The truffle is the best liked of mushrooms, especially on account of its perfume.

"To discover it under the ground, sometimes several feet deep, sight is no guide, for nothing above reveals the presence of the precious tubercle. Scent alone will do the work. But however pronounced the aroma of the truffle may be, it is not strong enough for us to perceive it through a thick layer of earth; we must have recourse to the scent of an animal much better endowed in this respect than we. The aid invoked in these circumstances is frequently the pig, itself very fond of truffles and quick to discover them, guided merely by their odor. At the beginning of winter, accordingly, the season of this mushroom's maturity, the pig is taken into the woods. Attracted by the odor that exhales from the ground, the animal digs with its snout wherever the truffles are concealed. But if allowed to finish its work, it would reach the tubercle, which would immediately disappear in its gluttonous maw. So the animal is drawn off at the right moment, while as a recompense and to encourage it in this good work it has a chestnut or an acorn thrown to it in place of the mushroom, and then the digging is finished with a small spade. This truffle-hunting requires, as you see, constant watchfulness, since the pig might, in an unguarded moment, unearth the truffle and straightway gobble it up. A grunt of satisfaction might announce the finding of the edible morsel, but it would be too late: the gluttonous beast would already have devoured the tidbit.

"Hence the dog is preferred to the pig, being more active than the latter, more docile, of keener scent, and seeking the truffles only for its master, with no selfish motive of its own. It is marvelous to see it at work. Nose to the earth, the better to catch the faint emanation from underground, it systematically explores the places that seem to it the most promising, such as copses of young oaks and thickets of brushwood. It scents something. Good! It is a truffle. With much tail-wagging in evidence of its joy the dog burrows a little with its paw to indicate the place. Man continues the digging with an iron tool. But the truffle is not always unearthed at the first attempt; the search involves uncertainties and the following of false leads. 'Let me look into this a little closer,' says the dog to itself. And it pokes its muzzle into the very bottom of the hole, with sniffings that powder its nose with earth. 'It is this way, master, to the left; dig again.' The man follows this advice and resumes operations; but no sign of a truffle. Fresh sniffings at the bottom of the hole. 'On the honor of a dog, the truffle is there, and a fine one. This way, master, a little more to the left.' At last the truffle is found, one of the largest of the gathering, and as a reward the dog gets a crust of bread.

"The pig hunts for truffles with no previous education, since it is its nature to burrow in the soil for the tubercles and roots on which it feeds; but the dog has to be taught the business so foreign to its own habits. The first step is to familiarize it with the savor of the truffle, which is done by making it eat a truffle omelet."

"A truffle omelet!" exclaimed Emile. "That's a dish much to be preferred to a bone."

"But not in the dog's opinion," rejoined his uncle. "Without showing any enthusiasm for this food that is so new to it, the dog accepts it at first partly as an act of obedience, then begins to like it, and finally would ask nothing better than to continue the diet for a long time. But the course of education in this dainty is of short duration, ending as soon as the odor to be remembered becomes familiar to the dog. Then a truffle is hidden in the ground, at first not very deep, to-morrow a little deeper, and the dog is trained in finding it. A caress, a piece of bread, are its recompense each time it does well. Such lessons, appropriately varied and repeated, at last produce the trained truffle-hunter, and the animal is then taken, from day to day, into the woods to perfect itself in its calling by actual practice. Of course this difficult work is the monopoly of dogs having the highest degree of intelligence, notably the water-spaniel."

"That's the one sure to be called upon wherever unusual ability is needed," Jules observed.

"We have just seen the dog rival the pig, even surpass it, in the art of unearthing the truffle. Now I will show him to you taking the donkey's place as a draft animal. An enormous dog harnessed to a light cart is not a rare sight in towns, where butchers especially make use of this singular equipage for the transport of their meat. But as I have something much more interesting to tell you I will not linger over this example. There is a country where the dog is the only draft animal, a country where it takes the horse's place for carrying the master on long journeys. That country is Greenland."

"Greenland is where they heat water in a leather bag by throwing in red-hot stones?" Jules interposed.

"And where they lick the piece of meat chosen for the distinguished guest?" added Emile.

"Yes, Greenland is the country."

"It must be a sorry sort of country."

"More so than you could imagine. In Greenland, as everywhere else near the Pole, winter with its snows and ice lasts two thirds of the year, and the cold is intense. Navigators who have passed the winter in that bitter climate tell us that wine, beer, and other fermented liquors turn to solid ice in their casks; that a glass of water thrown into the air falls in flakes of snow; that the breath from the lungs crystallizes at the opening of the nostrils into needles of rime; and that the beard, stuck to the clothing by a coating of ice, cannot be detached except with scissors. For whole months at a time the sun is not once seen above the horizon and there is no difference between day and night; or rather, a permanent night reigns, the same at midday as at midnight. However, when the weather is clear, the darkness is not complete: the light of the moon and stars, augmented by the whiteness of the snow, produces a sort of wan twilight, sufficient for seeing.

"Squat and under-sized, the inhabitant of these rigorous climes, the Eskimo, divides his time between hunting and fishing. The first furnishes him with skins for garments, the second with food. Dried fish, stored up in a half-rotten condition, and rancid whale-oil, viands repugnant to us, are the dainties familiar to his famished stomach. He depends also on his fishing for fuel to feed his lamp, this fuel being the fat of the seal, and for materials with which to make his sled, which is fashioned out of large fishbones. Wood, in short, is unknown there, no tree, however hardy, being able to withstand the rigors of winter. Willows and birches, dwarfed to the size of mere shrubs trailing on the ground, alone venture to the northern extremities of Lapland, where the growing of barley, the hardiest of cultivated plants, ceases. Nearer the Pole all woody vegetation ceases, and in summer only a few rare tufts of grass and moss are to be seen ripening their seeds hastily in the sheltered hollows of rocks. Still farther north the snow and ice cannot even melt entirely in summer, the ground is never visible, and no vegetation at all is possible."

"And there are people who give the dear name of home to those terrible countries?" asked Jules.

"There are people, the Eskimos, who inhabit them the year round, in winter living in snow-huts, in summer under tents of sealskin."

"They build houses of snow!" This from Emile.

"Not exactly houses like ours, but huts indeed that afford very good shelter. Regular slabs of snow are cut and piled one on another in a circular wall capped by a dome of the same material. A very low entrance, closed with skins, is left facing the south. To get daylight, they cut a round opening in the top of the dome, and fill it with a sheet of ice instead of a pane of glass. Finally, inside, all around the wall, a bench of snow is built, and it is covered with gravel, heather, and reindeer-skins. This bench is the sleeping-place for the family, the skins are the mattress, and the snow is the straw. In these dwellings there is never any fire: wood is wanting and, besides, with fire the dwelling would melt and come dripping down like rain on the inmates."

"That's so," said Emile. "Then where do they make the fire to heat the stones when they want hot water?"

"They do this outside, in the open air."

"And with what, if there isn't any wood in the country?"

"With slices of whale's fat and fishbones."

"They must freeze in those snow huts with no place for lighting a fire?"

"No, for a moss wick fed with seal oil burns continually in a little earthen pot to melt snow and give drinking-water. The small amount of heat thrown out suffices to maintain an endurable temperature in the dwelling, thanks to the thickness of the snow walls."

CHAPTER XXIII

THE ESKIMO DOG

"WHAT I have just told you will make it plain enough that no domestic animal dependent on vegetable food can be kept in that country. Where could one find a supply of forage for the ox, horse, or even donkey, when the ground is covered with a thick layer of snow the greater part of the year, and when during the three or four months of summer all the verdure consists of meager greensward where a sheep would hardly find enough herbage to browse? Besides, these animals would succumb to the severity of the winter. There is but one species of this sort that can live in these desolate regions, and that is the reindeer, which is about as large as the stag, but more robust and more thick-set. Its horns, or antlers, are divided each into two branches, the shorter one pointing forward, the other, the longer, pointing backward, and both ending in enlargements that spread out somewhat like the palm and fingers of an open hand."

"According to your description," observed Louis, "the reindeer must be a superb animal and must need plenty of food. Where does it find pasturage when everything is covered with snow?"

"If it needed the forage to which our cattle are accustomed, no doubt it would starve to death the first winter; but it is content with a kind of food that none of our animals would touch. It is a lichen, white in color and divided into a multitude of branches, close together and presenting the appearance of a little bush a few inches high. It grows on the ground, which it entirely covers for immense stretches. During the winter the reindeer scratch the snow with their fore hoofs and uncover the coarse plant,

REINDEER

softened by moisture; and this plant they browse. Thus it is that interminable fields of snow, the desolate abodes of famine, supply nevertheless sufficient pasturage for these animals. This lichen, last vegetable resource of the extreme north, is called reindeer moss, and is found everywhere, in the most arid lands, between the poles and the equator. Among the underbrush of our most barren hills you will find it in abundance, fresh and supple in winter, dried up and crackling under the feet in summer."

"The reindeer ought to live in our country," Jules remarked, "since there is lichen for it to feed on."

"The climate is much too warm for it. Hardly would it be able to endure the mildness of our winters; and how about the heat of our summers? It needs the snows and the harsh climate of the polar regions, away from which it rapidly dies out.

"In Lapland the reindeer is a domestic animal. There it fills the place of our cattle and serves at one and the same time as cow, sheep, and horse. The Laplander lives on reindeer milk and its products, and on the animal's flesh. He clothes himself with its warm fur, and makes a very soft leather out of its skin. When the ground is covered with snow, he harnesses the reindeer to his sled and travels as many as thirty leagues a day, his swift equipage with its broad runners gliding over the snow and hardly leaving a trace behind.

"The reindeer is not rare in Greenland, but there it lives in the wild state, for the Eskimo, much less civilized than the Laplander, has not yet learned how to win it to his uses and accustom it to domestic life. It runs at large and merely furnishes the game on which the Greenlanders count to vary somewhat their diet of fish. For domestic animals, then, what is there left to the Eskimo, since the only species able to live in that land of snow huts, the reindeer, is, in that desolate region, a wild animal approached by the hunter only with ruse and caution? There remains the dog, the faithful companion which, thanks to its kind of food, can accompany man everywhere, even on his most daring expeditions toward one or other of the poles. Where the reindeer would have to pause, lichen failing or being covered with too thick a layer of snow, the dog continues to go forward, since for food it needs only a fishbone, and the neighboring sea furnishes fish in plenty. The dog is the Eskimo's all, in the way of domestic animals."

"That all is very little," said Jules.

"Very little, certainly; but still without the dog the Eskimo could not live in his gloomy country. With the help of the dog he chases the wild reindeer, the flesh of which gives him food, and the skin furnishing for his hut; on the ice he attacks the white bear, whose fur will become a warm winter cloak; he makes himself master of the seal which will give him its intestines for ropes and its oily fat for fuel to feed his ever-burning lamp. In fact, the dog is to him not only a hunting companion, but also a draft animal able to transport him at a good rate of speed whithersoever he wishes to go.

"The Eskimo dog is about the size of our shepherd dog, but more robust in build. It has upstanding ears, tail coiled in a circle, hair thick and woolly, as it should be to resist the atrocious cold of the country it inhabits. No domestic species leads a harder life. At long intervals a meat-bone or a large fishbone for food, and nothing more; no shelter except the hole it may dig for itself in the snow; cuffs much oftener than caresses; after the fatigues of the chase the still more exhausting labor of drawing the sled—such is its life of hardship. Harsh treatment and constant hunger are not conducive to gentleness of disposition. So the Eskimo dogs are quarrelsome among themselves, surly toward man, always ready to show their teeth, and especially disposed to attack their victuals with voracity. Nowhere in the world are there more audacious pillagers: so extreme are the pangs of hunger that no punishment avails to prevent their snapping up any morsel unguardedly left within their reach."

"Not the most docile sort of companion, I should say," Jules remarked.

"The women, who treat them more gently, feed them, and take care of them when they are little, can easily make them obey. Nearly always, even when these poor animals suffer most cruelly from hunger, the women succeed in getting them together to be harnessed to the sled."

"I should like, Uncle," put in Emile, "before hearing the rest, to know just what an Eskimo sled is. I can't imagine exactly what it is like."

"The sled, as its name indicates, is a kind of light vehicle without wheels, designed for dragging over the ice or snow where sliding is easy. The Eskimo sled is rudely built. Imagine two strips of wood curving upward at each end and placed side by side at a certain distance from each other. They are the chief pieces, which are to support all the rest and themselves glide on the snow. Between the two is constructed a framework of light transverse bars, and on this framework rises a sort of niche lined with furs, where the traveler squats. That is the Eskimo sled.

"The two chief pieces, resembling long skates gliding over the hard snow, I said were of wood; but I hasten to add that generally they are made of other material, as wood is one of the rarest things in this country where there is not enough vegetation to furnish even a broomstick. All the wood in use is washed ashore by the sea, from far countries, at the time of heavy storms. So the Eskimo has not always at his disposal the two narrow strips necessary. He uses instead two long whalebones, chosen for their shape and curvature. If bones are lacking there remains one last resort. With the intestines of the seal or thongs of skin he ties large fish in two bundles, makes them of the desired shape, and exposes them to the frost, which hardens them like stone until summer comes again. Those are the two runners, the two chief pieces of the sled."

"What a queer country, where the people use bundles of frozen fish for runners!" Emile could not but exclaim.

"But the runner has not yet played out its part. After it has slidden all winter over the snowy plain, it thaws out with the return of warm weather and the fish composing it are popped into the bag of boiling water to cook."

"The people eat them?"

"Why, certainly, my friend; they eat the framework of the demolished sled."

"Once more, I say, if ever those people invite me to dinner I shall decline. I shouldn't relish their licking the food to clean it, nor should I care for fish that had been dragged about for months, nobody knows where."

"Now that you know about the sled, let us speak of the team. The dog's harness is composed of two thongs of reindeer skin, one going round the neck, the other round the breast, and both connected by a third thong passing between the fore legs. To this harness, near the shoulders, are attached two long leather straps which are fastened to the sled at the other end. The dog team numbers from twelve to fifteen. One dog, the most intelligent and with the keenest scent, goes along at the head of the pack; the others follow, several abreast, the novices nearest to the sled. Seated in the niche of his vehicle, one leg out this way, one the other, feet almost skimming the snow, the Eskimo drives his equipage with an enormously long whip, for this whip must be able to reach the farthest dog, seven or eight meters from the sled. But he refrains as much as possible from using it, since a lash from the whip is more likely to promote disorder than to increase the speed. The dog struck, not knowing whence the blow came, lays the blame on its neighbor and bites it; the latter passes the compliment along to another, which in turn hastens to worry the next; and in a moment, spreading through the pack, the rough-and-tumble fight becomes general. Then it is a task indeed to restore peace and get the broken or tangled harness straightened out.

"Hence the whip is but rarely called into service to correct a too unruly dog, and it is chiefly with the voice that the driver guides his team. The leading dog is particularly attentive to the master's word: he turns to the right, left, or goes straight ahead, increases or slackens speed, and the others govern themselves accordingly. Every time an order is given, the leader turns its head without stopping and looks at the master, as if to say, 'I understand.' If the route has been already traveled the driver has nothing to do: the leader follows the trail even when it is invisible to man. In black darkness, in the midst of violent snow-squalls, aided by its sense of smell and its astonishing sagacity, it continues to guide the rest of the team, and very seldom goes astray.

"In a single day 150 kilometers are thus made. If fatigue calls a halt, the Eskimo builds himself a shelter with snow piled up for walls and a large slab of ice for roof. Here he disposes himself as best he can for sleeping, after a frugal lunch of salt fish or flesh, thawed by the heat of a lamp. On awakening, a signal is given and immediately all about the hut little mounds of snow move and shake themselves. They are the dog-team, which has slept outside, covered by the falling snow. The Eskimo doles out to them a meager pittance, which is instantly swallowed, and without delay he harnesses the sled to resume his journey in quest of the white bear or the reindeer on which he has set his heart."

CHAPTER XXIV

THE DOG OF MONTARGIS

"THE DOG is much attached to its master; if it loses him it remembers him for a long time. I am going to give you an example so striking that it has been recorded in history.

"In the year 1371 there lived at the court of King Charles V a nobleman, the Chevalier Macaire, who, envious of the favor one of his companions, Aubry de Montdidier, enjoyed with the king, one day came upon his rival by surprise, when the latter was accompanied only by his dog, in a deserted corner of the forest of Montargis. Finding the occasion opportune for gratifying his odious rancor, he suddenly threw himself upon Aubry, killed him, and buried his body in the forest. The ill deed accomplished, he returned to court, where he bore himself as if nothing out of the ordinary had occurred."

"Oh, the hateful wretch!" cried Jules.

"In the meantime the dog couched on its master's grave, where night and day it howled with grief. When the pangs of hunger pressed too hard it returned to Paris, scratched at the door of its master's friends, hastily ate what was given it, and immediately went back to the wood to lie down again on the grave. Seeing it thus come and go alone, always oppressed with care and manifesting by doleful barks some deep grief, people followed it into the forest, watched its actions, and saw that it stopped on a mound of freshly turned earth, where its lamentations became still more plaintive."

"No doubt they dug and the crime was discovered?"

"Struck with the fresh mound of earth and the dog's howls at this spot, they dug and found the dead man, to whom a more honorable burial was then given; but there was nothing to make them suspect the author of the murder."

"And what became of the dog?" asked Emile.

"After having thus apprized Aubry's friends and relatives that its master had been miserably assassinated, there remained a more difficult task for it to accomplish; namely, to expose the murderer. A relative of the dead man had adopted the dog and was in the habit of taking the animal out with him when he went to walk. One day the dog chanced to spy the assassin, Macaire, in company with other gentlemen. To leap at his throat for the purpose of biting and strangling him, was the affair of an instant."

"Bravo! Good dog! Strangle the rascal!" cried Emile in great excitement.

"You are going too fast, my friend," his uncle remonstrated. "No one as yet suspected that Macaire was the author of the horrible crime. They draw off the dog, beat it, and drive it away. The animal keeps returning in a rage, and as it is not allowed to come near, it struggles, barks from a distance, and directs its threats toward the quarter where Macaire has disappeared.

"This performance is repeated again and again, and on each occasion the dog, perfectly gentle toward every other person, is seized with violent rage at the sight of the murderer and recommences its assaults. It is against Macaire alone that it nurses a grudge which neither threats nor blows can appease. Such is the creature's fury that finally the query arises whether the dog may not be actuated by a desire to avenge the death of its first master."

"Ha! now we are coming to it. Suspicion is aroused."

"They speak to the king about the affair; they tell him that a nobleman of his court was found buried, victim of an unknown assassin; they further inform him that the dead man's dog, with indomitable persistence, springs at the Chevalier Macaire every time it sees him. The king has the suspected person brought before him and orders him to remain hidden in the midst of a throng of other bystanders. Then the dog is brought in. Its sense of smell immediately warns it of the presence of the murderer. With its accustomed fury it spots its victim in the crowd and springs at him. As if reassured by the king's presence, it attacks with more boldness than ever, and by its plaintive barks seems to ask that justice be done it. There is hasty intervention, without which Macaire would be devoured by the animal."

"And it would have served him right."

"Wait: punishment will come. The dog's strange conduct, together with other suspicious circumstances, had made an impression on the king. Some days later Charles V had Macaire appear before him and pressed him by his questions to confess the truth. What foundation was there for the suspicions current in regard to him? How explain, if he were not guilty, the dog's repeated attacks and furious barking at sight of him? Seized with the fear of a shameful punishment, Macaire obstinately denied the crime.

"At this epoch, characterized by manners and customs little above barbarism, when the accuser affirmed and the accused denied, with no sufficient proof on either side, it was customary to decide the question by a mortal combat between the two. The one that succumbed was held to be in the wrong."

"But to be the weaker proves nothing against right," objected Jules. "One might be a thousand times right and yet be beaten by one's adversary."

"That is undeniably true, and I hope you will from day to day become more firmly convinced of this noble truth. In our lamentable age—you will learn this later, my friend—in our lamentable age it is a current maxim, a maxim of savagery, that might makes right! In the days of Charles V, rude as that period was, no one would have dared to say such a horrible thing; but nevertheless, under the influence of superstition, men really believed that the vanquished was in the wrong, because, they maintained, right can never succumb, upheld as it is by God. Therefore a judicial combat was called a judgment of God. Alas, alas, my friend, how far they were from sanity of mind! How far from it we ourselves are, with our duel, relic of ancient barbarism! What does a well-directed shot prove in favor of him who pulled the trigger? Nothing, unless it be that he is more adept in the use of firearms than his adversary, or that chance has been on his side. Thus it is, however, that men decide disputes involving our most precious possession, honor.

"The king, then, ordered the affair to be brought to an end and the truth determined by a combat between the man and the dog. A large field was laid out with seats for the king, all his court, and a numerous company besides. In the middle of the field were the two champions—the man with a large and heavy stick, the dog with the weapons that nature had given it, and with nothing but a leaky cask for a refuge and a sally-port."

"This cask was to serve it as shelter against the blows of the stick?" asked Emile.

"It was the citadel where, if the attack became too pressing, it could take refuge in order to escape the cudgel's blows. But the brave animal did not once make use of it. As soon as it was let loose it rushed at Macaire. But the nobleman's stick was big enough to fell his adversary with a single blow; so the dog began to run this way and that around the man to avoid the crushing descent of the club. Then, seizing its opportunity, with one bound it jumped at its enemy's throat and gripped it so firmly as to throw Macaire over backward. Half strangled, he cried for pity and begged to be freed from the animal, promising to confess everything. The guards drew off the dog and, the judges approaching by royal command, Macaire confessed his crime to them."

"And the assassin got off with nothing but a bite from the dog?"

"Macaire was hanged like the scoundrel that he was."

"That time, at least, might decided right," Jules declared with much satisfaction.

CHAPTER XXV

HYDROPHOBIA[5]

"**O**F ALL the ferocious animals that you know, at least by hearsay, which one would you most dread to meet?" asked Uncle Paul. Emile was the first to reply.

"For my part," said he, "if I went nutting in the woods I shouldn't at all like to meet a wolf, even if I had a stout stick with me."

"If I should meet a wolf," Jules declared, "I would just climb a tree and make fun of Mr. Wolf, for he doesn't know how to climb. But I should be more afraid of a bear, for that can climb trees better than we, and it hugs a man till it stifles him."

"As for me," said Louis, "the animal I should fear most would be the tiger; they say it is so ferocious. With a bound it springs on a man as the cat pounces on a mouse."

"The wolf is a coward," Uncle Paul assured his hearers. "Just threaten it in a loud voice, throw a stone or two at it, or shake a stick, and you put it to flight. Nevertheless, if it were pressed with hunger, it would take courage and one might pass a very bad quarter of an hour in its company. The bear is more dangerous. With it, retreat up a tree is of no avail, and precipitous flight has not much chance of success, for the bear is very nimble. What a terrible fate to find oneself held tight in a horrible embrace, and to feel the beast's warm breath on one's face! With the tiger it would be worse. Let its claws once get hold of a man, let its jaws once close on him, and he is torn to pieces. There is nothing so terrible as its sudden attack and its bloodthirsty ferocity."

"That's the animal most to be feared, as I said," Louis declared,

---

5   This was written before the days of inoculation as a preventive of hydrophobia.—*Translator.*

157

Tiger

"if it were found in our country. But luckily there are no tigers here."

"We have no tigers in our woods," assented Uncle Paul, "but we have in our very midst an animal that is still more formidable in certain circumstances. This terrible enemy that we are liable to encounter at any moment does not possess by a good deal the strength of the tiger or bear; most often it is not even so strong as the wolf; sometimes it is so feeble that a well-directed blow of the fist is enough to knock it down. Its nature is not sanguinary; its teeth and claws are not strong enough to frighten us."

"Well, then," Emile demanded, "why is this enemy so much to be feared?"

"Do not let this lack of strength reassure you. As for me, I shudder at the mere thought of the danger to which we are exposed. Against those other animals, however dangerous or strong they may be, defense is possible. With presence of mind and with weapons one may come out of the fight victorious; if one is injured by teeth or claws the wound may heal. But against this other creature presence of mind, skill, courage, weapons, help—all are useless; let it bite you only once, let the point of its tooth merely tear the skin so as to draw blood, making no more than a scratch, and it will suffice to endanger your very life. Better would it be to find yourself in the wolf's jaws or the bear's embrace. Vainly you get the upper hand and ward off the animal's assaults, vainly you kill it: a tiny scratch, insignificant enough from any other animal, will in the near future cause your death, a horrible death, more atrocious than any other in the world. As a result of that tiny wound a day will come, and it will come soon, when, seized all at once with a furious madness, shaken by horrible convulsions, frothing with drivel, and not recognizing either relatives or friends, you will spring upon them like a ferocious beast, to bite them savagely and give them your disease. No hope of restoring you to health, no way to alleviate your sufferings; you must be left to die, an object of horror and pity."

"What is that formidable animal?" Jules inquired. "Are we really ever likely to have a tussle with it?"

"We are daily exposed to this danger. No one is certain of not being attacked this very day, this very instant; for the terrible animal frequents our public places, wanders in our streets, makes our houses its home, and lives in close intimacy with us. In fact, it is no other than the dog."

"The dog, the most useful and most devoted of our servants!" exclaimed Jules incredulously.

"Yes, the dog. In proportion as it merits our attachment under usual conditions, so does it become the object of our just fear when seized with a malady called hydrophobia."

"They say, and I've often heard it, that mad dogs are very dangerous," remarked Louis. "How do they get this disease?"

"Its origin is unknown. Without any discoverable cause, from no motive that we can discern, the dog goes mad; the malady is spontaneous; that is to say, it makes its appearance unheralded by symptoms. Any dog may be attacked, the contented pet in a fine house as well as the poor homeless waif that hunts for a scrap in the sweepings at the street corner. I must add, however, that the sufferings of hunger and thirst, with bad treatment, tend to promote the disease, stray dogs being more subject than others to spontaneous madness. Here we have a new and very weighty reason why we should take good care of our dogs. To let them suffer cruelly is to expose them to the inroads of a horrible ailment that may perhaps be our own destruction.

"Spontaneous madness once developed in a dog, the malady, unless precautions are taken, is propagated in others with frightful rapidity. Ten dogs, a hundred dogs, can in a short time themselves become mad. An animal attacked with rabies is, in short, tormented with an irresistible desire to bite others. Wild-eyed, tail between its legs, hair erect, lip frothing, it springs with lowered head on the first dog it meets, bites it, and immediately springs at another, then another, as many as it comes across. Now, every dog bitten becomes itself mad in a few days, some sooner, some later, and propagates the evil in the same way unless energetic measures cut this scourge short.

"The disease is communicated to man also by the bite. A mad dog bites animals and human beings without distinction; it springs furiously at passers-by, and even springs at its master, whom it no longer recognizes. If the tooth, moistened with saliva, pierces the skin so as to draw blood, it is all over with the victim: hydrophobia has been communicated."

"It is the same here, then, as with the viper's venom?" asked Jules.

"Exactly the same. From the mad dog's mouth runs a deadly saliva, a real venom which, mingling with the blood through an open wound, causes madness at the end of a certain time. On unbroken skin this saliva has no effect; but on the slightest bleeding scratch it operates in its peculiarly terrible fashion. In short, like other venoms, the saliva of rabies, as it is called, must infiltrate into the blood in order to act.

"This shows you that the bite is less dangerous if made through clothing, especially thick clothing. The fabric can wipe the dog's teeth on the way and retain the venomous saliva; it can even arrest somewhat the action of the jaws and prevent the animal's teeth from going in so far. If there is but a slight wound that fails to draw blood, the saliva has not penetrated and there is no danger.

"The conditions necessary for the development of rabies, namely the mingling of the dog's saliva with our blood and its introduction into our veins, should always be in our minds if we wish to avoid a danger that threatens us even in the midst of seeming security. It is to be noted that in the first stage of the disease the dog is more demonstrative in its affection than usual: the poor beast seems to wish once more to lavish its tokens of attachment on those it loves, before abandoning itself to the transports of fury that will soon be beyond its control. Let us suppose that at this moment you have a slight wound on your hand, and the dog comes, docile and fawning, and lovingly licks the little wound. Its tongue mixes the saliva with your blood; the terrible venom infiltrates into your veins. Fatal caress! Rabies and all its horrors perhaps will be the consequence. Take this as a warning: never allow a dog, however reassuring its demeanor may be, to lick you on a place where the skin is broken. No one can affirm with certainty that the atrocious malady is not already developing in the animal, and you might fall a victim to your excess of confidence.

"Hydrophobia shows itself in man usually in from thirty to forty days after the bite. It begins with headache, deep depression, continued uneasiness, troubled sleep, and bad dreams; then come convulsions and delirium. The face expresses great terror; the lips turn blue and are covered with foam; the throat contracts so as to render swallowing impossible. The sight of liquids inspires the patient with insurmountable aversion, and a drop of water placed in the mouth would produce frightful strangulation. Then come fits of madness during which the patient struggles furiously to bite and rend the one who is taking care of him. The disease has changed him to a wild beast. At last death comes and puts an end to this horrible agony."

"Then there is no remedy for hydrophobia?" asked Jules.

"Medicine as yet knows absolutely none. All it can do is to let the sufferer die—banishing forever the execrable notions that formerly prevailed, and perhaps still do at present. To get rid of the incurable and dangerous patient it was necessary, they said, to smother him between two mattresses. Whoever should to-day commit such a barbarous act would be pursued by justice and punished as a murderer."[6]

6   Today post exposure treatment is almost 100% effective.

"Formerly they smothered the patient between two mattresses, now they let him die—no great advance," observed Louis.

"Pardon, my friend; it is no small advance to have banished forever from the sick-bed the senseless brutalities of ignorance, pending the day, which will come, I hope, when science shall gain the upper hand of the terrible disease.

"Hydrophobia, when it has once set in, cannot, I say, so far as we know, be cured; but at least, by means of certain precautions, we can anticipate it and prevent the mad dog's bite from leading to fatal results. The saliva of rabies acts in poisoning the blood precisely as does the venom of dangerous serpents. The precautions to be taken are then, in both cases, about the same: the saliva must be prevented from entering the veins; it must be destroyed in the wound. To this end it is customary to bind the bitten part above the wound, so as to arrest the circulation; then the torn flesh is made to bleed and is afterward washed in order to remove as much as possible of the venomous humor; finally, and as soon as may be, the wound is cauterized with iron heated white-hot."

"Oh, what a frightful remedy!" cried Emile. "Is there no other?"

"It is the only one, and it must be applied with the least delay possible, and boldly. Life is at stake. These precautions taken, especially the cauterization, one can feel some reassurance that the malady will not make its appearance. Of course the operation would succeed better in a doctor's hands, which are more experienced than ours; but if his help cannot be got at once, let us proceed without him, for here promptitude offers the best chance of success."

"I shudder at the thought of that white-hot iron making the wound sizzle," said Jules. "All the same I would submit to being burned in order to escape the most terrible of fates."

"If there's no other way, I would submit, too," Emile declared. "But still I say, plague take dogs for making us have to endure the hot iron if we wish to escape something worse. Can't they keep these animals from going mad?"

"To prevent all outbreaks of rabies is not in our power, but it rests with us to make mad dogs scarce enough not to cause us too much anxiety. When this malady threatens, notably in the heat of midsummer, police regulations require the muzzling of all dogs permitted to go from home. Furthermore, little poisoned balls are scattered in the street to get rid of stray dogs. To these measures of the police we ought to add our own watchfulness; we ought always to have an eye on our dogs, if we have any, for, living with us as they do, they will be the first to expose us to danger. It is most important, then, for us to know by what signs incipient rabies can be detected. That is what I am going to teach you according to the masters who have made a thorough study of this grave subject.

"First of all, I will refute two erroneous assumptions that are widely held and that might become fatal by imparting a false security. It is generally believed that a mad dog is always in a state of fury. That this frenzied condition shows itself when the disease is at its height, is very true; but also nothing is more utterly false as to the first stages of the malady. Far from being seized with attacks of fury, the dog just beginning to be infected shows, on the contrary, an excess of affectionate feelings: by multiplied caresses it seems to beg of man some sort of help against the vague terrors with which it is tormented. Secondly, it is popularly maintained that a mad dog does not drink and manifests a great horror of water, and that no dog seen in the act of drinking can be mad. This notion is so deeply rooted in most minds that, to designate rabies there has been formed, from two Greek words, the special term, hydrophobia, signifying horror of water. Well, my friends, never forget this: no matter what the Greek term says, a mad dog drinks very well; it drinks greedily every time it has the chance, without manifesting any aversion whatever toward the water. Later, when the animal is near its end, the throat contracts and swallowing becomes impossible. Then, and not till then, the dog shuns drink with horror. Therefore, far from reassuring us, it is on the contrary an added cause for alarm when we see a dog becoming more affectionate than usual and drinking with unaccustomed avidity.

"It is in restlessness and agitation without apparent cause

that the first signs of the inroads of rabies manifest themselves. The dog cannot stay in one place, it goes without any object from one spot to another, and retires to a corner where it turns round without being able to find a position that suits it. Its look expresses gloom and sadness. It seems obsessed by a fixed idea from which the call of a loved voice may draw it for a moment; then it relapses into sadness.

"Food is not yet refused. On the contrary, the dog pounces gluttonously on the food set before it; sometimes its depraved appetite is such that it even devours substances having no nutriment, such as wood, straw, and anything found in its way, even its own excrement. Water is drunk with the same avidity. As soon as this unreasonable agitation, this deep sadness, this excess of affection, and this depraved appetite show themselves, the dog should be suspected of rabies; prudence demands that it be chained and closely watched.

"Suspicion becomes complete certainty if the animal from time to time utters a peculiar and quite characteristic cry, which is called the mad-dog howl. In the midst of one of these attacks of lugubrious sadness, all at once the dog springs with a bound at an imaginary enemy. Then, muzzle uplifted, it gives an ordinary bark that ends bruskly and peculiarly in a piercing howl. At this discordant sound one might be reminded of the manner in which roosters sometimes crow, at least so far as the extremely hoarse and cracked tone is concerned."

"A dog often howls for want of something else to do, when it is shut up," remarked Louis. "That would not be a sign of madness?"

"No, my friend. Ordinary howling denotes a passing feeling of gloom, ennui, fright; and this cry cannot be confounded with the veritable howl of rabies, the characteristics of which are very different. This latter begins with a perfect bark and suddenly passes into a sharp and prolonged howl comparable to the cock's crow.

"As long as the furious madness that will end the progress of the malady is not declared, the animal is harmless; but it is unnecessary, it would even be dangerous, to wait so long. If the peculiar howl of rabies is heard, doubt is no longer possible: the dog is unquestionably mad. For our safety and also to spare the poor animal the tortures awaiting it, the dog should be killed at once. In the animal's interest as well as our own, it is a kind action."

"Poor dog!" murmured Jules. "The master gives it a last look of regret, and, with tears in his eyes, lodges a ball in its head."

CHAPTER XXVI

THE CAT

"THE CAT entered our household long after the dog; nevertheless its domestication took place very early. The East, whence we received it, has possessed it from time immemorial. Ancient Egypt, the old land of the Pharaohs, has transmitted to us the most curious documents on this subject.

"In that country, celebrated for its profound veneration for domestic animals, honors almost divine were paid to the ox, dog, cat, and many other creatures. Nearer the primitive ages than we, and still remembering the miseries from which the domestic animals had freed man, the Egyptians no doubt showed their gratitude by these honors, which seem to us to-day the height of superstition. The ox, turning up the farmer's soil with the plow, was accorded the highest position. A magnificent white bull, called the bull Apis, was kept at the expense of the State in a sumptuous temple of granite and marble, and cared for by a retinue of attendants who approached it with reverence, wearing rich costumes of ceremony, swinging the censer, and, in short, observing all the forms of deep veneration."

"Just to change the straw and fill the rack with hay, they went censer in hand and with bent knees?" Emile asked with incredulity.

"Yes, my friend."

"Then times are greatly changed for the ox. Nowadays the ox-tender lets the animal go disgracefully dirty with dung and lie on a miserly allowance of straw; and he isn't at all sparing of the goad to quicken the ox's pace."

"On great fête-days, when the bull Apis went out escorted by its retinue of servants, the crowd prostrated itself to the ground

MUMMY OF THE BULL APIS

along the way, with foreheads in the dust. At its death, mourning was general throughout Egypt. An immense granite coffin, masterpiece of art and patience, the work of a thousand artisans, received the sacred remains, which were then placed in a sepulchral chamber hollowed out in the heart of a mountain and sumptuously adorned with the finest examples of sculpture and painting."

"And did other domestic animals receive like honors?" asked Jules.

"All were honored, but none so signally as the ox. In regard to the cat, for instance, it was deemed sufficient to embalm it with aromatics after its death, swathe it in bands of fine linen, and place the body thus prepared in a chest of sweet-scented wood adorned with gildings, paintings, and inscriptions. These chests were then arranged on shelves in the niches of a sepulchral chamber excavated to a great depth in the solid rock.

"In some of these chambers, with decorations as fresh as if made yesterday, we find to-day, after the lapse of three and four thousand years, a prodigious number of bodies of cats and other animals, sufficiently preserved to be recognized, thanks to the aromatic bitumen with which they were impregnated. Well, the examination of these old relics conveys information on one point of great interest: it shows us that the domestic animals of those remote times did not differ from those of our own day. As were the ox, dog, cat, four thousand years ago, such they are to-day.

"The cat—since it is the cat I am going to tell you about to-day—the cat in particular is like ours in every way. The rat-hunter of forty centuries ago differs in nothing from our tom-cat. But where did it come from, so long, long ago, in the houses of the Egyptians? Of what country was it a native?

"To the south of Egypt lies Abyssinia, where we have already found the wild dog, from which probably came our greyhound.

There, too, is still found, sometimes wild in the heart of the forest, sometimes domesticated, a kind of cat, called the gloved cat, that presents a striking resemblance to our domestic variety. It is generally agreed that this is the parent stock of our cats, though perhaps only in part, since there is reason to believe that a second species, Asiatic according to all appearance, has a place in the pedigree of our domestic cat as we now know it. Briefly, the cat came to us from Eastern Africa.

"In the old forests of Europe, and notably in those of the east of France, there is found, in no great numbers, a kind of cat called the wildcat, but which cannot be regarded as the progenitor of the domestic cat, in spite of current opinion to the contrary. Fitted by nature for violent exercise, for fighting and tree-climbing, and for making long leaps, it has longer and stronger legs than the common cat, a larger head, and more powerful jaws. The tail, very furry and variegated with black rings, is more expanded at the end than at the base. The coat is a warm fur of yellowish gray with large black stripes, transverse and encircling the body, thus imitating a little the tiger's coat. A dark band extends the entire length of the spine from the nape of the neck to the tail. Finally, the fleshy balls of the soles of the feet, and also the lips and nose, are black.

"The domestic cat, on the contrary, generally has red lips as well as nose and balls of the feet. It also has on the front of the neck and breast a band of light color sometimes extending under the stomach. Similar coloring of nose, lips, feet, and front of the neck is found, in exact detail, in the wild species of Abyssinia or the gloved cat; and that is one of the reasons for regarding this species as the source, or at least as one of the sources, of the domestic cat."

"But I have often seen domestic cats with black lips," objected Louis. "Where do they come from?"

"They are apparently in some way related to the wildcats of our woods. The female cats of isolated dwellings near our large forests sometimes mate with wildcats, it is said. The young of these parents bear inscribed on the nose and lips their paternal origin, and transmit these family traits to their descendants.

But if this crossing gives new vigor to our cat, it is far from improving its disposition. The wildcat of our woods is in fact an intractable animal, unruly despite all the care we bestow upon it. It is an implacable destroyer of game and, if chance offers, a more formidable ravager of the hen-roost than the fox.

"It is believed that one of our domestic varieties, known as the tiger-cat, counts this bandit among its ancestors; at any rate, it has the wildcat's black lips and zebra coat. It also has its disposition to a certain degree. The tiger-cat is the least tame of all, the most distrustful, the most inclined to plunder. No other is so ready with its claws if you try to take hold of it or merely stroke it on the back. But these peculiarities of savagery ought not to make us forget its good qualities: there is no more spirited hunter of mice. It is true that cheese forgotten on the table and game hung too low in the kitchen attract its attention a little too readily.

"I much prefer the Spanish or tortoise-shell cat, which is more civilized, of gentler disposition, and not less adept at catching mice. It is in this variety, one of the most widely diffused, that the original feline characteristics are the best preserved, that is to say those of the gloved cat of Abyssinia. The Spanish cat has rather short and brightly colored fur, the balls of the feet, the lips, and the nose red, the front of the neck light-colored. Its coat is generally spotted with irregular patches of pure white, black, and bright red. But, singularly enough, the three colors are never found united except in the female; the male is limited to two colors at most, generally white and red."

"Then every cat with three colors to its fur is a she-cat?" asked Jules.

"So far I have met with no exception to this strange rule."

"It is very queer, that unequal division of colors—three for the Tabby and only two at most for the Tom-cat. Other animals show nothing of the sort."

"The Angora cat forms a third variety. It is a magnificent animal, of majestic carriage, with silky and very long hair, especially around the neck, under the stomach, and on the tail. But its qualities do not equal the fineness of its fur. The Angora is the friend

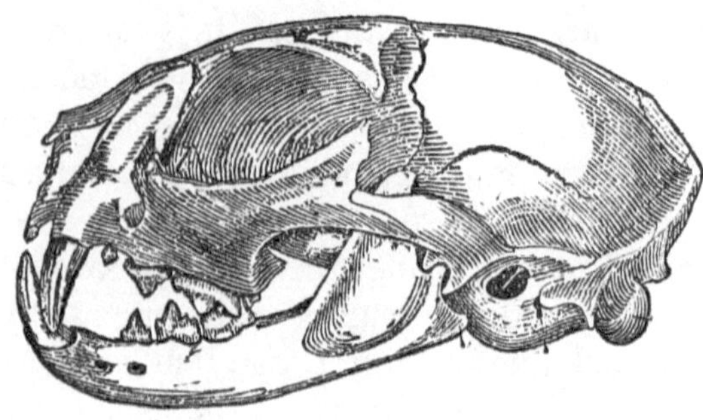

of sweet idleness, fond of prolonged siestas in drawing-room arm-chairs. Do not try to make it watch patiently for a mouse in the garret. Pampered by its mistress, assured of its saucer of milk, it finds the business of hunting too arduous. Repose and caresses and a soft bed are its lot. That is all I have to say about this lazy-bones.

"Let us pass on to the cat's weapons, its teeth and claws. In telling you the story of the Auxiliaries I pointed out to you the arrangement of the cat's teeth, so admirably adapted for coping with live prey. I will refresh your memory on this subject by showing you a sketch of these teeth. How well formed for cutting flesh are those molars, with their sharp points that play one against another like the blades of a pair of scissors! And those canine teeth, so long and sharp—aren't they veritable daggers for the cat to stab the mouse with? How horribly they must pierce the poor little victim's body! A mere glance at this set of teeth is enough to assure one that it belongs to a fierce hunter.

"It is by surprise and stealth that the cat seizes its prey. Hence it must have special foot-gear to render its approach noiseless, to deaden completely the sound of its footsteps. And that reminds me of something. When you were younger, you were told the wonderful exploits of Puss-in-Boots, how Puss caught partridges and offered them to the king, as a gift from the cat's master, the future Marquis of Carabas."

"Oh, yes," cried Emile, "I remember. The artful creature, with a grain of wheat in its paw and the bag open, lay in wait for the partridges in a furrow. What astounding success we credited it with! The giddy partridges and innocent quails, and foolish young rabbits ran helter-skelter into the bag. According to us, the game of the entire canton was bagged. One day the cat defied the ogre to take the form of every kind of animal in turn, as he pretended he had the power to do. The stupid ogre hastened to change himself into a lion first, then into a mouse. But in a half a jiffy out shoot the cat's claws, the mouse is caught, and the ogre is gobbled up. Thenceforth the castle belongs to the miller's son, who has become the Marquis of Carabas, as true as can be. Then the wedding is celebrated with great magnificence. Isn't that the way it goes, Uncle?"

"Precisely; only I must say to you that I object to the boots in that performance. How, with such foot-gear thumping and creaking on the gravel in the road, can the cat approach the game without being heard?"

"That's so. Let us take off the boots. We will suppose the cat leaves them at the mill while it is out hunting, and that it only wears them on great occasions."

"How much wiser the real cat is than the one in the story! It would not wear noisy boots and run the risk of making the garret floor creak under its footsteps. If the mouse heard the slightest sound of hard soles, it would never come out of its hole. What the cat really needs is slippers and not boots or wooden shoes—slippers thick and soft so as to muffle the footfall completely.

"Let us examine the underside of the cat's paw. You will see under each toe a little ball of flesh, a real cushion softly stuffed. Another ball, much larger, occupies the center. In addition, tufts of down fill up the intervening spaces. Thus shod, the cat walks as if on tow or wadding, and no ear can hear it coming. Have we not there, I ask you, slippers of silence, marvelously adapted to surprise attacks?"

"It is a fact," assented Louis, "that we never hear the cat coming."

"The dog, too," added Jules, "has similar little cushions, only larger, under its paws. Nevertheless we hear its footsteps, perhaps on account of the claws scraping the ground a little."

"Your 'perhaps' is superfluous," his uncle rejoined. "It is certainly the claws scraping the ground that make the dog's walk heard in spite of the fleshy balls."

"How does the cat manage, then?" asked Jules. "It has claws and very strong ones."

"That is the cat's secret. When walking and sleeping it keeps its claws drawn back in a sheath at the extremity of the toes; it has then what we call velvet paws. Thus drawn into their case, the claws do not project beyond the paw and cannot strike the ground. To this first advantage of not making any noise in walking is added another not less useful to the cat. Completely hidden inside their sheaths, the claws do not get blunt; they preserve their sharpness and fine point for the attack. They are excellent weapons, and the animal keeps them in a case until they are needed. Then the claws shoot out of their sheaths as if pushed by a spring, and the velvet paw of a moment ago becomes a horrible harpoon that implants itself in the flesh and rends the prey in most sanguinary fashion."

"If I give the cat's paw a little squeeze with my fingers," said Emile, "the claws come out of their sheaths; if I stop squeezing, the claws go in again."

"That is just what the cat can do at will. Let us examine this curious mechanism more closely. The little terminal bone of the toes, the one that bears the claw, is fastened to the preceding little bone by an elastic ligament, the effect of which, in a state of repose, is to raise the first bone and rest it on top of the second. Suppose that the tips of your fingers had play enough to fold back: there you have an exact representation of the process. In this position of the terminal bone the claw is held upright, half sunk in a fold of the skin and hidden under the thick fur of the paw."

"I understand," said Jules; "then it is a velvet paw; the claws are in their sheaths."

"Promptly, at the call to arms, the cat has but to will it, and its claws spring out. Look at this picture of a cat's paw and notice what appears to be a network of cords. Those are the tendons which, whenever the animal so desires, are pulled by the muscles situated higher up. They are fastened each to the

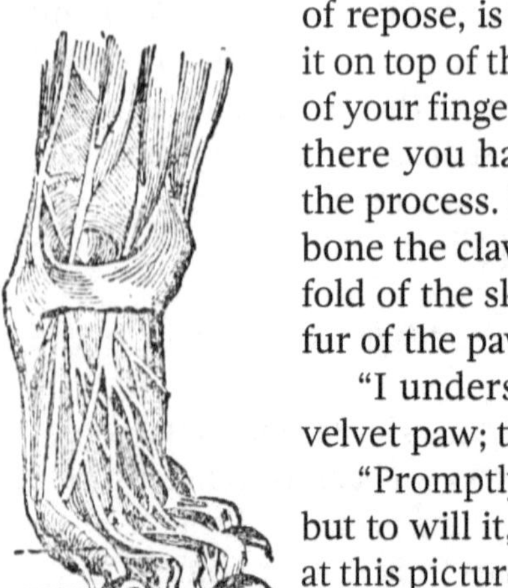

CAT'S CLAWS
AND TENDONS

lower side of one of the terminal bones of the toes. Pulled by its tendon, this terminal bone pivots, as if on a hinge, on the extremity of the preceding bone, and gets in a straight line with it. At the same time the pointed end of the claw comes out of the paw."

"Then the cat's claws are worked by cords and pulleys!" exclaimed Emile. "It is enough to bewilder one, it is so complicated. But I understand it in the main. To make velvet paws the cat doesn't have to do anything at all; the claws go in of their own accord and stay in their sheaths; and if they have to be drawn out, the cords or tendons give a pull, and the thing is done."

"To be shod with soft slippers which both admit of a noiseless approach to the hunted prey and can, on the instant, change into terrible weapons of attack, is not alone sufficient for the hunter's success; he must also have eyes to guide him in the darkness of midnight, the hour most favorable for an ambuscade. In this respect the cat is admirably equipped. Its eyes are formed for receiving more or less light as may be necessary for seeing.

"Notice a cat in the sun. You will see the pupil of the eyes reduced to a narrow slit resembling a black line. Not to be dazzled by too great light, the animal has closed the passage to the rays of light; it has closed the pupil while leaving the eyes wide open. Take the cat into the shade: the slit of the eyes will enlarge and become an oval. Put it in a semi-dark place: the oval opening will dilate to a circle and this circle will grow larger as the light diminishes.

"Thanks to these pupils, which open very wide and can thus still manage to receive a little light where for others it would be pitch-dark, the cat guides itself in the dark and hunts at night even better than in broad daylight, since it remains invisible to the mice while it can see them well enough. Nevertheless, if there were no light, if the darkness were absolute, the cat could not see anything. In this connection, recall what we were saying a while ago about nocturnal birds of prey. Some maintain that a cat sees distinctly in complete darkness; I have shown you, on the contrary, that for every animal without exception sight becomes impossible as soon as there ceases to be even the faintest ray of light."

"The cat cannot see without some light, I haven't the slightest doubt," assented Jules. "But all the same I have known it to hunt in places where not a glimmer of light could get in."

"Then its mustaches served to guide it; these are frequently made use of by the cat when it cannot see."

"Mustaches!" Emile exclaimed. "Oh, what a queer guide! And how can those long hairs that stand out on its lip tell it where it is?"

"Perhaps you think the cat wears mustaches simply as a bit of swagger. Undeceive yourself: they are a valuable item of its equipment for hunting by night. With them it feels the ground, gets its bearings, explores nooks and corners. Let a mouse so much as graze one of those long hairs sticking out in all directions, and that is enough to warn the cat. Immediately the jaw snaps and the claw seizes. Moral: never cut a cat's mustaches; you would place it in a sad predicament, seriously impairing its efficiency as a mouser."

"That's what I've heard said," Louis remarked, "though I didn't know the reason for it. Now I see that to deprive a cat of its mustaches, out of childish mischievousness, is like depriving a blind man of his cane."

"In my humble opinion," Uncle Paul continued, "the cat has been slandered. The eloquent historian of animals, Buffon, speaks thus about the cat: 'It is an unfaithful servant, kept only out of necessity, as the enemy of another and still more troublesome inhabitant of our houses, otherwise not to be got rid of.' "

"Buffon means the rat and mouse?" was Emile's query.

"Evidently. 'Although cats,' says he, 'especially when young, have pretty ways, they have at the same time an innate malice, a treacherous disposition, a perverse nature, which age increases and education only masks. From being determined thieves they become, under domestication, docile and fawning rogues: they have the same skill, the same cleverness, the same taste for mischief, the same tendency to petty pilfering, as have rogues. Like them, they know how to cover their tracks, dissimulate their purpose, watch for their opportunity, lie in wait, choose their time, seize the right moment for their stroke, then steal away and escape punishment, scamper off and keep out of sight until they are called back. They make a show of attachment, nothing more, as one can see in their sly movements and shifty eyes. They never look the loved one in the face; whether from distrust or falsity, they take a roundabout way of approach and of winning the caresses which they value only for the momentary pleasure they themselves receive. It cannot be said that cats, although living in our homes, are thoroughly domesticated. The best tamed among them are no whit more brought under control than the rest; one might even say that they are entirely beyond control. They do only what they choose, and nothing in the world would avail to keep them for a moment in a place they desired to leave. Furthermore, most of them are still half wild, do not know their masters, frequent only garrets and roofs, and sometimes the kitchen and pantry when they are hungry. They are less attached to persons than to houses.' "

"To my mind," commented Jules, "that accusation amounts to no more than this, that Buffon did not like cats."

"Oh, perhaps," suggested Louis, "he wrote it when he was vexed at some misdeed committed by his tom-cats."

"I, for my part," Uncle Paul replied, "will say this to you: treat the cat well, and it will not be wild; feed it, and it will not turn thief; show it a little attention, and it will return the compliment. But what a miserable fate it often has! It is allowed to grow thin with hunger under the pretense that then it will hunt rats better. If it comes into the kitchen, mewing for something to eat, it is driven out with a broom; if it ventures into the dining-room to gather up the crumbs fallen from the table, the dog, suspecting designs on the bone it holds between its paws, growls and makes a move to throttle the invader. As a last resort the poor animal takes to pilfering. Who would go so far as to call this a crime? Certainly not Uncle Paul."

"Nor I either," chimed in Jules; "for it must eat."

"Buffon says the cat does not become attached to its master, that it shows no signs of affection. I appeal the case to your own memories of the matter. When Minette, our gentle cat, installs herself with loud purrings on Emile's knees in the chimney-corner and rubs her pretty red nose on his cheeks, then on his forehead, and higher still until it makes his cap fall off, are not those, I ask you, kisses and caresses of the most affectionate sort? Emile is transported with delight when his cap tumbles to the floor under the poking of that delicate nose. He puts it on again and the friendly rubbing begins afresh."

"Certainly," Emile assented, "the cat gives me caress for caress. Her look is affectionate, not treacherous and distrustful, as the author says, that you have just been reading. And then Minette never steals, and always has velvet paws for me. She hasn't once given me a scratch in all the time we have played together."

"Emile forgets one very good quality," put in Jules. "Minette is a splendid hunter. Let her hear the slightest rustle anywhere, and there she will sit for hours and hours on the watch, motionless, patient, all eyes and ears. A mouse heard is for her a mouse caught. But it isn't hunger that gives her that love of hunting, for she kills her mouse and then leaves it lying there, with no desire to eat it."

"Minette has other talents too," Emile hastened to add. "When there is going to be a change in the weather, she licks her paws and washes her ears and nose over and over. Then you say, that is a sign of snow, or a sign of storm. And the cat's prediction is hardly ever wrong. When the north wind blows cold and dry, I like to rub my hand over her fur and make the bright sparks fly. In the evening I like to hear her *rerr-rerr*, which makes me sleepy."

"Why," asked Uncle Paul in conclusion, "do not Minette's good qualities agree with what Buffon says? Because you love the cat and the cat loves you in return. Animals, my dear children, are what people make them. Good master, good servant."

CHAPTER XXVII

SHEEP

"CONCERNING THE cat's origin there are surmises, probabilities; concerning the sheep's origin nothing is yet known. But if we are ignorant from what wild species the sheep descends, we are at least certain it came to us from Asia, where man has raised flocks of these useful animals from the earliest recorded times."

"The East gave us the dog, cat, and sheep," Jules here interposed, "and from what you said in some of our former talks, I got the impression that the other domestic animals also came from Asia."

"The Asiatic origin of our oldest known and most important domestic animals is a truth that all the records of history affirm without a shadow of doubt. We owe to the East the ox, horse, donkey, sheep, goat, pig, dog, cat, hen. Civilization, in fact, had its cradle in the lands of central Asia, where already there were flourishing peoples versed in sheep-raising and agriculture when in our western countries man, still plunged in wretched barbarism, lived only by the chase and hunted the bear and urus with his stone weapons."

"Then those ancient peoples of the East came and settled here and brought the first domestic animals with them?" asked Jules.

"That is just how it happened, and hence the Asiatic origin of our oldest domestic animals."

"Doubtless the sheep was with the new-comers?"

"Very likely; for its habits to-day show the sheep to have been dependent on man a very long time. No species has undergone so radical a change from its primitive character; and this indicates a very early domestication.

"In the beginning, when it wandered wild on the grassy plateaus of Asia, the sheep must have had means of defense against its enemies, since otherwise the species would have become extinct. It was not enough for it to crop the greensward; it must also have been able to hold its own when menaced, or at least to escape from danger by flight. The other domestic species shared the same risks as a necessary concomitant of freedom; but all knew how to defend themselves, and all, under man's protection, have nevertheless kept the use of their own means of protection. Left to itself, the dog, by its courage and its murderous jaws, valiantly copes with any assailant; the horse flees at full gallop or breaks the enemy's bones with a vigorous kick; the cat climbs trees and from her lofty fortress braves the foe; bulls group themselves in a circle, the weak ones in the center, the strong at the circumference, with horns pointing out, and woe then to any creature that dares to approach; the goat overthrows the aggressor by butting with lowered head. What can the sheep do in its turn when in danger? Nothing. With no thought of defending itself, imbecile and stupid, it waits for the wolf to come and devour it.

"Look at a flock of sheep, startled by some unusual noise. They rush headlong, bewildered with fear; they crowd together, press against one another, lower their heads to the ground, then await, motionless, the issue of the event. The wolf, if it be a wolf that has caused the panic, has only to choose its victim out of this compact mass: there will be no thought of resistance or flight. What would become of the poor creatures if shepherds and dogs were not there to protect them? In a few days they would all perish, sacrificing their last drop of blood to the wolf. See them again in the open country in bad weather. They press close to one another and refuse to budge, enduring rain and snow, shivering with wet and cold, while not one of them so much as thinks of seeking shelter. Their stupidity is such that they do not even seem to notice how unfavorable their situation is; they come to a standstill wherever they may happen to be, and obstinately stay there. To make them go and to conduct them to a more suitable spot, the shepherd is obliged to chase them before him and give them a leader taught to walk in front.

"Certainly, in its primitive freedom the sheep could not have been the actual animal of our folds; it must have possessed the qualities necessary to sustain its existence; it must have found in itself means of protection and must at least have imitated the goat, which resolutely faces danger, or, if too weak, scales with unerring foot the ledges of rock and there takes refuge. The sheep, as we have it to-day, is absolutely incapable of living without man's protection; left to itself, the whole species would soon perish, the victim of carnivorous animals and inclement weather. To lose thus all its native instincts and descend to the lowest degree of stupidity, how many centuries of servitude must it not have undergone? I would not venture to say; but at least I see that, after the dog, the sheep was one of the first animals tamed by man.

"No other species, the dog alone excepted, has undergone so complete a transformation at our hands. Let me tell you some of the strange results obtained. In Africa, Madagascar, and India there is found a breed of sheep in which the tail, loaded with a heavy mass of fat on each side, right and left, is transformed into a sort of ponderous battledore, broader at its base than the body itself. The weight of this inconvenient appendage amounts to and even exceeds thirty pounds."

"Inconvenient appendage I should say it would be," remarked Louis. "The sheep cannot walk very easily with that heavy battledore knocking against its hocks. The tallow from that tail would make a good many candles, but it is a very troublesome sort of treasure when one has to run away from a wolf."

"This breed is called the broad-tailed sheep. Other sheep, particularly in southern Russia, have tails of moderate size, like the tails of our sheep, but very long so that they drag on the ground."

"Again a hindrance when fleeing from the wolf," Jules observed. "In its primitive state the sheep certainly had neither this long trailing tail catching in the bushes, nor that other one in the shape of a heavy load of tallow."

"Neither had it the singular horns that it sometimes bears to-day. Some sheep have horns of excessive length and twisted

LEICESTER SHEEP

in long spirals that sometimes stand erect on the top of the forehead, and sometimes point sidewise. Those weapons are more threatening than serviceable: they needlessly overburden the head and are a serious source of annoyance to the animal when it has to pass through a thicket of underbrush. As if to hamper themselves still more in the brambles, other breeds wear an addition to this inconvenient ornament. The sheep of the island of Cyprus have two pairs of horns, one standing straight up on the forehead, the other curving back behind the ears. Those of the Faroe Islands have three pairs, all arranged spirally and pointing backward. Our sheep, as a rule, have only two horns, rather small and making barely one turn at the sides of the head; apparently that is how the primitive species wore them. In fact the greater part of our flocks is composed of entirely hornless sheep. It is best for the animal, which is thus relieved of a useless load.

"These horns, double or triple in number, and twisting in curious fashion, this tail so long that it trails on the ground, or else swollen with tallow and broad beyond measure, while showing us what singular modifications the body of the sheep is capable of, are of no use to us whatever. It is much to be preferred that the animal, profiting by the care we bestow upon it, should gain in weight and furnish more abundant food material. The English, who are great meat-eaters, were the first to ask themselves this question: how to make the sheep an abundant source of mutton chops and legs of mutton, or, in other words, how to increase to the utmost the proportion of it that can be eaten and at the same time diminish or even reduce to nothing that which cannot?

"A celebrated breeder, a benefactor to humanity—Bakewell was his name—solved the problem in England about a century ago. He said to himself. The sheep that I want as a producer of legs of mutton must have no horns, for these useless ornaments would mean so much pure loss in the total weight of the animal; the food required for the growth and maintenance of the horns would be better employed in producing flesh. For the same reason it should have only just enough wool to clothe it and protect it from the cold. The bones I cannot eliminate, the more's the pity, as in their place I should prefer something of greater nutritive value. But as a matter of fact they are necessary to the animal: they are the indispensable framework for the flesh. If I cannot eliminate them, the bones shall at least be light, thin, reduced in weight and size. When the leg of mutton is served at table, the knife must be able to penetrate it like a ball of butter and find in the center only a small, hard drum-stick. I will reduce in like manner all that is not meat and leave the sheep only what is strictly necessary for the functions of life."

"And that came to pass as the breeder wished?" asked Jules.

"That came to pass just as Bakewell foresaw. In his sheepfolds the animal was transformed into an opulent source of meat, such as had never been seen before; it became a pair of enormous legs of mutton and a pair of enormous shoulders, led to pasture by a small head on four thin legs."

"With large mutton chops mixed in?" Emile inquired.

"To be sure. A few figures will show you the importance of the result obtained. The gross weight of our ordinary sheep averages thirty kilograms, representing about twenty kilograms net of meat. The Leicester sheep, as the perfected breed developed by Bakewell's exertions is called, weighs from sixty to one hundred and sometimes one hundred and fifty kilograms; and its net yield in meat varies from fifty to one hundred kilograms; that is, at the very lowest, two and a half times as much meat as our common sheep produces, and at the highest, which is exceptional, I admit, five times as much."

"Then man can do what he likes with his domestic animals to change them as he pleases?" asked Louis.

"He does not do exactly as he likes, for the organization is from its very nature bounded by definite limits which no effort of ours can set aside; but by holding one end constantly in view and bending every exertion toward its attainment he can do much. The great means used by Bakewell on the breeding of sheep, and utilized since for the improvement of various other domestic animals, consists above all in selection, which I have already told you something about in speaking of the dog. Selection is called into play when the breeder singles out and sets apart for the propagation of the species those individuals that show in the highest degree the qualities he desires. These qualities, however feeble at first, are capable of great development in the course of several generations; for the offspring inherit the parents' qualities, keep them, and add to this inheritance certain qualities of their own."

"You compared that to a snowball increasing in size as it rolls," said Jules.

"Yes, my friend; the succeeding generations, always chosen from among the best, are the successive layers that bring their complement to the increase of the ball."

"The Leicester sheep must have acted on the snowball wonderfully, to increase its weight from thirty kilograms to one hundred and fifty."

"I admit that such a transformation is not brought about in a single year, and that Bakewell must have had great confidence in his method to devote his whole life to the pursuit of the end foreseen by his genius."

"What is this famous Leicester sheep like?" asked Emile.

"Its trunk is all of a size, almost cylindrical. The head is small, bald, and without horns. It is supported by a neck so slender and short that the head appears to spring directly from the trunk."

"To judge by the picture you are showing us, one would say that the head came out of a hole made in the middle of the fleece."

"That comes from the smallness of the neck. The wool, long and coarse, takes the form of pointed locks hanging down and not very close together, so that the whole fleece weighs much less than one would suppose from the size of the animal. The four legs are thin and naked. All the bones in short, are remarkably light, having only enough solidity to support the animal's massive bulk of flesh."

"Is this breed found in France?" Louis asked.

"With us it is represented by the Flemish breed, raised in Flanders, Normandy, and Poitou. It is the most corpulent of the French varieties, furnishing sheep that weigh as much as sixty kilograms, and more. In the second class for size comes the Picardy breed, scattered over Picardy, Brie, and Beauce. The sylvan breed of Touraine, Sologne, Bourgogne, Anjou, in short a great part of central France, is smaller still. It is remarkable for the fineness of its wool and the excellence of its flesh. By its side may be placed the Provence breed, occupying Roussillon, Provence, and Languedoc. Immense flocks of this variety graze during the winter in the salt marshes bordering the Mediterranean, notably in the vast pebbly plain of Crau and in the island of Camargue which the forks of the Rhone form at the mouth of that river. After the cold weather is past, these flocks move up to the high mountains of Dauphiny, where they pass the whole summer out of doors. I will come back in a few moments to their interesting migrations.

"Besides meat, the sheep furnishes us wool, which is still more important, since it is the best material for our clothing. Other animals, the ox and pig for example, feed us with their flesh; only the sheep can clothe us. With wool we make mattresses and weave cloth, flannel, serge, in fact all the different fabrics best adapted for protecting us from the cold. It is far and away the most suitable material for clothing; cotton, despite its importance, takes only second place; and silk, with all its fine qualities, is very inferior to wool for actual service. The sheep's coat, more than anything else, we use for clothing; we cover ourselves with its fleece after converting it by spinning and weaving into magnificent cloth."

"All the same," objected Emile, "wool is not in the least beautiful when it is on the animal's back; it is dirty, badly combed, often completely covered with filth. To be changed into the fleece suitable for cloth it must go through a good many processes."

"A good many, indeed. We will speak only of the first, for the others would lead us too far from our subject.

"As it is found on the sheep, the wool is soiled by the sweat of the animal and by dust, which together form a layer of dirt called natural grease. An energetic washing is necessary to remove these impurities. The best way is to wash the sheep itself before shearing. The flock is driven to the edge of a stream, not so cold as to endanger the health of the animals, and there each sheep is seized in turn by men who plunge it into the water and rub and squeeze the fleece with their hands until the grease has disappeared and the water runs clear from the tufts of wool. That is what is called washing on the back, because the wool is cleaned on the body itself, on the animal's back.

"At other times the sheep is shorn without having been washed first, just as it comes out of the fold, with all its coating of dust and sweat. The wool thus obtained is called greasy wool, while the washed fleece is known as greaseless wool. The greasy wool is too dirty to be used as it is, even for making mattresses; it is washed in a stream of running water, and then it is like the wool taken from a washed sheep.

"To shear a sheep, the animal is tied fast by all four legs to keep it from moving and perhaps getting cut during the operation; then it is placed on a table about as high as a man is tall, and with large, wide-bladed shears the wool is clipped off as close as possible to the skin without at the same time cutting the poor animal. As the locks of wool are naturally curly and entangled, the fleece comes off all in one piece.

"Sheep are white, brown, and black. White wool can be

dyed any shade, from the lightest to the darkest, whereas black or brown will only take dark colors. White wool, therefore, is always preferred to any other; but however beautiful it may be after all impurities have been removed by washing, it is still far from possessing the degree of whiteness that it should have if it is to be used without dyeing. Accordingly it is bleached by being exposed in a closed room to the suffocating vapor that comes from burning sulphur.

"Wool varies in value according to the sheep that produced it; there are different degrees of coarseness and fineness and length. The best wool, that which is reserved for the finest stuffs, comes from a breed of sheep raised principally in Spain and known by the name of merino. This breed has a squat, short, thick body, legs strong and short, large head furnished with stout horns that fall in a spiral behind the ear, woolly forehead, and a very snub nose. The skin, fine and pink, forms at different parts of the body, chiefly around the neck, ample folds which give room for additional fleece. Wool covers the whole body, except the muzzle, from the edge of the hoofs to a rim around the eyes. It is fine, curly, elastic, and short. The grease with which it is impregnated is very abundant, so that the dust sticking to it forms on the surface of the fleece a grayish crust, a sort of plate-armor, which splits open here and there with a slight crackling sound when the animal moves, and closes of itself when the animal is at rest. By washing, these impurities all disappear and merino wool then shows the whiteness of snow and has a softness that rivals silk.

"In Spain the merino flocks pass the winter in the fertile plains of the South, in a climate remarkable for its mildness. At the beginning of April they start for the high mountains of the North, which they reach after a journey of a month or six weeks. All through the summer they remain in the highland pastures, rich in savory greensward which the summer sun never dries up, and at the end of September they descend again to the plains of the South. These traveling flocks, changing from plain to mountain and from mountain to plain, according to the season, are called migratory flocks. Some of them number as many as ten thousand animals, tended by fifty shepherds and as many dogs."

"It must be very interesting," said Jules, "to see those immense flocks in motion along the highways when they go to or from their mountain pasture."

"What takes place in the south of France can give us some idea of this. I told you that the vast plains of the Mediterranean coast, the plains of Crau and Camargue, support flocks of considerable size, which emigrate to the mountains of Dauphiny when warm weather comes, and return home on the approach of cold."

"Are those sheep merinos?" Jules asked.

"No, my friend: they are ordinary sheep; but, like the merinos, they travel alternately from the plain to the mountains and from the mountains to the plain; in a word, they are migratory flocks. Let us look at them on their return journey.

"At the head are the donkeys laden with clothing and provisions. Large and heavy bells hang from their collars, each collar being made of a big sheet of bent deal. If they spy a thistle beside the road, they turn out and with a grimace crop the savory mouthful with a movement of their lips, after which they at once return to their posts of file-leaders. In large panniers of plaited grass one of them carries the lambs born on the journey, too weak to follow the flock. The poor little things bleat, their heads nodding to the movements of their nags, and the mothers answer from the midst of the throng. Next come the ill-smelling, high-horned, flat-nosed, cross-eyed he-goats; the bells attached to the wooden collars ring under their thick beards. After them come the she-goats, their heavy udders, swollen with milk, striking against their hams. By their side caper the giddy band of young kids and goats, already beginning to butt with their foreheads. Such is the vanguard.

"Who is this with holly stick cut from an alpine hedge and large drugget cloak draped over his shoulder? It is the head shepherd, the one responsible for the flock. At his heels come the rams, leaders of the stupid common sheep. Their horns, twisted into a pointed spiral, make three and four turns. They have deal collars like those of the he-goats and asses; but their large bells, sign of honor, have a wolf's tooth for tongue. Tufts of red wool, another sign of distinction, are fastened to their fleece on the sides and back. In the midst of a cloud of dust comes now the main flock, its members crowded close together and bleating, their countless little hoofs striking the ground with a noise like that of a storm. In the rear straggle the loiterers, the lame, the crippled, the ewes accompanied by their lambs. These last, at the briefest stop, bend their knees, take the teat in their mouth, and, while their tail trembles and wriggles, butt the udder with their forehead to start the flow of milk. The shepherds bring up the rear, urging on the slow ones with their cries and giving orders to the dogs, their lieutenants that go and come on the flanks of the army and watch that none go astray. If all is in good order, the dogs walk beside their masters, pensive, fully appreciating the seriousness of their functions, and perhaps thinking of the woods they came from, the dark woods where there are bears."

CHAPTER XXVIII

THE GOAT

"IN THE hilly regions of Persia there are found herds of wild goats of a kind that is universally regarded as the parent stock of the domestic variety. This goat closely resembles our own in size and form. It has a grayish fawn-colored coat with a black line on the backbone. The tail and forehead are black, the cheeks red, the beard and throat brown. The horns have sharp edges on the front side and are short in the female, very long in the male, always erect on the forehead, and not rolling back behind the ears like those of the ram.

"In domestication the goat has preserved its primitive instincts, no doubt because, being of less value than the sheep, it has not been so carefully and completely tamed by man. It has remained with us much as it was on the bare rocks of its native country, lively, wandering, adventurous, fond of lonely and steep places, delighting in rocky summits, sleeping on the edge of precipices, and always ready to use its horns at the slightest appearance of hostility.

"Willingly it accompanies the sheep to pasture, but without mixing with the flock, the stupid society of which is not to its taste. It walks at the head, staying its impatience on the way by browsing an occasional twig in the hedgerow."

"That's the way the he-goats of the emigrating flock go, the captains of the company," put in Jules. "The she-goats follow pell-mell with the kids. Left to themselves, they would walk at the head and occupy the post of honor held by the donkeys and he-goats."

"Arrived at the pasture, the sheep begin peacefully cropping the grass without straying too far from the spot chosen by the shepherd. Besides, the dog is there to call to order any that might tend to wander away."

"But the goats don't listen to the dog's warning: their wish is to go and flock apart, is it not?" asked Emile.

"Precisely. The turf is green, smooth as a carpet; the grass thick and tender. What more could be desired? But no, the goats will have none of it. The rich grass and the company of the timid sheep are not what they are after. Away up yonder, on the top of the hill, are some great rocks, cleft and overturned in disorder. In the clefts, where a handful of earth has lodged, there are thin tufts of grass half dried up by the sun; between the fragments of stone a few pitiful shrubs with scanty foliage manage to find room for their roots. Those are the goat's haunts of delight. Nothing can keep it from them; away it goes.

"Soon you will see it on the steep slope of the rocks, moving about with ease where any other animal would break its neck, and sometimes having no more secure support than a narrow ledge that offers barely room enough for its four hoofs. From this perilous position it stretches its neck in an effort to reach the neighboring bush, a bush no better than countless others that are in places easy of access; but the difficulty gives it an added charm, and to get it the goat risks its life on slopes that would be its destruction if it should chance to slip. But don't worry about that: the goat will not fall; its sinewy leg is of unequalled surety, and its head, giddy though it seems, is never seized with vertigo on the brink of a precipice. The coveted bit of foliage is reached, the bush twisted out of shape in its attainment, and the ascent continues from one projection to another. The goat is at the top of the rock. It proclaims its prowess to the surrounding world with bleatings. The sheep are down there, beneath its feet. Proudly it surveys them, saying perhaps to itself: Poor, timid creatures, they will never climb up here!

"I must tell you, my friends, that the goat is very hard to keep in flocks. Its wandering propensity always impels it to stray, and its predilection for precipices leads it to places where it would be dangerous for the shepherd to follow. It has a still worse caprice. I have pictured the goat to you as abandoning at the first opportunity the rich grass in which the sheep delights, to scale the rocky summit and crop the sparse shrubbery growing on some perilous ledge. It is an undoubted fact that to the tender grass of the best pasture it prefers hard turf, yellowed in the sun, dried and trodden, and especially the young woody sprouts of the shrub and bush. Thus far all is for the best, since such tastes enable us to gain profit from the most sterile soil and even from the bare rock. Where the sheep would die of want, the goat finds the wherewithal to fill its udder with milk. Unfortunately its passion for the bitter bark of the shrub has evil consequences. Cultivated grounds, gardens, orchards, quickset hedges, copses, and woods have no more terrible enemy than the goat. The young shoots are eagerly browsed, the bark is gnawed, and all shrubbery within reach is destroyed. Accordingly, to prevent these ravages, severe laws forbid flocks of goats access to all wooded tracts."

"I shouldn't like such gnawers of branches and bark among the pear trees in the garden," remarked Jules. "If any goats got in there, it would be good-by forever to those delicious juicy pears."

"I have told you the goat's bad qualities; now let us look at its good ones. The goat is much more intelligent than the sheep. It comes to us of its own accord, makes friends with us readily, is responsive to caresses and capable of attachment. In households where it furnishes the milk supply it is the companion of the children, who know how to win its friendship by a few handfuls of choice grass. It takes part in their games and amuses them with its frolicsome gambols."

"It also runs with lowered head at its playmates as if it meant to knock them over with a butt of its horns," added Emile; "but it is only in fun. They hold out an open hand, and the goat strikes the palm very softly without hurting it, provided they are good friends. If not, I shouldn't like to find myself facing the goat's horns."

"The goat is always friendly if well treated. Its butting is then harmless, and play does not degenerate into a fight.

"To appreciate fully the kindness of the goat, one must have witnessed the following illustration of it. When a nursing baby has had the misfortune to lose its mother, it sometimes happens that the she-goat is substituted as a nurse. In this function the excellent animal is truly admirable; the tenderest mother is not more vigilant or more assiduous. To the wailing of the beloved baby it responds with a gentle bleating and runs to it in all haste, lying on its side the better to present its udder to the nursling. If there is any delay in putting the baby within reach, the goat by its restless movements, trembling voice, I might almost say by its gestures, begs that the infant be allowed to suck. How shall I express it, my friends? The animal in this action is sublime in its devotion.

"Should you like now to see the goat giving proof of its tame, trustful nature? I will tell you how the milk-peddlers of our southern towns are in the habit of leading their flocks of goats through the streets, to sell from door to door the milk freshly drawn under the buyer's very eyes. What would the timid sheep do if led thus through the turmoil and confusion of a populous town? It would take fright and run away, and in its foolish terror it would get crushed under the wheels of passing vehicles. The goat is not alarmed at anything. Throngs of people, the noise of traffic, the barking of quarrelsome dogs, to all this it is quite indifferent. The horned company, its approach heralded by the tinkling of little bells, moves with a confident and familiar air in the midst of all this hustle and bustle, as if in the perfect solitude of the mountains. With graceful coquetry it looks at its reflection in the large shop-windows and strikes the flag-stones of the pavement with ringing hoof. At the customers' doors, which the flock never fails to remember, it comes to a halt. Each goat in its turn is taken in hand by the milkmaid, and the warm milk spurts foaming from the udder into the tin measure. They go on through the crowd to another customer, and so it continues, a measure of milk at a time, until the flock has exhausted its day's supply."

"Is there anything gained by leading the goats from door to door?" asked Jules.

"Unquestionably: the buyer cannot doubt the freshness and purity of the milk when he sees it drawn under his eyes; and the milkmaid finds in the confidence of her customers remuneration for her extra trouble."

"That's so. No one can say the milk is watered if it comes fresh from the udder."

"Goat's milk is light and very nourishing; it agrees with weak stomachs better than the heavier milk of the sheep or cow. It is remarkably abundant, too, considering the smallness of the animal. Two liters of milk a day, from six to nine months in the year, make but a moderate yield. There are goats that, when well-fed, give three and four liters a day.

"Thus the goat, so easily maintained, is a valuable resource in mountainous and arid countries; it takes the place of the milch cow in the poor man's hut, as the donkey serves instead of the horse.

"This abundant milk supply is about the only merit of the goat, for its stringy flesh is tasteless and of no value. Only the kid is prized for eating, especially in the South, where the aromatic vegetation of the hills takes away its natural tastelessness. The goat's fleece, though used for certain coarse fabrics, is not of much importance, either, and cannot in any way take the place of sheep's wool. But a breed native in the hilly regions of Central Asia, the Cashmere goat, furnishes a down of incomparable fineness, from which precious stuffs are made. This goat, under a thick fur of long hair, bears an abundant down that protects it from the rigors of cold and is shed naturally every spring. When that season comes the animal is combed with a long toothed comb that gathers from the rest of the fleece the fine down detached from the skin.

"Another breed, the Angora goat, almost rivals the Cashmere in fineness of down. It takes its name from the town of Angora in Turkey in Asia. Nothing could be more seductive in form, nothing more graceful, than these little goats with their long silky fleece, always pure white. From the same country come the Angora cat and the Angora rabbit, both furnished, like the goat, their compatriot, with long, silky, white fur."

CHAPTER XXIX

THE OX

"THE TAMING of the ox took place in Asia a very long time ago when our western countries were covered with wild forests in which a few miserable tattooed tribes wandered, living by the chase. Bringing the ox under subjection must have been one of the most memorable of events for the native of the Orient, since thereby the animal's powerful shoulders lent themselves to the labors of agriculture, and the tiller of the soil profited accordingly. It must also have been a very dangerous undertaking, no doubt impossible without the help of the dog. The friendly goat perhaps came to man of its own accord; the peaceful sheep let itself be folded without resistance; but the ox, terrible in power and anger, throwing the disemboweled enemy heavenward with a toss of its horns, certainly did not let itself be led from its native forest to the stable without a fight. No account has come down to us of the brave men who first dared to attack the formidable beast with the hope of subjugating it; nor does any record remain of the difficult training which, perhaps prolonged through centuries, finally reduced the wild creature to a state of docility. The very first historical reference to the ox in the earliest annals of our race shows him to us as a patient, docile beast, submissive to the yoke, and in short no other than he is to-day.

"But if these bull-tamers of ancient times remain unknown, all the East preserves the memory of their invaluable achievement. The man was forgotten, but the animal was fêted, here in one way, there in another, according to the fancy of a simple, imaginative people striving in every possible manner to evince gratitude for services rendered. I have told you of ancient

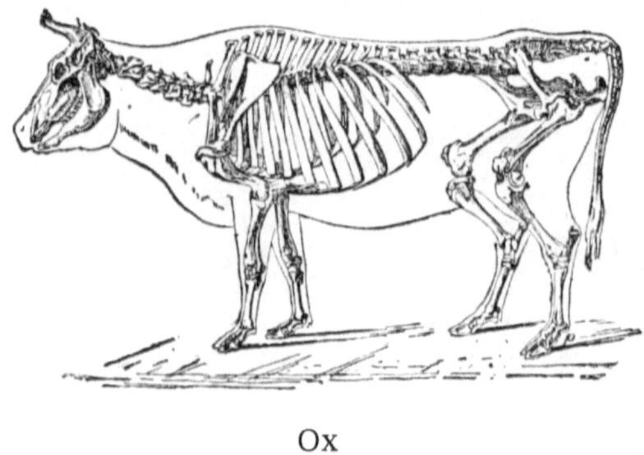

Ox

Egypt and its raising of marble temples to the bull, and I have also described its practice of bowing the forehead to the dust when the majestic beast passed with its retinue of attendants. Elsewhere it was enjoined on every one as a religious duty of the most sacred kind to raise at least one ox; and, again, in still another country, where horned cattle were not yet plentiful enough to make it permissible to use them for food, the laws punished with death anybody who killed or even maltreated one of these animals. In our day, in India, the cow is a thrice-sacred animal. Its tail, symbol of honor, is carried as a standard before the great; and to win favors from Heaven the people believe there is no surer way than to smear the body with cow's dung and then go and wash in the waters of the Ganges. These anointings with the holy dung make you smile, children; in me they arouse serious reflections. From what depths of misery must not the domestic animals have raised us if the Hindu of our time still preserves in these strange rites some vestiges of the ancient veneration of the entire Orient for one of these animals, and that one the most important, the ox?"

"I should say it was a strange rite," declared Jules, "to daub oneself with dung in honor of the cow. They might have hit on a better way."

"In every age and in every land popular imagination has easily lent itself and still lends itself to extravagant notions. In the most important city of the South I have seen, I, Uncle Paul, the people leading through the streets, in triumphal procession, the fattened ox that was to be sacrificed on Easter Eve. A laurel branch on its forehead, many-colored ribbons on its horns, the peaceful beast bore on its shoulders a pretty little child, rosy, plump, clothed in a lamb's skin. A retinue accompanied it in bright-colored costumes. Is not that a vague reminder of the procession of the bull Apis, with this difference that the Egyptian bull returned after the ceremony to its perfumed manger, while ours meets its end in the heavy blow awaiting it at the slaughter-house? It is the custom for the be-ribboned ox to be led from door to door, where its escort never fails to present the basin for offerings, great and small; for it is to be noted that at the bottom of every superstition is found the quest of the piece of coin. Thus takes place throughout all France, with more or less pomp, the procession of the fattened ox.

"But here is a peculiarity worthy of note. If the house has a wide enough entrance door, the ox is led into the vestibule, where its presence is supposed to confer honor; and if by good luck at that moment the animal deposits on the floor some of the material used by the Hindu for smearing himself, it is the greatest possible blessing for the visited. A prosperous future is presaged by a few spans' breadth of this dung, according to the hope and belief of the simple folk. You see, my friends, without leaving home we find, under a little different form, the Indian customs that make you smile so. I cannot but see therein the survivals of the ancient honors paid to the bull. Without explaining these customs to themselves, without knowing their origin, without understanding their significance, the people perpetuate them among us."

"The survivals from those old customs," remarked Jules, "prove clearly that the acquisition of the ox left an ineffaceable trace on man's mind; but, once more, why didn't they hit on some better way to honor the ox?"

"Well, if you want something better as a mark of honor, perhaps this will satisfy you: the invaluable animal has its name written forever among the stars, those jewels of the sky. I will explain myself. History tells us that we owe the invention of astronomy to the shepherds of the East, who spent their leisure night-hours, under the mildest of skies, in deciphering the secrets of the stars while their flocks rested in the open air. To get their bearings in the midst of the infinite multitude of stars, these shepherds gave to the principal groups or constellations names that have been perpetuated and that science still uses. Man's most precious possession received at that time a celestial consecration by having its name given to such and such a part of the sky. One of the constellations was called Taurus (the bull); and that is what it still is and always will be called. In this group are seen stars that form an angle, the two branches of which represent the animal's horns; there is also a superb star that darts red fire and suggests the sparkling eye of an infuriated bull. What greater honor could the bull receive than to be thus placed among the splendors of the sky?"

"The shepherds' idea fully satisfies me; nothing better could be imagined for the glorification of the ox. Other domestic animals doubtless have had places assigned them in the firmament?"

"Of course. Another constellation is called Aries (the ram), another Capricornus (goat-horned)."

"And how about the dog?" Emile asked.

"The dog was not to be forgotten: is it not man's earliest ally, the courageous servant that made possible the taming of the herd? Its name has been given to a magnificent constellation in which shines the brightest star in the sky."

"And the others, the cat, horse, pig, and donkey?"

"None of them received from the ancient shepherds the honor of a place in the firmament, their acquisition being undoubtedly more recent and of less importance. Briefly, my friends, the most esteemed and the most ancient of our domestic animals have been glorified by honors never bestowed upon prince, emperor, or monarch. Man's gratitude has placed them among the splendors of the firmament.

"In Asia, where it originated, the ox is no longer found wild; but in the pampas of South America the species has resumed its primitive freedom and, mingled with horses that have become equally wild, lives in vast herds beyond the supervision of man. *Pampas* is the name given to the immense plains extending from Buenos Aires to the foot of the Cordilleras of the Andes. During the rainy season they furnish rich pasturage of tall grass, but in the dry season verdure disappears and the soil becomes a powdery plain where thistles wave. Nothing, not even a tree, breaks the uniformity of these plains, the limits of which cannot be seen in any direction. There lives the wild ox, descendant of the domesticated ox that the Spaniards brought to this part of the New World, for the species did not exist anywhere in America before the arrival of Europeans.

"The few pairs that escaped from their stables or were left to themselves in the pastures of the pampas three or four centuries ago, have multiplied so rapidly that to-day the number of cattle there is incalculable. More than two hundred thousand are slaughtered every year, and still the herds show no sign of diminution. The carnage has long been and still continues to be carried on for the sake of the hides, or at least this is in great part the purpose."

"They kill the cattle just for the hides?" asked Jules incredulously. "Then the meat isn't good for anything?"

"It is excellent, but they do not know what to do with it, there is so much. The population of the country not being sufficient to consume this enormous quantity of food, the cattle are slaughtered, the hides removed and cured, after which they can be kept indefinitely, and the flesh is left behind as a useless encumbrance. This is a waste much to be regretted, for with us meat is becoming scarcer every day, and our food problem would find a ready solution in the pampas cattle that now feed only carnivorous animals.

"It is true that attempts are made to save a part of this copious supply of provision. The meat is cut into strips which are dried in the sun or salted or smoked, as a means of preservation; and in this state commerce carries them to all parts of the world. Unfortunately, I must acknowledge, this meat preserved by salting, smoking, or drying is not very palatable eating. Let us hope that improved methods of preserving will be introduced, and that some day South America will furnish Europe a rich supply of butcher's meat.

"In the present state of things the pampas cattle are hunted principally for their hides. I say hunted, for the cattle of the grassy plains of Buenos Aires may be called veritable game, since these animals do not fall, as do our cattle, under the blow of the butcher's hammer, but are pursued in the open pasture and killed on the spot. The hunter is on horseback. For weapon he has the lasso; that is to say, a very long and tough leather thong, fastened at one end to the saddle-bow, armed at the other with balls of lead. When the hunted animal is within reach, the hunter throws the perfidious leather thong, which, whistling and following the course of the lead, encircles the animal's horns and neck. At the touch of the spur the horse gallops off, putting forth all its strength, and drags the half-strangled ox after it. A plunge of the dagger in the heart finishes the beast. After removing the skin and rolling it up on the crupper of his horse, the cattle-hunter resumes his quest, leaving to the birds of prey the dead bodies whose bones, whitened by rain and sun, will serve him on future expeditions as material for building himself a hut."

"A hut of bones!" exclaimed Emile.

"Yes, my friend. On those vast plains wood is lacking as well as stones. Therefore bones, piled one on top of another, serve the hunter of the pampas for building him a shelter, where he rests under a grass roof. The skull of an ox with long horns serves him as a seat by day and a pillow at night."

"It seems to me I shouldn't sleep very well with my head between the two horns of an ox's skull."

"The hardened hunter of the pampas sleeps on it as on feathers."

"And what do they do with all those hides that they get by hunting the ox?" asked Jules.

"There is an extensive commerce in those hides. Ships bring them to us, well salted, so that they will keep. In our tanneries the salt is washed out, and then with oak-bark they are made into leather for boots and shoes."

"Then the leather of our shoes may come from some ox strangled by the lasso on the pampas?" Louis queried.

"There is nothing impossible in that. I would not say positively that we are not wearing shoes made from the hide of a wild ox, for Buenos Aires supplies a considerable part of our deficiency in leather. It may be, on the other hand, that our shoes come simply from the domestic ox, whose hide is put to the same use as that of the South American bullock. You are at liberty to ascribe your footwear to either source."

"For my part," Emile declared, "I choose the wild ox, and perhaps its body is now being used by some hunter for his hut."

"To finish the subject of tame cattle that have run wild, I will say a few words about the herds of Camargue. A little below Arles, about seven leagues from the sea, the Rhone forks and encloses between its two branches and the Mediterranean a large triangular plain. That is Camargue, a shifting tract subject to the action of both fresh and salt water, receiving the alluvial deposits of the river and the sands of the sea. There are three different regions to be distinguished in going from the riverbanks to the interior of the island, where there is a large pond known as the Vaccarès Pond. These regions comprise the cultivated territory, the pasture land, and the group of ponds. The first, running the length of the two outlets of the Rhone, is wonderfully fertile, being made so by the annual deposits of silt. Rich harvests gild these strips of land along the river, the current of which prevents the infiltration of salt from the sea. Going further, one comes to the salt marshes, and finally, from the center of the island to the sea, stretches the region of ponds. This last is merely dry land in the making, a plain in the process of formation, with the river constantly adding its accretions of soil and the sea forever washing them away.

"In the portion devoted to pasturage roam thousands of bullocks that have reverted to the wild state, unprovided with shelter of any sort and free from all surveillance except such as is exercised by mounted keepers who, at long intervals, come and round up the unruly herds with the aid of a trident. Black, small, and stocky, with fierce eyes and menacing horns, they have resumed the primitive characteristics of the race. Bad luck to whoever should come and disturb them at their sport among the reeds. Only the herdsman, mounted on a fast horse and equipped with a trident for pricking the nostrils of the beasts, can control the wild herd. In one particular alone are we reminded that they are still man's servants, victims destined for his slaughter-houses and sometimes also, alas, set apart for his entertainment in the barbaric bull-fight: on their shoulders the mark of the proprietor is branded with red-hot iron.

"Over the same prairies gallop, heedless of bad weather and proud of their freedom, horses descended from those that the Arabs, once masters of the south of France, left in these regions. They are white in color, small, active, and skittish. Their mouth knows not the bit, nor their hoof the shoe. At harvest time they are led up from their pasture-ground to tread the threshing-floor and thresh the wheat. The work finished, they are set free again.

"Of all our domestic animals the ox is certainly the most useful. During its lifetime it draws the cart in mountainous regions and works at the plow in the tillage of the fields; furthermore, the cow furnishes milk in abundance. Given over to the butcher, the animal becomes a source of manifold products, each part of its body having a value of its own. The flesh is highly nutritious; the skin is made into leather for harness and shoes; the hair furnishes stuffing for saddles; the tallow serves for making candles and soap; the bones, half calcined, give a kind of charcoal or bone-black used especially for refining sugar and making it perfectly white; this charcoal, after being thus used, is a very rich agricultural fertilizer; heated in water to a high temperature, the same bones yield the glue used by carpenters; the largest and thickest bones go to the turner's shop, where they are manufactured into buttons and other small objects; the horns are fashioned by the maker of small-wares into snuff-boxes and powder-boxes; the blood is used concurrently with the bone-black in refining sugar; the intestines, cured, twisted, and dried, are made into strings for musical instruments; finally, the gall is frequently turned to account by dyers and cleaners in cleaning fabrics and partially restoring their original luster.

"But this does not exhaust the list of the animal's merits. Under man's care, under the influence of climate, soil, and manner of living, the ox has become modified and has given us many different breeds that have adapted themselves to the most varied conditions of existence; one breed furnishing more work, another more meat, and still another more dairy food, according to our choice. Among the breeds scattered over France I will limit myself to the following.

"A stocky body, large and strong head, short, thick horns, short and massive neck, powerful legs, bold appearance, quick walk, medium-sized and well-shaped body—these natural endowments make the Gascon breed one of the best for work. Its coat, generally brown or tawny, is always lighter along the back. The chief source of this breed is the department of Gers.

"The Salers breed is originally from the department of Cantal. Its coat is bright red, often with white splashes on the rump and belly. The horns are large, smooth, black at the tips, of symmetrical shape, and pointing a little backward. Very rustic, sober, intelligent, vigorous, inured to toil, the Salers ox is an excellent worker. When fattened at the end of its toilsome service, it gives abundant, firm, and savory meat. The cow, if well fed, can furnish as much as twenty liters of milk a day.

"The Breton breed stocks the five departments of ancient Brittany. It is characterized by smallness of body, readiness for work, and remarkable excellence of milk, which is rich in butter-fat. The cow's coat is spotted with white and black in large splashes, and she has a black muzzle, slender horns, bright eyes, and determined gait. The ox, similarly spotted with black and white, has powerful and very pointed horns; but the peaceful beast never dreams of using its formidable weapons.

"The Normandy breed furnishes animals of enormous size, little adapted to work, and hence reserved for the butcher. Some of these gigantic animals raised in the rich pastures of Normandy are said to have attained the weight of 1970 kilograms. In the Normandy ox the head is long and heavy, muzzle broad, the mouth deeply cut, the skin thick and hard, the hair close, sometimes red, sometimes brown, sometimes black and white. The horns are rather short and are borne well forward on the forehead. On an average the cow gives 3000 liters of milk a year.

"The Garonne breed, occupying the basin of the Garonne River from Toulouse to Bordeaux, is likewise tall, corpulent, and almost as highly esteemed for butchering as the Normandy breed. Its coat is uniform in shade, resembling in color the yellow of wheat. The horns, which turn forward, are white all over; the edge of the eyelids and the nose are pale pink. In fact, the whole physiognomy of the animal has something remarkably peaceful about it."

CHAPTER XXX

MILK

MOTHER AMBROISINE had just milked the goat for breakfast. While Emile and Jules were crumbling their bread each in a cup of milk, foamy and still warm, Uncle Paul, who takes advantage of every occasion for enriching the intelligence of his young nephews with new ideas, thus began the conversation:

"What a priceless resource we have in milk; what delicious breakfasts with this food so nourishing, so light, so appetizing! To judge by the reception you are giving it at this moment, you know well how to appreciate its value."

"For my part," Emile declared, "I like milk better than anything else Mother Ambroisine can give us, especially when the bread is toasted a little over the coals."

"I don't need anything of that sort," said Jules, "to make the milk first-rate."

"Since you like milk so much, you shall learn something about it; then your breakfast will give you a double benefit, food for the body and food for the mind.

"Let us speak first of a property the effects of which you have doubtless seen more than once without paying attention to them. At times the milk turns, as they say; in other words, it curdles. Why is that? You do not know. I will tell you.

"Here is a glass of milk just as it came from the goat. It is of irreproachable fluidity without the slightest trace of curdling. I squeeze into it a drop of lemon juice, one only, and stir the liquid. Immediately a great change is effected: one part of the milk clots and rises to the surface in thick white flakes; another part remains liquid, but loses its whiteness and becomes like slightly turbid water. If I let the glass stand for some time, the curd collects at the surface and floats on a clear liquid. With a drop of lemon juice I have just made the milk turn quickly."

Emile examined with lively interest the contents of the glass thus speedily transformed. His uncle, whom nothing escapes, perceived it. "What is it you are looking at so attentively?" he asked.

"Your experiment," Emile answered, "reminds me of what happened to my milk one day at breakfast. To my toasted bread, which Jules turns up his nose at, I wanted to add something still better. I had an orange and I took it into my head to squeeze the juice into my cup of milk, thinking to make a delicious drink of the mixture. Who was the fool that time? It was giddy Emile. The milk instantly curdled, just like this when you squeezed the lemon juice into it. Trying to improve my cup of milk, I only made it so that I had to throw it all away, it had gone so bad."

"I wish I could have seen the face Emile made," said Jules, "when he saw the result of his improvement."

"I was much surprised, I admit," Emile rejoined, "to find how two things, orange juice and milk, each excellent by itself, could make such a nasty drink when mixed."

"In future, my friends, you will know that anything sour makes milk turn. What I brought about with lemon juice you effected with orange, which contains, though in small quantity and masked by the sweet flavor of the fruit, exactly the same ingredient that gives the lemon its sour taste.

"The juice of sorrel leaves, that of green grapes, and of unripe fruits in general, vinegar, and in fact everything with a similar taste, make milk turn at once. These sour-tasting substances are called acids. Vinegar is an acid; that which gives its sourness to the lemon is another; green grapes contain a third; sorrel leaves furnish a fourth. The number of acids is very considerable. All those that we need to know anything about have this same sharp flavor, sometimes stronger, sometimes weaker; all, in short, make milk curdle just as I showed you with the acid of the lemon.

"From theory let us turn to practice. Cleanliness in everything is of the first importance, but in the care of milk especially must one be scrupulous in this particular. The vessels for holding it and keeping it any length of time must be carefully and thoroughly cleaned as often as they are used, if one would avoid the risk of its turning. Suppose a few drops of old milk or some remnants of any kind of food are left in a pot, tucked away where they are hard to get at: these impurities soon turn sour, especially in warm weather, and the milk, finding an acid substance in the vessel, quickly spoils and curdles. How often the milk itself is blamed for this accident when want of cleanliness is the sole cause!

"Milk contains three principal substances, namely: cream, or fatty matter from which butter is made; casein, or curds, used for making cheese; and, finally, a substance with a slightly sweet taste called sugar of milk. These three ingredients taken away, hardly anything is left but water. To separate these three, one proceeds as follows:

"Left standing in a cool place and exposed to the air, milk becomes covered, sooner or later, according to the season, with a thick oily layer that takes the name of cream. This is the material from which butter is made. It rises to the surface unaided and separates when simply exposed to the air. It is removed with a skimmer.

"What is left is skimmed milk, of the same whiteness, the same appearance, as the original milk, but deprived of its fatty matter. Into this skimmed milk let us pour a few drops of some acid, lemon juice for example. The milk turns and thick white flakes are formed. Those flakes are the curd, the casein, in short the material of which cheese is composed.

"After the casein has been removed there remains nothing but a transparent liquid that might be taken for water slightly tinted with yellow. This liquid is called whey. It contains little besides water with a small quantity of sugar of milk which gives it a slightly sweet taste. It is especially in Switzerland that sugar of milk is obtained on a large scale by the evaporation of the liquid that remains after removing the cream and curds from the milk. In spite of its name this substance has nothing in common with ordinary sugar, the white loaf-sugar we use;

it is a dull-white substance, rather hard, crunching under the teeth, and of a slightly sugary taste. It is used only in pharmacy.

"Cream and casein constitute the nutritive ingredients of milk, and determine its food value. The milk that is richest in these constituents is sheep's milk, next comes goats' milk, and last of all cows' milk. Although of little value to us, sugar of milk claims our attention for a moment on account of the change it undergoes to the great detriment of the milk itself. Little by little, especially when exposed to the heat of summer, this sugary matter sours and becomes an acid. That is what makes milk sour if kept too long. Of course when this sourness shows itself the milk soon curdles. Coagulation takes place as if an acid had been added to the milk. Hence, to keep milk for some time and prevent its turning sour of its own accord, this acidulation of the sugar of milk must be delayed. This is done by taking care to boil the milk a little every day."

CHAPTER XXXI

BUTTER

"FROM MILK," continued Uncle Paul, "we make butter and cheese. I have just explained to you in a few words how the ingredients composing them—that is, cream and casein—are obtained in their separate forms; but further details are now called for, and I will give them to you, beginning with butter.

"The material necessary for making butter is cream, a fatty substance disseminated through the milk in excessively fine and almost invisible particles. When milk is left undisturbed in a cool place and exposed to the air, these particles of fat rise to the surface little by little and collect there in a layer of cream. An example taken from things familiar to you will explain the cause of this spontaneous separation.

"Oil, you know, cannot in any way be made to dissolve in water. If a mixture of the two liquids is well shaken, the oil divides into an infinity of tiny globules uniformly distributed, and the whole takes on a whitish tint that looks something like milk. But this condition is only temporary. If you stop heating or shaking the mixture, the oil, the lighter part, comes to the surface, globule by globule, and soon the two liquids are completely separated, the oil on top, the water at the bottom. If a little gum were added to the water to make it sticky, the separation of the oil would be less easily effected and the mixture would retain its milky appearance for a longer time; nevertheless the two liquids would always end by separating.

"The fatty matter composing butter behaves in the same way as the oil of our experiment. It is not dissolved by the milk; it is simply divided into very minute particles that are held in place by a liquid thickened with casein, just as water thickened with gum holds for a long time the tiny drops of oil. Left undisturbed long enough, these oily particles free themselves and rise to the surface."

"Cream rises to the top of milk," observed Jules, "just as oil that has been shaken up with water rises to the surface; only the separation is slower on account of the casein that thickens the liquid."

"That is the secret of this curious separation. Milk is placed in large earthen nappies[7], smaller at the bottom than at the top, and thus a large surface is exposed to the cooling action of the air, which hastens the separation of the cream. The full nappy is put in a cool and very quiet place. In summer half a day is long enough for the rising of the cream; in winter it takes at least twenty-four hours. When the separation is finished, the cream is removed with a skimmer or a large almost flat spoon.

"Cream is yellowish white, oily to the touch on account of its greasy matter, and sweet and very pleasant to the taste, having the flavor of both fresh butter and cheese. It is most delicious eating."

"We know that," Emile assented, "from those capital sandwiches Mother Ambroisine makes for us with cream on feast days."

"That delicacy," remarked his uncle, "cannot be allowed every day, for the cream is needed for butter for the family."

"Once I helped Mother Ambroisine work the little butter machine, a kind of small cask called a churn. Why do we have to thump so long to get the butter?"

"That is what I am going to explain to you. In cream the particles of butter are simply grouped side by side, without forming a united body. Besides, a layer of moisture, coming from the whey, isolates them and prevents their uniting. To combine all these particles into a compact mass of butter, it is necessary to squeeze out the milk and knead them together. This is accomplished by prolonged beating.

"The implement used is called a churn. The simplest consists

7   A wide, shallow, earthenware bowl or pan.

of a kind of small cask larger at the bottom than at the top. The cover is pierced with an opening through which runs a rod carrying a perforated wooden disc on the end inside the churn. After the cream has been poured into the churn, the operator takes the rod in both hands and vigorously raises it and plunges it down in alternate strokes, thus causing the terminal disc to rise and fall in the creamy mass. By this prolonged beating the fatty particles unite and become butter. Sometimes the churn is made of a small cask in which turns—by means of a crank—an axle bearing perforated wings or blades which beat the cream in their rotation.

"Some precautions must be taken to carry this delicate operation through successfully. During the heat of summer churning should be done only in the morning and in a cool place. It is even well to set the churn in a tub of cold water. If this is neglected the butter may turn sour in the process of churning. In winter, on the contrary, the churn should be kept a little warm by wrapping it in warmed cloths and working it near the fire. Cold hardens the fatty particles and prevents their uniting. If nothing is done to raise the temperature enough to soften them they will be slow in turning to butter and the operation will be long.

"As soon as all the fatty particles are well stuck together the butter is made. It is taken out of the churn and put into cold water, in which it is kneaded over and over again with a large wooden spoon to press out the whey with which it is impregnated.

"If the butter is to be eaten soon, it suffices to keep it in water that is changed every day for the sake of freshness and to prevent the butter's souring. But if it is to be kept for a long time, more thorough-going means of preservation are necessary. The most simple method consists in kneading it with kitchen salt, well dried in the oven and reduced to fine powder. After salting, the butter is put in earthen jars and the surface covered with a layer of salt.

"Another way to keep butter is to melt it. I must tell you, to begin with, that butter, however carefully prepared it may be, always contains a certain quantity of whey and casein. These are the substances that, changing later by contact with the air, make butter sour and finally rancid. If the fatty matter were all by itself, if it could be completely rid of the casein and whey that go with it, we could keep it much longer. This result is attained by melting.

"The butter is placed in a kettle over a bright fire that is even and moderate. Melting soon begins. The moisture of the whey is evaporated, this process being hastened by stirring the melted mass. A part of the casein rises to the surface and forms a scum which is removed; another part collects at the bottom of the kettle. When the melted butter looks like oil and when a drop of it thrown on the coals takes fire without crackling, thus proving that it is quite free from moisture, the operation is finished. The kettle is taken off the fire, the liquid is left standing a few minutes to give the casein time to settle at the bottom, and finally the butter is poured by spoonfuls into earthen jars carefully dried in the oven. These jars should be of small capacity and narrow opening, so as to prevent as much as possible the access of air, the cause of change in all our food substances. It is advisable to put on top of the butter, as soon as it hardens, a layer of salt, as is done with salted butter. Finally the jars are closed with parchment, which is tied on with string."

CHAPTER XXXII

RENNET

"IN THE making of cheese the first step is to cause the milk to curdle. Lemon juice, vinegar, or any other acid would bring about this result, as we have already seen; but it is customary to make use of another and much more efficacious liquid called rennet. Let us learn first what this liquid consists of. That calls for certain explanations apparently foreign to our subject, but nevertheless leading directly to it.

"Among our domestic animals three—the ox, goat and sheep—are remarkable for their horns and split hoofs. All three have a way of eating very different from that of other kinds of animals. The dog, for example, after masticating its food sufficiently, swallows it once for all and passes it into a single digestive cavity called the stomach, where it becomes a fluid mass suitable for nutrition. On the contrary, the goat, sheep, and ox chew and swallow the same food twice; at two different times, with a rather long interval between, the same fodder is subjected to mastication and passed down the throat.

"Animals are characterized as 'ruminant' that, after chewing their food once and letting it pass into the digestive cavity, bring it back into the mouth for a more complete trituration. The ox, goat, and sheep are ruminants. Instead of only one stomach they have four, that is to say four membranous pouches where the alimentary matter passes from one to another before being converted into a sort of nutritive soup.

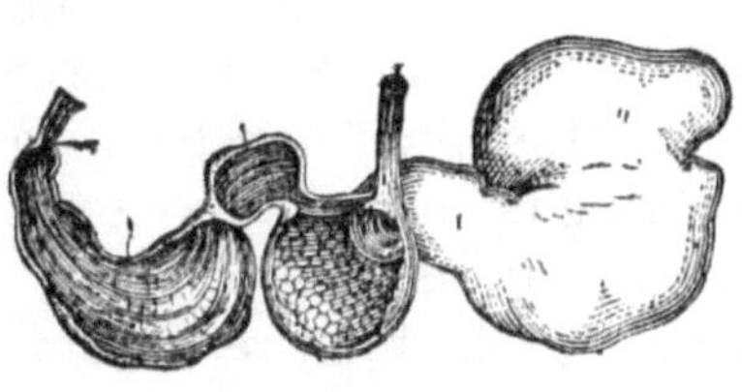
TYPICAL RUMINANT STOMACH

"The first of these pouches

is called the paunch. It is a spacious cavity in which the animal accumulates the fodder that has been hastily browsed and not thoroughly chewed. Its inside surface is thickly covered with short flat filaments that give it the appearance of coarse velvet.

"Watch the ox and sheep in the pasture. They crop the grass without stopping, without a moment's rest; they chew very slightly, very hastily, and then swallow; one mouthful does not wait on another. It is the time for filling the paunch without losing a bite by prolonged chewing. Later, in the hours of repose, there will be leisure for bringing up again the food swallowed and for grinding it to the proper fineness.

"This receptacle known as the paunch having received its due supply of fodder, the animal retires to a quiet spot, lies down in a comfortable position, and takes up at its ease, for hours at a time, the work of chewing. This second stage in the preparation of the food under the millstone of the teeth is called rumination. The ox is then seen patiently chewing, with an air of gentle satisfaction, without taking anything from outside. What is it eating thus, when there is apparently no fodder within reach? It is re-eating what has been stored up in the paunch, and which now comes up from the bottom of the stomach in little mouthfuls. Then the motion of the jaws ceases, the mouthful is swallowed, and immediately after something round and bulging is seen making its way upward under the skin of the neck. It is a fresh alimentary ball coming up from the paunch to the mouth to be chewed. Ball by ball, the mass of fodder accumulated in the paunch comes back thus to be ground by the teeth to the right degree of fineness and then swallowed for good."

"That's a clever way to eat," was Emile's comment. "In order not to lose a moment of their time in the pasture, the sheep, goat, and ox do not stop to do their chewing there: they browse without stopping and store up a good supply. Then, lying down comfortably in the shade, they bring up again the contents of the paunch and grind it at their ease, little by little."

"The second stomachic cavity is called the reticulum, its inner surface presenting a reticulated appearance, with an arrangement of dentate and laminate folds forming, all together, an elaborate network of meshes. This curious formation cannot fail to strike you if you look for a moment at a piece of tripe, one of our countless articles of food; for what is called tripe is nothing but the collective stomach of the ox."

"I remember having seen that beautiful honeycomb network," said Jules, "and the coarse velvet lining of the paunch. They were very interesting."

"The office of the honeycomb is to receive, in small portions, the food already somewhat softened in the paunch, and to mold it into balls, which rise one at a time to the ruminant's mouth. That in fact is where the alimentary balls are made that we see gliding from below upward, under the skin of the neck of the ruminating ox.

"After being re-chewed to the proper fineness the food does not return to the paunch, where it would mix with material not yet similarly prepared; it goes to the third stomach, or manyplies, so named on account of its numerous and wide parallel folds, having some resemblance in arrangement to the leaves of a book.

"From the manyplies the food passes finally to a fourth and last stomach called the rennet-bag. After this come the intestines. Now guess whence we get that significant name of rennet, knowing as you do what I have especially in mind in this connection?"

"You have in mind," answered Jules, "a certain liquid, rennet, that makes milk curdle quickly. The word rennet, or runnet, as it is also written, must be connected with the verb run, in the sense of dropping, coagulating. Can it be, then, that from this fourth stomach or rennet-bag of ruminants we get the liquid rennet that is used for curdling milk?"

"You have said it yourself," declared Uncle Paul, much pleased at his nephew's clear explanation of the matter. "It is from the fourth stomach of ruminant animals that we obtain rennet, the most efficacious substance known for curdling milk.

"Preferably it is the rennet-bag of a young calf that is selected; then it is cleaned carefully, salted, and dried. Thus treated, it keeps a long time. When it is required for use, a piece as large as your two fingers is cut off and put to soak in a glass of water or whey. The next morning two or three spoonfuls of this liquid, called rennet, is added to each liter of milk. In a very short time, if kept moderately warm, the milk turns to a mass of fresh cheese."

CHAPTER XXXIII

CHEESE

"THE CHIEF constituent of cheese is casein coagulated by the action of rennet. But, prepared from casein alone, cheese would be coarse and almost tasteless, and when dry would become as hard as stone. To give tenderness and flavor to the paste-like mass, the cream is commonly retained in milk used for making cheese. The casein furnishes the main substance of the product, while the cream contributes what might be called the seasoning.

"Hence we have two principal varieties of cheese: one, prepared with milk from which the cream has been taken, contains only casein; the second, made from unskimmed milk, contains both casein and cream. The first kind, known as cottage cheese, white cheese, or, more expressively, skim-milk cheese, has little food value and is not made for its own sake, but in order to put to some use the milk that has already served to make butter. The second kind, called cream cheese, is what commonly appears on our tables in different varieties and varying appearance, according to the quality of the milk and the mode of preparation.

"To make cheese still more unctuous and to give it a finer flavor, we do not always content ourselves with using milk in its natural state; to the cream that it naturally contains we often add some more from milk skimmed expressly for the purpose. The cheeses thus enriched with fatty matter are the most delicate of all. Again, we occasionally adopt a middle course, using neither natural milk nor entirely creamless milk, but of two equal parts of milk we keep one just as it is and skim the other, mixing them together afterward.

"By adding or withdrawing, in varying quantities, this fatty constituent of the milk, we obtain as many different varieties of cheese. If also we bear in mind that sheep's milk has not exactly the same properties as goats' milk, nor goats' milk the same properties as cows' milk; if we remember, further, that the same animal's milk varies according to the nature of its feed and the care given to the herd; and if, finally, we take into account the different methods of manufacture, of one sort in one place, of another sort somewhere else, we shall understand how numerous may be, and in fact are, the various kinds of cheese."

"For my part," Jules interposed, "I know at least half a dozen kinds. There is Roquefort, a pasty cheese streaked with blue and of a sharp flavor; Gruyère, riddled with large round holes and yellowish in color, and clear like quartz; Auvergne, as large as a big millstone and not very delicate in flavor; Brie, in thin, wide cakes that sweat a kind of ill-smelling cream; Mont d'Or, packed with a little straw in a round deal box; and a lot of others that I can't remember now."

"Jules has just told us the best known kinds of cheese; I will add a few words on the way they are made.

"Fresh cheeses are those that are eaten soon after being made. They are white and soft. They are made of either skimmed or unskimmed milk, and in the latter case they are incomparably better. When the rennet has brought about coagulation, the curdled milk is poured into round molds of tin or glazed earthenware, with holes in the bottom for the escape of the whey contained in the curdled mass. As soon as this has drained enough and is sufficiently firm, the cheese is done, and it is taken from the mold ready for the table without any other preparation."

"That's the cheese I like best," Emile declared. "It's the kind we spread on slices of bread to make those delicious sandwiches."

"That is very true, but it has the fault of not keeping long. In a few days it turns sour and uneatable. All the other cheeses would do the same, all would spoil and become sour if certain measures were not taken to prevent this. These measures consist in the use of salt, which is rubbed and sprinkled on the outside of the cheese, and sometimes even mixed with the curd itself.

All cheeses, then, that are to be kept a long time receive more or less salt, while fresh cheese is not salted at all.

"Of these salted cheeses some are soft, some hard. That of Brie, named from the district where the best is made, in the department of Seine-et-Marne, is a large and thin soft cake, made of sheep's milk. It is salted on both sides with finely powdered salt, and is left to soak for two or three days in the salted liquid that drips from it. The salting finished, the cheeses are packed in a cask with alternate layers of straw, and are left alone for several months. Then there starts a kind of fermentation, which is the beginning of putrefaction, and which develops new qualities. The curd loses its odor and insipid taste of milk-food, to acquire the heightened flavor and strong smell of cheese; its mass becomes more oily, even partially fluid, and changes under the rind to a liquid pap of creamy appearance. This work of modification is called refining. It has gone just far enough when the liquid part under the rind is of a pleasant taste. The cheeses are then taken out of the cask and are ready for eating.

"This first example shows us that cheese acquires its peculiar qualities through an incipient deterioration. Before this putrefaction sets in the cheese is simply curd, sweetish, insipid, without pronounced odor; after this process it has the odor, the taste, in fact all that is required to make it really cheese. But the putrefaction, once started artificially, does not stop where we should like it to stop. It goes on all the time, slowly indeed if we take some precautions, and the cheese, smelling more and more, and tasting stronger and stronger, ends by becoming a mass of rottenness. All cheese, therefore, when it gets too old, is sure at last to go bad; it spoils by continuing to excess the kind of deterioration that in the beginning gave it precisely the qualities desired.

"From its appetizing flavor and fine texture Roquefort is the king of cheeses, the prominent feature in any well-appointed dessert. Its renown extends all over the world."

"That's the cheese that is so strong and takes so much bread to go with it?" asked Emile.

"Yes, that is it. Its pronounced flavor and its blue streaks make it easy to recognize. It is made in a village of Aveyron called Roquefort, and is obtained from sheep's milk only, the best of all milk on account of its richness in casein and butter."

"Brie cheese also," observed Louis, "is made of sheep's milk; yet it doesn't compare in quality with Roquefort."

"That marked difference shows us how much the method of making it determines the quality of cheese. You have just seen what pains are taken with Brie cheese; now see how much care is given to Roquefort.

"The cakes of curd are not thin in this case, but as thick as they are wide. They are stored for months in grottoes hollowed in the heart of a rock, either by nature or by man, in the environs of the village of Roquefort. These grottoes are remarkable for the strong currents of air that circulate through them, and for the coolness of their temperature. During the summer, while the thermometer outside marks thirty degrees,[8] it shows but five inside the cheese caves. The difference is that between the heat of an oppressive summer and the cold of a severe winter. It is in the depths of these cold caves that the cheeses acquire their peculiar qualities. The only care given them is an occasional rubbing with salt and a scraping of their surface to remove whatever moldiness may have developed. This moldiness even gets into the inside by degrees, where it forms blue veins. But that is in no way detrimental; on the contrary, the flavor of the cheese gains by the formation of this mold, which is merely another kind of rotting that adds its energies to those of the usual change undergone by cheese. Hence the makers are not content with letting nature produce these signs of moldiness: they hasten the process by mixing with the fresh curd a little powdered moldy bread. The cheese would be better if left to its own working, but this addition accelerates the result, and to-day, alas, in the making of Roquefort, as in so many other branches of industry, there is greater eagerness for quick results than for excellence.

"The cheese called Auvergne is made in the mountains of Cantal. Cows' milk is used. When the curd has formed, the

---

8   Centigrade, not Fahrenheit.—*Translator.*

dairyman, legs and arms bare, mounts a table and tramples and compresses with feet and hands the mass of fresh cheese to squeeze out the whey. The curd is then separated, mixed with pounded salt, and pressed in large round molds containing up to fifty kilograms. These enormous cheeses are finally left in cellars to the action of fermentation, which perfects them.

"Gruyère cheese owes its name to a little village in the canton of Fribourg in Switzerland. In the Vosges, Jura, and Ain a great quantity of this cheese is made. This too is made of cows' milk. The milk, after a third of its cream has been skimmed off, is slightly warmed in large kettles over a brisk fire. Then the rennet is poured in. When the curd has formed, it is separated as much as possible by being stirred in the kettle with a wide paddle, after which it is warmed still further. Finally the curd is collected, placed in a mold, and subjected to strong pressure. The cheese thus produced is next rubbed several times with salt, and then stored in a cellar and left undisturbed for two or three months. It is during its stay in the cellar that the holes or eyes characteristic of Gruyère cheese make their appearance; they are due to bubbles of gas released from the fermenting substance of the cheese. You will notice in the making of this kind of cheese the application of heat. The milk is warmed over the fire just before the rennet is added, which is not done in the other kinds. Hence Gruyère cheese is called cooked cheese.

"If kept too long, all cheeses are sooner or later invaded, first on the outside and then within, by mold, yellowish white at first, then blue or greenish, and finally brick red. At the same time the cheese decays and acquires a repulsive odor and a taste so acrid as to make the lips sore. The cheese is then a mere mass of putrefaction to be thrown on the dung-hill. The rate of decay is proportioned to the softness of the cheese and its permeability by the air. Therefore, in order that it may keep well, it must be carefully dried and also reduced to a compact mass by strong pressure. That is why so much force is exerted in pressing the large cheeses of Gruyère and Auvergne in their molds. But it is nothing in comparison with certain cheeses, called Dutch cheeses, which are noted for their extraordinary lasting qualities. They become so hard and dry that before they can be eaten they sometimes have to be broken up with a hammer and put to soften again in a cloth wet with white wine."

"Those very hard cheeses, as solid as a rock, can't be of much use," commented Emile.

"That is where you are mistaken. Cooks use this hard cheese to season certain dishes, after grating it to a powder. It is also in favor on shipboard as a valuable article of food on long voyages. The Dutch cheese is round like a ball, and has a reddish rind. It takes its name from the country where it is made."

CHAPTER XXXIV

THE PIG

"THERE IS every reason to believe that the domestic pig is descended from one or another of the numerous kinds of wild boar scattered over Asia—perhaps even from several of them. But the Asiatic wild boar bears so close a resemblance in shape and habits to the European that it will suffice for me to acquaint you with the latter in order to give you a correct idea of the former, and thus show you what the pig must have been in its primitive state.

"Though very numerous in early times throughout the forests of France, wild boars are from day to day diminishing in number with us, and are destined sooner or later to disappear altogether, as they have already disappeared from England, where they have now been exterminated to the last one, as is the case also with wolves. This complete extermination is explained by the situation of the country. England is entirely surrounded by the sea. If then the wolf and boar, hunted down as two undesirable neighbors, are at last entirely destroyed, the two species are forever annihilated in the island, since the sea interposes an impassable barrier against new arrivals."

"That is perfectly clear," assented Emile. "As soon as the last wolf and boar have been killed, the English, protected by the sea that surrounds them, are rid of these animals once for all."

"If we could only rid ourselves of wolves like that!" Louis exclaimed. "Gladly would I see the skin of the last one stuffed with straw and paraded from farm to farm. I will say nothing of the boar, as I don't know its manner of living."

"The wild boar is also a formidable foe, not to flocks, but to cultivated fields, where it does great damage; besides, it is a

221

brutal beast, rather dangerous to meet in the depths of a forest. In size and shape it closely resembles the common pig, the chief difference being in the boar's coarse, blackish-red coat; its dorsal bristles, stiff and strong and standing up in anger in a horrible looking mane; its head, longer and more curved; its ears, smaller, more erect, and very mobile; its thick and shorter legs; and, finally, the great stockiness of the body as a whole. The eyes are small but not without expression, becoming quite fiery and ferocious in anger. The eye-teeth of each jaw project in a threatening manner beyond the lips, the lower ones being very long, with a backward curve, sharp edges, and pointed ends, the upper ones shorter and rubbing against the first in such a manner as to serve them as whetstones. From this peculiar function the upper tusks are in fact sometimes likened to grindstones and hence go by the name of grinders, while the lower tusks, terrible in combat, are called defenders. With its powerful muzzle or snout the boar strikes and overthrows an opponent; with its sharp tusks it rips open and disembowels. The female, or sow, has no tusks, but her bite is most formidable; she accompanies it with a ferocious gnashing of the teeth and an infuriated stamping of the hoofs that would alone prove fatal to the trampled adversary. The cry of both consists in an obstreperous snort, a signal of alarm and surprise; but except in case of danger the brute is usually silent.

"The wild boar is fond of vast forests, in which it seeks the darkest and most retired spots where it will not be disturbed by man's presence. In the daytime it lies in its retreat or lair amid the thickest of brushwood and bushes. In the neighborhood there is generally some sort of muddy pool where it wallows with delight. Toward nightfall it leaves its retreat in search of food. With its snout it plows the ground, always in a straight line, to unearth fleshy roots; it gathers the fruit fallen to the ground, the kernels of cereals, also chestnuts, beech-nuts, hazel-nuts, and acorns, especially the last, its favorite food. But a vegetable diet fails to satisfy its voracity. If it knows of a fish-pond, it plows up the banks to get the eels lurking in the mud; if it knows of a rabbit-burrow, it ransacks it by hollowing out a deep ditch and upturning stones with its powerful snout. It surprises the partridge on its nest and devours mother and brood; it crunches young rabbits in their snug retreat; it lays hold of young fawns in their sleep. Finally, if live prey is wanting, it gorges itself with carrion. The whole night is passed in predatory raids of this sort, after which the beast regains its lair at the dawn of day.

"A wild sow's litter numbers from three to eight little ones, sometimes called grice. They are white, with tawny or brown stripes running lengthwise. At the age of six months their hair becomes darker, a sort of dirty gray, and they outgrow the name of grice. When two years old their tusks begin to be dangerous, and at an age ranging from three to five years the animal attains its maximum size and strength and is entitled to the name of wild boar. After this, until twenty-five or thirty, the ordinary limit of its life, it is called an old boar or an old hermit, on account of the isolation in which it lives. Then the tusks become blunted and turn in toward the eyes.

"Boar-hunting is not without its dangers. If the boar finds itself hard pressed by the pack of hounds pursuing it, the animal takes refuge in some dense thicket of brambles and holly, and forces a passage through the thorny rampart where no other would dare to penetrate. Through the opening thus made rush the dogs, vying with one another in ardor and in barking. There are eight, twelve, fifteen of them; no matter, the boar awaits with firmness its numerous assailants. Backing up against a gnarled stump which protects it in the rear, it sharpens its tusks and works its drivelling jaws. Its mane stands erect on head and back; its little eyes, inflamed with fury, resemble two glowing coals. The boldest dogs rush to seize it by the ears; it disperses them with a few vigorous blows from its snout, dealt with startling promptness. Some fall back with belly split open, from which the entrails protrude and catch on the bushes; others have a leg broken, a shoulder dislocated, or at least one or two flesh wounds. The dying stretch their legs in the last convulsions of agony, the wounded howl with pain, the least crippled beat a hasty retreat. But reinforcements arrive, bringing back the fugitives to the charge. Then, from the midst of the thicket, an indescribable uproar is heard. To the cries of the pack, howling, barking, and growling in various keys, and to the wild boar's grunts of rage, are added the crashing sound of underbrush broken in the fierce scrimmage and the shrill notes of the magpies that have flown in all haste to the scene of tumult and from the surrounding tree-tops noisily discuss the event. Finally the boar emerges from the thicket and, drunk with carnage, takes its turn as pursuer. Woe then to the inexperienced hunter who loses his presence of mind or whose shot misses its mark: he might forfeit his life for his unwariness and lack of skill. But let us hope that a bullet, cleverly aimed between the beast's eyes, will put an end to a battle that has already cost the lives of the best dogs in the pack."

"I see that this is no tame rabbit-hunt," said Jules. "If any one should come within reach of the fierce brute that the dogs are worrying, he would not, as they say, have much of a picnic."

"Nevertheless there are men of dauntless courage who go straight for the furious beast and plunge their hunting knife into its heart. But usually the thing is attended with less peril and with no such atrocious ripping-up of the dogs, a sport for the grand *seigneurs*. Ambushed in a safe place, the hunter awaits the boar and gives it a couple of bullets as it passes; and that is the end of it. If the attack is less spectacular, at least it spares the life of the dog and does not endanger man's."

"Then I give it preference," Jules declared, "to that in which a whole pack might be killed. I don't like that slaughter of dogs, with the boar's tusks ripping them open there in the underbrush."

"And what do they do with the beast after they have killed him?" asked Louis.

"It is a piece of game," replied Uncle Paul, "that surpasses anything else to be found in our woods. Such a boar, old hermit-boar, as we call him, may weigh as much as two hundred kilograms. That is enough for a feast, I should hope, and all the more so as the flesh is excellent. The piece of honor is the head, the famous boar's head.

"The Asiatic wild boar, from which the domestic pig descends, does not differ from ours in its habits; it is, like ours, a ferocious, coarse, vigorous, bold, voracious animal, a formidable creature to encounter in the dark woods. How has this intractable beast become the pig that we raise? By what care, what gentle treatment, has it been made to lose its ancient savagery? To these questions there is no further answer than in the case of the dog and the ox. After centuries and centuries of domestication, the first steps in this process of redemption from the wild state have become lost in oblivion.

"Despite all its improvement the pig still remains a coarse animal, resembling the wild boar in more than one trait. Like the latter, it feeds on anything and everything; and even more than the latter is it addicted to gluttony. The perils attending its wild state no longer existing, it devotes itself unreservedly to the gratification of its voracious appetite. The pig is a fat-factory: it lives only to eat, digest, and fatten. Its gluttony extends even to the devouring of kitchen refuse, greasy dishwater, nasty leavings, garbage; in fact everything even to excrementitious matter. Ill effects can result from its nosing about in filth to satisfy its gluttony, since it is thus liable to a horrible disease of which we will speak later. Not satisfied with acorns and other viands that go to fill its trough, it turns up the earth with its snout in quest of roots, worms, and fat larvæ. It is always either sleeping, stretched out on its side in the full enjoyment of digestion, or rooting in the ground in the hope of some chance additional tidbit, however small. In the cultivated fields, in prairies and grass-lands, devastation makes rapid progress with such a miner tearing up the ground. To check this mania for excavating, the end of the snout is pierced with two holes through each of which is passed a piece of iron wire, which is then bent into a ring."

"Oh, I know," cried Jules. "I have often seen little rings of iron wire at the end of a pig's snout. I didn't know what they were for, but now I see. If the pig wants to dig, the iron wire is pressed against the earth and bruises the raw flesh through which it passes; and the pain forces the animal to stop."

"Yes, that is the part played by the rings fixed in the end of the snout."

"And we see pigs, too, with a kind of large wooden triangle around the neck," Emile put in.

"As the pig is not very tractable and pays little heed to the drover's voice, it is customary, when a number of these animals are taken to the fields, to put around their neck a large triangular wooden collar, which prevents their getting through hedges and overrunning the neighboring cultivated fields.

"The pig's gluttony is proverbial. But let us beware of reproaching it for this. Its voracious appetite transmutes into savory meat and fat, quantities of refuse that none of the other domestic animals would eat, and that would be wasted but for its intervention; out of otherwise worthless scraps its strong stomach, which turns at nothing, makes those delectable articles of food so much enjoyed by all of you when they appear in the form of sausages and sausage-cakes. Let us not reproach it, either, for its passionate love of mud, in which it wallows to reduce its temperature. In that it simply inherits the habits of its ancestor, the wild boar, which also delights in the luxury of a mud-bath. Besides, it is more our fault than the pig's taste. The pig likes a cold bath; it submits with every indication of satisfaction to being washed and brushed by its keeper. So fond is it of cleanliness that it alone of all the domestic animals hesitates to soil its bed with its excrement. Why then does the word pig suggest the idea of dirtiness? Here we are to blame, more often than not. Let the pig be given clean water for its bath, and it will turn its back on the foul mud that it contents itself with for want of something better; let its premises be kept clean, and the poor animal will be highly delighted, much preferring a sanitary straw bed to a filthy hole. By these attentions to cleanliness the animal will be the gainer, and we shall profit likewise.

"In lifetime the pig is of no use to us, unless it be in hunting for truffles, an exercise in which it excels by reason of the extraordinary development of its nose and the keenness of its scent. Yet even for this service the dog is preferred, as being better fitted for exploring uneven ground, more active, and more intelligent. It is after its death that the pig pays us for the care bestowed upon it. Let us be present at this event, a festive occasion for the family.

"Fattened for a long time on potatoes, excellent for making flesh, and on acorns, which give firmness and savor to the meat, the porker can hardly stand on its short legs. It sleeps and digests in a reclining posture, lying lazily on its side. From its neck hang three and four great cushions of fat; under its belly are seen ponderous masses of lard; the rump is well rounded, the back padded with fat. The animal is ripe for the knife. At the break of day it is aroused from its sweet repose and sacrificed in the midst of piercing cries of protest against so cruel a fate. With torches of burning straw the bristles are burnt off, after which the body is well scraped and washed, then opened and cut up. Now the housewife proceeds to the work of salting and curing this rich store of provision. Every member of the family comes to her aid. Here, over a big fire, in a resplendent copper kettle, the lard is tried out and poured into pots, where it hardens and turns as white as snow. Yonder the black puddings are hardening in boiling water. Over there some one is busily plying a big chopping-knife, mincing the meat that is to go into sausages, which will be wound in a long garland about two laths and hung from the ceiling opposite the fireplace to get a good drying. In still another place the ham is being made ready for wrapping in linen and hanging in a corner under the chimney mantel to assure its preservation. On a screen are spread the most important parts of the animal, the chine and flanks, covered with a layer of salt. And the housewife's heart is filled with content as she views her cupboards and larders stored with provisions for a year to come.

"Now, these provisions, on which the housekeeper's hopes are based, would speedily decay and become unfit for food without the use of salt. A piece of meat left to itself soon gives out a bad smell and undergoes putrefaction. The higher the temperature and the damper the air, the more rapid the rate of decay. That is why the approach of winter and as far as possible a dry time are chosen for the annual pig-killing. Salt in liberal quantities is used for preserving the meat, lard, and fat. Salted meat dries without becoming tainted, and keeps for a long time, though not indefinitely, since sooner or later it turns rancid. Nevertheless salting is the best way to preserve meat.

"Another process, discovered long ago and very efficacious, consists in exposing the meat to the action of smoke from burning wood. That is why salted hams are hung in the chimney-corner. But on the farm it usually happens that too little attention is paid to this method of curing: it is deemed sufficient to place the hams within reach of the smoke from the fireplace without any covering to protect them. Hence the meat becomes covered with soot, black juices permeate it, and putrefaction sets in. To avoid this mishap it is enough to wrap the hams in two layers of linen, which sifts the smoke, keeps out the soot, and admits only the vapors really adapted to the preservation of the meat without blackening it and giving it a disagreeable taste.

"In various countries, Germany and England for example, smoking is practised on a large scale for curing beef as well as pork. Three or four rooms with low ceilings and communicating with one another by means of openings are connected with a fireplace at some distance, in which oak shavings and aromatic plants are burnt. The largest pieces are hung in the first room on poles or iron hooks, the medium-sized pieces are hung in the second, and the smallest are relegated to the last room. The smoke, on account of the comparative remoteness of the fireplace, is cold when it reaches the first compartment, where it acts with full force on the large pieces of meat, the hardest to penetrate. Thence it passes to the second compartment, and finally to the third, thus in proportion to its loss of strength encountering pieces less resistant to its action. As food, smoked meat is preferable to salted: it tastes better and is easier to digest.

"Smoking is also applied to fish. You have a well-known example in the herring. This fish, as it comes from the grocer, is sometimes silvery white, sometimes golden red. In the first state he calls it white herring; in the second, red herring. The difference is in the way it is cured. Directly after being caught, the herrings are opened, cleaned, washed, and put to soak in brine, that is to say in a strong solution of salt. About fifteen hours later they are taken out, put to drip, and finally packed in casks in regular layers. The product of this process is the white herring, so named because the fish, simply salted and put up in casks, keeps its beautiful silvery color. Smoking produces the so-called red herring, recognizable from its golden-yellow tint and smoky smell. The fresh fish are first of all strongly salted by being left thirty hours in the brine; then they are attached to small twigs or branches passed through the gills, after which they are hung in a sort of fireplace where green wood is burnt, which gives out little flame and torrents of smoke. It is here that the herring takes on its red color and its slightly smoky smell."

CHAPTER XXXV

PIG'S MEASLES

JEAN HAD come to market to sell his pig; Mathieu, on his part, had gone thither to buy one. Jean's animal pleased him. After some talk in which all sorts of finesse were employed on the part of the seller to heighten the value of his merchandise, on the part of the buyer to lower it, they came to an agreement on the price and shook hands to bind the bargain.

But before taking out his purse and counting out the crowns Mathieu wished, as was his right, to make sure that the pig was sound. A man was called whose business it was to decide such questions. He took the animal by the legs and threw it over on its side. Whereas Jean and Mathieu stood in some awe of the animal, he made no ceremony about forcing a stick, as a sort of lever, between the pig's teeth and prying the jaws apart. Then he plunged his hand in between those terrible jaws and felt about with his fingers to the right, to the left, and especially under the tongue. Meanwhile the pig was giving forth heartbreaking cries, and with raucous grunts all its companions in the market voiced their sympathy in its distress. The whole square was in an uproar. The ordeal over, the animal was let loose and immediately everything became quiet again. The pig was found to be in good condition.

Emile was passing at the time of this performance. What are they doing to that poor animal with the big stick thrust between its jaws? Why are they feeling in its mouth? Couldn't they leave the creature in peace instead of making it squeal worse than if they were slaughtering it? Such were the questions that passed through Emile's mind as he found himself almost seized with terror at the piercing cries of the animal and the chorus of alarmed grunts from its companions. In the evening the conversation turned upon this event.

"The man who felt with his hand in the pig's mouth," Uncle Paul explained, "while the stick kept the formidable jaws apart, had a definite purpose, which was to assure himself that the animal was free from measles. For the pig is subject to a strange disease thus named, which makes its flesh unwholesome and even dangerous. When the animal is afflicted with this malady, its flesh is filled with a multitude of round white granules from the size of a pinhead to that of a pea, or larger; these granules are called hydatids. Their number is sometimes so great that in a piece of fat no larger than the five fingers of my hand they can be counted by hundreds. To determine whether a pig is thus affected, it is of course out of the question to explore the flesh of the living body. What do they do then? They feel the soft parts accessible to the hand—the walls of the mouth and especially the under side of the tongue, a favorite haunt of the hydatids. If hard granules are felt by the fingers, the pig is affected and its market value greatly lowered; if no such granules are found, the animal is healthy and will bring its full price. That is the reason of the operation that so puzzled Emile this morning in the market. The man that was feeling of the animal's tongue was an inspector. His office is to examine all pigs offered for sale and to determine from the feeling of the tongue whether the animal has the measles. Hence he is commonly called a tongue-tester, a word that will now explain itself to you."

"I see very well," Jules interposed, "how the word came to be used in connection with the examination of the pig's tongue, but I don't yet in the least understand how those hard white granules that the tongue-tester looks for, those hydatids as you call them, can make the meat unwholesome and dangerous."

"You will soon see. Each of those granules is a lodge, a cell, a little chamber if you like, in which lives a sort of worm, richly fed by the pig's animal substance. You are familiar with the worm that inhabits the juicy pulp of cherries, with the one that gnaws the kernel of nuts, with the one that makes its home in the heart of the pear and apple, and with countless others in fact that I told you about when we were on the subject of harmful insects. Well, fruit is not the only thing to harbor such troublesome guests; every animal has its parasites to devour it while it is still alive. The pig in its turn has a great many, especially when its gluttonous habits lead it to feed on excrement. One of these parasites is the worm I have mentioned.

"It is the most curious creature one could possibly imagine. Picture to yourselves a little bladder full of liquid as clear as water; on this bladder a very short and wrinkled neck; finally, at the extremity of this neck a round head bearing on the sides four suckers and at the end thirty-two hooks arranged in the shape of a crown in a double ring. That is the worm, the hydatid. Each one is enclosed in a sort of little pouch, a firm and semi-transparent cell which derives its substance from the flesh of the pig itself. Commonly the tiny creature is entirely hidden in its snug retreat; at other times, through an opening in the pouch, it stretches its neck and pushes its head out a little, doubtless to feed on the adjacent fluid matter by means of its four suckers. As to the little bladder forming the other part of the worm, it never leaves its cell, the cavity of which it fills exactly. Hence the animal never changes its place."

"That must be a very dull sort of life," was Emile's comment. "No exercise for the little worm except occasionally sticking its head out of the bag that holds it, and then drawing it in again and shutting the door. Is this bag very large?"

"There are different-sized ones, according to the worm's degree of development, for as it grows its dwelling also becomes larger. The usual shape of these cells is that of a small egg, the greatest dimension of which might be as much as two centimeters, and the smallest five or six millimeters.

"Hydatids live in the flesh of a live pig; they live there by thousands and thousands, in such multitudes that sometimes not a piece of fat the size of a nut could be found free from these little parasites. Each one, snugly ensconced in its retreat, its strongly-walled cell, grows in peace, sheltered from all attack, and makes predatory raids in the immediate vicinity with its crown of hooked claws and its four suckers."

"What a miserable fate is the pig's," Emile exclaimed, "to be eaten up alive like that, all full of the ravenous vermin and unable to get rid of them! The poor animal must soon succumb."

"Not exactly. It wastes away, it is true, but it resists for a long time, being very tenacious of life."

"I can't think without horror," said Jules, "of the terrible itching such an army of vermin must cause, biting and boring into the creature's flesh all over its body."

"Your horror would redouble if you knew that this vermin only awaits a favorable opportunity to emigrate to our bodies even, and to ravage us in our turn."

"What! Those horrid pig worms have designs on us?"

"And designs, alas, too often accomplished, if we are not careful. That is what we are now about to consider."

CHAPTER XXXVI

A PERSISTENT PARASITE

"MANY MEMBERS of the animal kingdom change their form in the course of their existence, and with the new structure adopt also a new way of living. Thus the caterpillar and the butterfly, for example, are in reality the same creature, but very different in shape and habits. The caterpillar drags itself heavily over the plant, gnawing the foliage; the butterfly, furnished with light and graceful wings, flies from flower to flower, imbibing a sugary liquor from each with its long proboscis. The cherry worm grows in the midst of the juice that feeds it; after attaining full size it falls from the tree with the damaged fruit and hastens to bury itself in the ground, there to undergo its transformation. Next spring it comes forth in the form of an elegant fly that lives on honey from the flowers and never again touches a cherry except to deposit its eggs therein, one by one. In the same way, again, the nut worm, after finishing its growth, bores a hole in the firm shell, emerges from its fortress, and buries itself for a time in the soil. There it becomes a beetle with a long proboscis, the so-called nut weevil, which leaves its subterranean retreat in the spring and takes up its quarters on the foliage of a nut tree, where it lays its eggs in the growing nuts.

"All species of animal life that change their shape act in this way. In the first half of their existence, under their initial form, they have certain habits and certain dwelling-places; in the second half, under their final form, they have habits and abodes that are quite different.

"Well, the worm that makes its home in the white cells or granules of the diseased pig's flesh is also subject to transformation. It has to change its form, but before doing so it must first change its abode. The cherry worm would never turn into a fly so long as it remained in the cherry; the nut weevil would never become a beetle if it continued to abide in the nut. Both must emigrate and hollow out a home for themselves in the earth if they would cease to be worms and become a fly in one case, a beetle in the other. In like manner, the parasites of the diseased pig would never attain their final form in the flesh that they inhabit; it is absolutely necessary for them to change their abode in order that the transformation may take place. But as they cannot leave their cells of their own accord and transport themselves to their new abode, which is difficult of access, as you will see, they wait patiently, whole years if necessary, for a favorable opportunity to emigrate."

"Where then is this new abode?" asked Jules.

"In us, my poor child, in us exclusively. The cherry worm and the nut weevil are content, for the purposes of their metamorphosis, with a hole in the sand; but the odious worm of the diseased pig must have the human body for its new home—nothing else."

"It can't be that the abominable creature really gets into us."

"It gets there very easily, and it is we ourselves who unconsciously open the door to the perfidious enemy. Some day or other the pig is killed for our nourishment. Its four legs become hams, other parts are made into sausages, its fat is tried out and stored away. All these various pork products are well salted, carefully dried, or sometimes smoked; nothing is neglected that will assure long keeping. Now in all this thorough treatment, this salting and drying and smoking, what do you think becomes of the little worms inhabiting the diseased flesh?"

"They must die, surely."

"That is where you are mistaken. They are very tenacious of life, the accursed things! The strongest saline solution leaves them unaffected; but if some or even a great many should perish, there would always be plenty of survivors, for they are numerous beyond counting. Behold, then, our food infected with the vermin that at the first opportunity will invade our bodies. You eat a sausage the size of your finger, or a slice of ham, and the thing is done: with the appetizing mouthful you have just swallowed the horrible creature. Henceforth the enemy is with you, at home; it will grow, develop, be transformed, and cause no end of mischief."

"But the stomach will digest it, I hope, as it would digest anything else; and the hateful intruder will perish."

"Not at all. The digestive energies of the stomach make no impression on it. It passes through quite untouched, protected perhaps by its resistant shell, and goes farther on to establish itself definitively in the intestines.

"And now all the conditions are the best possible for the worm. The situation is quiet, disturbance from without is not to be apprehended, and the best food in our power to furnish is supplied in abundance. With its double ring of hooks, each one shaped like the fluke of an anchor, the organism fastens itself to the wall of its abode and straightway begins to develop. On its arrival it was a very short and wrinkled little worm, terminating at one end in a small round head, at the other in a spacious bladder. In a short time it will turn into a sort of ribbon that may attain the enormous length of four or five meters."

"Oh, how horrible!" cried Louis. "Can it be that we serve as a dwelling for such a guest?"

"Say rather for a number of such guests, since as a rule they are not found singly. They are commonly called solitary worms, an improper term, as you see, since there are generally several of them together. Their real name is tænia, or tape-worm, from their ribbon-like form.

"Imagine a narrow tape or band of a dull white color, a sort of ribbon of variable length that may measure as much as five meters; imagine this ribbon almost as small as a hair near the creature's head, then broadening little by little and attaining the width of a centimeter; picture to yourself the entire length of the creature divided into sections or joints, some square, others oblong, placed end to end like the beads of a chaplet, or, better, like pumpkin seeds strung one after another, and you will have a sufficiently good idea of the tænia or tape-worm.

"The number of these joints is sometimes as many as a thousand, and, what is more, new ones are always forming, for the tænia has the singular faculty of producing them indefinitely in a row, each one growing out of the preceding. All are full of eggs, detestable seed of the original malady in the pig, and then of the tape-worm in man. The terminal sections or joints, the oldest and ripest, become detached from time to time in chaplets and are expelled. Any pig nosing about in the excrement containing them is pretty sure to become infected from the eggs contained in these joints, for each one is the germ of a hydatid. These eggs will hatch in the animal's intestines; and, as soon as hatched, the young worms, opening a passage for themselves here and there with their crown of hooks, will go and lodge wherever they please, some in the lean flesh, some in the fat, there to encase themselves in a resistant shell, a cell built out of the pig's substance, and there they will await the moment favorable for their emigration to the human body.

"These frequent losses in chaplets of discarded sections do not in the least impair the tape-worm's vigor; new sections grow, and the frightful length of the creature is maintained. Were it to lose almost its entire length, that would in no wise trouble it; let only the head remain, firmly held in place by its hooks, and new joints will form until the worm is as long as ever. Until the head is got rid of there is no hope of deliverance. I could not describe to you, my children, the atrocious sufferings of a person afflicted with this formidable parasite so difficult to dislodge."

"You give us goose-flesh," said Emile, "with that five-meters-long worm that keeps growing again, each time stronger than before, provided its head is left."

"It must need very serious precaution," Louis remarked, "not to be attacked by the creature."

"The precaution is very simple. Since the tape-worm has its origin in the diseased pig, let us beware of all pork thus infected. This infection, as I told you, is recognizable in the white granules abounding in the flesh, each granule being the abode of a little worm, the first form of the tænia. Raw meats, such as ham and sausage, are the only ones to fear, because salting and drying leave, if not all, at least some of these worms alive. But meat perfectly cooked, either boiled or baked, is absolutely without any danger even if infested with a multitude of these little granules, because heat of a sufficient intensity kills whatever worms they contain.

"The rule to follow, therefore, is plain: if a pig is diseased, it need not be summarily thrown away; its flesh, although of inferior quality, its lard and bacon, can very well be utilized, but care must be taken never to use any of this food without first thoroughly cooking it at a heat intense enough to destroy every dangerous germ. As for the pig itself, it can be kept from the measles by cleanliness, and especially by seeing that it eats no excrement. Every pig that wanders about and feeds on filth deposited along walls may find under its snout some pieces of tænia, swallow them with the dirty food, and thus become infected with hydatids.

"To finish this subject, I will tell you of another tænia which in its tape-worm form inhabits the dog's intestines, and in its bladder-like or hydatid stage has its home in the sheep's brain. Grass defiled by the excrement of dogs affected with this tænia receives the eggs of the expelled ripened sections. A sheep comes to browse this grass, and in a few weeks a terrible disease shows itself in the poor animal. With wild eye, driveling mouth, and heavy head, the animal turns round and round, always the same way, and falls gasping on its side. Food no longer tempts it, the blade of grass stops on its bleeding lips. All its efforts to stand up are powerless; it keeps looking for a support, especially for its head, and if this support is lacking it falls after a few turns. This strange disease is called the staggers, from the animal's tendency to turn and turn with staggering motions.

"Now if we open the brain of a sheep that has died of the staggers, we invariably find in the cerebral substance one or more limpid bladders from the size of a pea to that of a hen's egg."

"And these horrid worms in the bladder," queried Jules, "no doubt destroy the brain matter, little by little."

"They grow at the expense of the brain."

"I can well believe then, that the sheep is unable to stand."

"Each of these little bladders is a tænia in its first stage of development, and comes from the germ sown by the severed link or joint that the dog ejects with its excrement. As indisputable proof of this, if lambs are made to swallow some of the tænia links ejected by the dog, these lambs soon show themselves to be seized with the staggers, and in their brains are found the bladder-like organisms that cause the disease. The germs contained in the severed pieces of the tænia must therefore hatch in the lamb's intestines, and the worms thus brought into being must make their way, through a thousand obstacles, to the animal's brain, the only part of its body adapted to the development of the parasite."

"Then it is in the brain that the little worms grow and become bladders as large as hens' eggs?"

"It is only there that they can flourish. But these bladder-shaped worms are only incomplete beings, comparable to the larvæ of insects; and as long as they remain in the sheep's brain their final development will not be attained. To acquire their final form, to become tænias, tape-worms, these larvæ must pass into the dog's intestines. A conclusive experiment shows it. If a dog is made to take with its food some vesicular worms from a sheep's brain, the animal soon gives unequivocal signs of the presence of the tænia: its excrement contains chaplets, more or less long, of ripe joints. Furthermore, by sacrificing the dog so as to be able to decide the question more conclusively, one finds in the intestines the vesicular worms converted into veritable tænias or tape-worms. So the dog gives the sheep the germs that develop in the brain into vesicular worms; and the sheep gives the dog back these vesicular worms, which change into tape-worms in the intestines."

"But how," asked Louis, "can the dog become infected with vesicular worms when they are not expressly given to it with its food, as an experiment?"

"Nothing easier. The sheep affected with the staggers is slaughtered, and its head, the seat of the disease, is thrown away. The dog that finds it feasts on it."

"And there we have shepherd dogs attacked by tænia," said Louis. "Their excrement will spread the staggers among the flock."

"We must, then," concluded Uncle Paul, "as is recommended by those who have studied this subject experimentally in veterinary schools, exercise careful supervision over shepherd dogs and exclude from the flock those that are attacked with the tænia; finally, if the infection shows itself in the sheep, we must bury beyond the reach of any dog the heads of the slaughtered animals."

CHAPTER XXXVII

THE HORSE

"**W**OULD YOU like to hear some eloquent words written about the horse several thousand years ago? I take them from the book of Job, the just man, whose admirable history is related in the Bible."

"It was Job wasn't it," asked Jules, "who was tried by the hand of God, lost his health, family, all his goods, and was reduced to such misery that, lying on a dung-hill, he scraped his boils and vermin with a potsherd? His faith in God gave him back his former prosperity."

"Yes, my friend. The just man whose faith in God even the direst misfortunes could not shake has left us these beautiful words on the horse:

" 'Hast Thou given the horse strength? Hast Thou clothed his neck with thunder? Canst Thou make him afraid as a grasshopper? The glory of his nostrils is terrible. He paweth in the valley, and rejoiceth in his strength: he goeth on to meet the armed men. He mocketh at fear, and is not affrighted; neither turneth he back from the sword. The quiver rattleth against him, the glittering spear and the shield. He swalloweth the ground with fierceness and rage: neither believeth he that it is the sound of the trumpet. He saith among the trumpets, Ha, ha; and he smelleth the battle afar off, the thunder of the captains, and the shouting.'

"Thus spake Job in the ancient days while around his camel's-skin tent bounded mares and colts under the shade of the palm trees. Now let us listen to our great historian of animals, Buffon, who, in his turn, draws in a few splendid phrases the portrait of the horse.

" 'The noblest conquest man has ever made is that of this proud and spirited animal that shares with him the fatigues of war and the glory of battle. As intrepid as its master, the horse sees danger and shrinks not; it becomes accustomed to the clash of arms, loves it, seeks it, and is fired with the same ardor. It also shares his pleasure in the chase, in the tournament, and in racing. But, no less docile than courageous, it does not let its ardor run away with it; it knows how to control its impulses. Not only does it obey the hand that guides it, but it seems to consult that hand's wishes; always responding to its touch, it quickens or slackens its pace, or stops altogether, compliant in its every act. It is a creature which renounces itself to exist only by the will of another; which by the promptness and precision of its movements expresses and executes that will; which feels as much as it is desired to and only renders what is asked; which surrenders itself unreservedly, refuses nothing, serves with all its strength, wears itself out, and even dies to obey the better.' Thus Buffon expresses himself in regard to the horse."

"I like Job's way of saying it a good deal better," Jules declared.

"I too," his uncle assented. "To my mind, no one has said it better than the old author who lived in the land of palms. In a few sublimely energetic words he paints for us the character of the horse."

"I'm too young," said Emile, "to have an opinion on such a lofty subject; at the same time I will confess, Uncle, that I get lost very easily in Buffon's long sentences."

"In the form in which I have quoted them to you, do not call them long, for on your account I took the liberty to cut them up into separate clauses. In the author's exact words the whole makes but one sentence. From beginning to end, the sonorous period does not give one a chance to take breath."

"All the same, in spite of the cutting, I still lose my way."

"Let us return then to your uncle's simple manner of talking. The appearance of the horse denotes agility combined with strength. The body is powerful, the chest broad, the rump well rounded, the head somewhat heavy but sustained by strong neck and shoulders; the thighs and shoulders are muscular, legs slender, hocks vigorous and supple. A graceful mane falling on one side runs along the neck; the tail bears a thick growth of long hair which the animal uses to drive troublesome flies from its flanks. The eyes are large, set near the surface, and very expressive; the ears, remarkable for their mobility, point and open in any desired direction in order the better to catch the sound in their trumpet-shaped exterior. The nostrils are full and also very mobile; the upper lip projects and folds over to seize the food, arrange it in a convenient mouthful, and carry it to the teeth, just as a hand would. The whole surface of the skin, which is extremely sensitive, quivers and shakes at the slightest touch. Let us not forget a characteristic peculiar to the horse and other animals that most nearly resemble it, such as the zebra and donkey: on the forelegs, and sometimes the hind ones as well, there is a bare spot, hard as horn, and known as a callus.

"The horse's neigh or whinny, as it is called, varies according to the feelings expressed. The whinny of delight is rather long, rising little by little, and ending in a shrill note. At the same time the animal kicks out, but not violently or with any desire to do harm—merely as a sign of joy. To express desire the whinny is longer, ends on a lower key, and is not accompanied with any kicking movement. On these occasions the horse sometimes shows its teeth and seems to laugh. The neigh of anger is short and sharp. Vigorous kicks accompany it, the lips are distorted in a grimace, showing the teeth, and the ears lie close to the head and point backward. This last sign shows an intention to bite. The neigh of fear is pitched low and is hoarse and short. It seems to be produced chiefly by blowing through the nostrils, and slightly resembles the lion's roar. The animal's chief mode of defense, kicking, is sure to accompany it. Finally, the note of pain is a deep groan, becoming weaker and weaker, subsiding and then coming again with the alternate inspiration and expiration."

"So when the horse shows its big teeth and seems to laugh, it wants something," Emile broke in.

"Yes, my friend. It is hungry and tired, and it thinks of the repose of the stable, of the crib filled with hay, of the manger with its savory peck of oats. Perhaps it has heard the joyful neighing of its mates and wishes to join them. Horses that are most given to neighing with eagerness or desire are the best horses, the most spirited."

"And if they lay their ears back they want to bite?"

"Yes, that is their way of giving notice that they are going to have revenge for some ill-treatment, by biting.

"In our talk on the Auxiliaries, I have already told you of the remarkable structure of their teeth; in particular I showed you how the horse's molars, or grinders, are arranged so as to grind the tough fodder like mill-stones. A very hard substance called enamel, capable of striking fire like flint, covers the teeth and extends into the underlying and less resistant mass of ivory, forming on the crown of each molar a number of sinuous folds. These hard folds constitute a kind of strong file which tears in pieces the blades of forage when the opposite molar is brought into play. Need I go over all this again?"

"No, Uncle," replied Jules; "we all remember how ivory wears away by degrees, but the folds of enamel cap this softer substance and keep the molars in a proper condition for crushing the food."

"Then I will continue by showing you how by examining a horse's incisors we may learn the animal's age. These incisors are six in number in each jaw. They are accompanied in the upper and often also in the lower jaw by two small canine teeth having the shape of pointed nipples. Beyond these, and until the row of molars begins, the jaw is toothless, and this part is called the bar."

"I know," broke in Louis; "it is in the bar that the bit is placed with which the horse is guided."

"Let us return to the incisors. The two in the middle of the jaw are called the first or central incisors; the next two, one on the right and the other on the left of the first ones, are called the second incisors; finally, the two last, one on each side, are called the third incisors. Remember these names; they will save us the trouble of roundabout expressions.

"A few days after birth the central incisors show themselves in each of the foal's jaws. In one or two months the second incisors appear, and in six or eight months the third incisors pierce the gum. These are the first or milk teeth, as they are called. When the animal is between two and a half and three years old they fall out and are replaced by the second teeth, which make their appearance in the same order as the preceding ones: first the central incisors, then the second incisors, and lastly the third incisors. The three pairs succeed one another at intervals of about a year. I will add that the milk teeth are whiter and narrower than the others. You already see that by examining the incisors and noting whether they are first or second teeth we can tell the age of a young horse; but there are other distinctive marks which we must now learn.

"Here is a picture of the longitudinal section of a horse's incisor. In the lower part, or root, of the tooth is a cavity occupied by the nerve which gives sensitiveness to the tooth and which carries to it, in the blood, the materials for its growth and maintenance. The upper part, or crown, likewise contains a depression, which is called the pit or cavity of the crown, and is filled with blackish matter. A layer of enamel covers the outside of the tooth, folds over the crown, and extends into the cavity, the walls of which it lines. The rest of the tooth is composed of ivory.

"From this structure you will see that the enamel, continuing uninterruptedly from the outside to the inside, forms a sharp ridge on the edges of the coronal cavity. But this condition does not last long and is found only in incisors of recent formation. In fact, by the grinding of the teeth one against another when the animal chews its forage, the edge of the enamel first crumbles, then wears off little by little, and finally disappears altogether, leaving the ivory exposed on the

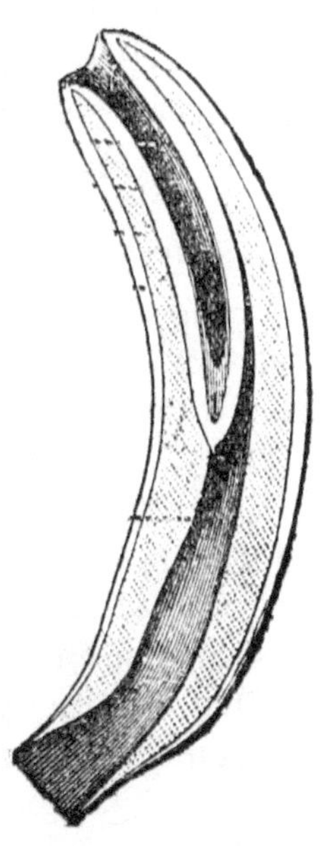

LONGITUDINAL SECTION OF A HORSE'S INCISOR

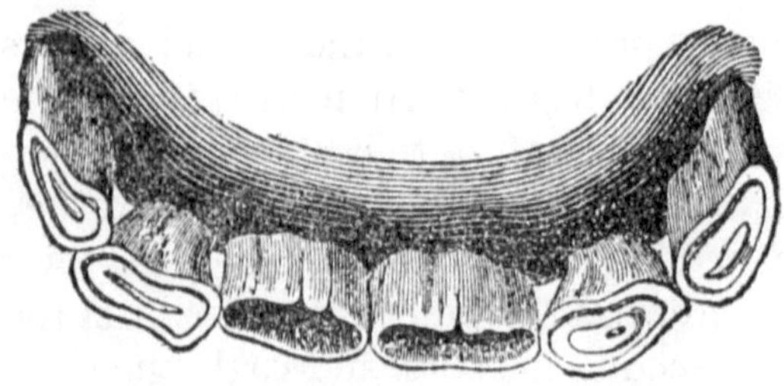

Teeth of a Three-Year-Old Horse

top of the crown. This friction always going on, the coronal cavity or pit becomes less and less deep until at last there is nothing of it left. The upper face of the crown is then flat instead of hollowed-out as it was at first. This gradual obliteration of the hollow or pit in the crown of the incisor, whether in the first or in the second set of teeth, furnishes a means of determining the horse's age. I have just told you when the milk teeth make their appearance; I will now add what is to be said about their wearing down. The central incisors of the first set of teeth are worn down so that their crowns are flat in ten months, the second incisors in one year, and the third incisors in from fifteen months to two years. Let us next consider how the horse's age may be determined at a later period.

"I here show you a picture of the incisors of the lower jaw. What do you see that will help you to estimate the horse's age?"

"I see in the first place," answered Jules, "that the teeth are not all of the same age. The two in the middle, the central incisors as you call them, are newer, since the cavities in their crowns are in good condition, with their sharp edges of enamel. The others are older; their crowns are blunted by friction; in fact, they are a good deal worn down."

"Are all six of the same cutting?"

"Evidently not, for if they were, the middle incisors would show the most wear, as they come first; but exactly the opposite is the case. Since they are quite new and those on each side are already worn, they must belong to the second cutting."

"That is quite right. Now find the animal's age."

"Let me think a moment. I have it. When the horse is between two and a half and three years old the shedding of the milk teeth begins. The first to be replaced are the central incisors. The jaw you show me has these teeth of the second set quite new. Consequently the horse is about three years old."

"The answer leaves nothing to be desired: the horse is in fact three years old. Now, Louis, what have you to

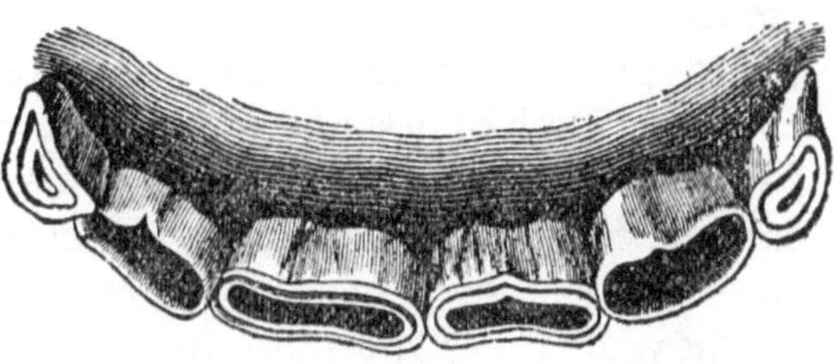

TEETH OF A FOUR-YEAR-OLD HORSE

say about this jaw that I next show you?"

"Here, too, the teeth are of different sets, since the central incisors and those next to them are less worn than the others. Moreover, the second incisors are newer than the middle ones, as can be seen from their sharper edges. These second incisors are second teeth; so are the central incisors, which are a little worn because they appeared the preceding year. The third incisors, which show the most wear of all, are milk teeth."

"All that is correct. And the animal's age?"

"It must be four years old. At three the second set of central incisors has grown, and now at four come the incisors next to them."

"Your opinion is mine too: the horse is four years old. Now it is Emile's turn. I will ask him to examine this third picture of a horse's jaw, and I hope he will show his usual perspicacity."

"These teeth," said Emile after some study, "are too large to be milk teeth. All six belong to the second set, and as the newest are the outside incisors the animal must be a year older than the preceding one; that is to say, five years."

"Very good, Emile," applauded his uncle. "You have handled the

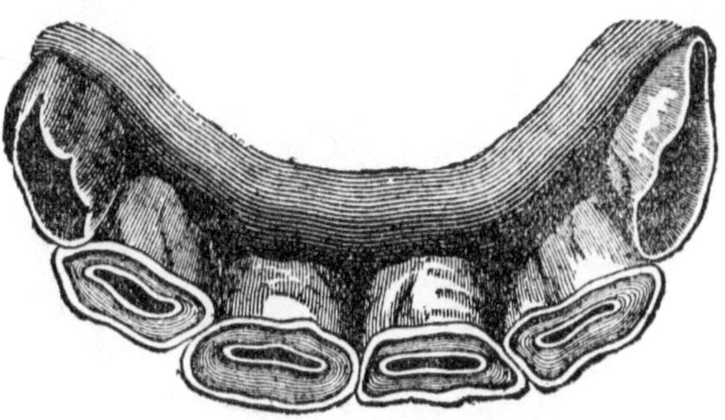

TEETH OF A FIVE-YEAR-OLD HORSE

case like a master. At five years the entire second set of incisors has pushed through and it is too late to learn anything by comparing teeth of first and second sets; henceforth the degree of wear in the different incisors is our sole guide. Thus at six years the coronal pit in the central incisors has entirely disappeared, while it is still plainly seen in the third incisors. Finally, at eight years these latter are worn down so that their crowns are smooth. It is then said that the horse no longer shows its age by its teeth. Nevertheless an expert can still detect, on the surface of the incisors as they become more and more worn, certain marks that enable him to estimate, at least pretty nearly, the age of the horse up to the twentieth year and beyond."

"That must be a difficult undertaking," commented Jules.

"Very difficult; therefore I will not dwell on it any longer."

CHAPTER XXXVIII

THE HORSE
(Continued)

"Now let us say a few words about the horse's coat, the growth of hair that covers its body. This may be of uniform color or of two or more different colors. Coats of uniform color are the white, the black, and the chestnut. The two first do not need any explanation. A horse is chestnut when its coat is of a reddish or yellowish tint.

"Among the composite coats, the following are distinguished. The horse is piebald if the coloring is in large splashes, some white, others black or red. It is flee-bitten gray if the coat is a mixture of white, black, and red, over the whole body, legs and all; but if the legs are black while the body presents a combination of the three tints, the horse is roan. Bay horses have a chestnut-colored coat, that is to say reddish or yellowish, with the legs, the mane, and the tail brown or black. The coat is dappled when it is thickly sprinkled with light spots on a darker background of uniform color. Dappled gray is common. It is dun when the color is yellowish with a brown stripe on the back, a peculiarity rather common in the donkey and mule. A number of other terms are used in describing a horse's coat in detail. Thus the term white-foot is applied to the white marking sometimes found just above the hoof. A white spot in the middle of the forehead is called a blaze if it is round, a star if angular.

"The horse's mode of progress is called its gait, and may be either natural or artificial, depending on whether the animal is untrained or trained. The natural gaits are the walk, the trot, and the gallop. In the walk the legs move in what may be termed a diagonal sequence, as follows: the right fore leg, the left hind leg, the left fore leg, the right hind leg. If the horse is well formed the hind foot steps exactly into the track left by the fore foot on the same side.

"In the trot the feet are lifted and put down two by two in diagonal pairs, the right fore foot with the left hind foot, and the left fore foot with the right hind foot. This gait is more rapid than the preceding, but is also harder for the rider as well as for the horse, because of the shock sustained when two feet strike the ground at the same time.

"The gallop is of several kinds, the simplest and swiftest consisting of a succession of forward bounds. The two fore feet are lifted at the same time, then the two hind feet, which push the animal with a sudden spring. That is the racer's gait.

"Among the artificial gaits I will mention the amble, in which the legs move in pairs on the same side, the two left at the same time, then the two right, alternately. The horse thus maintains a sort of oscillation, furnishing a gentle and easy motion for the rider. The amble is, however, rapid, for as there is no support on the side of the two uplifted legs the animal keeps from falling only by the rapidity of its motion.

"In galloping, a horse covers ten meters a second, or at most fifteen when going at top speed. In trotting it covers from three to four meters, and in walking, from one to two."

"Let me reckon up what that would be in an hour," Emile interposed. "I will take the highest figures." With his pencil he wrote some figures on a piece of paper, and then said: "That would make, by the hour, thirteen leagues of four kilometers each for the horse at its fastest gallop; only three leagues for the horse when trotting; and a league and a half when walking."

"I must inform you, my friend," rejoined his uncle, "that though a horse can keep up a trot for whole hours at a time, it is impossible for it to gallop even one hour without stopping. The speed that would give the enormous distance of thirteen leagues an hour lasts fifteen minutes at the most in racing, after which the animal is exhausted. Note in passing the superiority of the railway engine, the locomotive, in regard to rapidity. This speed of thirteen leagues an hour, which blows a horse in a quarter of an hour's race, the locomotive keeps up and even exceeds as long as may be desired. No comparison, you see, is possible between the iron steed and the steed of flesh and blood.

"Let us turn to the subject of the horse's strength. A riding horse carries on an average from 100 to 175 kilograms at a slow gait. If the load is a rider of 80 kilograms, the horse can travel seven hours and cover ten leagues of four kilometers each. But its strength is much better employed if instead of carrying the weight on its back the animal draws it in a vehicle. Then an expenditure of energy represented by the weight of five kilograms is sufficient to move a load of 1000 kilograms if the wheels of the vehicle run on a railway track. For the same load on a smooth, level road an expenditure of energy represented by 33 kilograms is needed; finally, if the road is paved with stone the required energy will be 70 kilograms. On an excellent road, stagecoach horses draw each a load of 800 kilograms and cover six leagues in two hours, after which they are replaced by others.

"Let us compare these figures once more with those relating to the steam engine. A passenger locomotive draws with a speed of a dozen leagues an hour a train having a total weight of as much as 150,000 kilograms. A freight locomotive draws at the rate of seven leagues an hour a total weight of 650,000 kilograms. More than 1300 horses would be needed to take the place of the first locomotive, and more than 2000 for the second, if they were used to transport similar loads the same distance at the same rate of speed, using cars running on rails. How many more would be needed with wagons on ordinary roads, where the surface inequalities cause such waste of energy!

"The domestication of the horse goes back to the first communities of the East. After the herd they must soon have had, first, the ass to carry the baggage of the nomadic tribe, then the horse, man's valiant comrade in the chase and in war. What is still to be observed to-day shows us how easily this valuable animal submitted to man's domination. The grassy plains of Tartary abound in wild horses, and probably the species originated in these Asiatic regions. The pampas of South America feed innumerable herds of them, mingled with the wild cattle that I have told you about. Both descend from domestic animals brought to the New World by Europeans. Each herd follows a leader of tried strength and courage. If danger arises, if there is menace from some ferocious wild beast, such as a wolf, panther, or jaguar, the horses crowd together and press against one another for their common defense. Their haughty look and their kicking are generally sufficient to put the aggressor to flight. But if the enemy charges them, counting on an easy prey, the leader of the herd rears and falls on the beast with all its weight, crushing the assailant with its fore hoofs; then with its powerful jaws seizes the shattered body and throws it to the colts, which finish it and caracole on its body."

"An animal that defends itself like that," remarked Jules, "must be rather hard to tame into a docile servant."

"No, the difficulty is not, after all, very great. What happens to-day on the pampas when it is desired to master a wild horse is of a nature to show us how the ancient horse-tamers accomplished the same object. A herd of horses, skilfully turned aside from its feeding ground and surrounded little by little on all sides, is driven without suspecting the ruse into a large enclosure called a corral. There those of finest appearance are selected. Immediately a dexterous hand throws the lasso, the long leather thong weighted with balls of lead, which catches them round the neck and legs and prevents their moving. A halter is quickly put on the captive. A practised horseman wearing sharp spurs mounts the animal, the fettering lasso is removed by helpers, and there stands the animal, free, but trembling after its misadventure."

"Now the horseman had better look out," said Jules.

"Certainly, the first moment is not without danger. The indignant animal rears, kicks, bounds, and tries to roll on the ground to get rid of its burden; but the horseman masters this rage with the bleeding prick of the spur; he keeps his seat as if he were one with his mount. Then the gate of the enclosure is opened, and the horse darts out and gallops away at breakneck speed until utterly winded. This unbridled run suffices to tame the animal, after which the horseman rides it back, unresisting and already obedient to bit and spur, to the corral. Henceforth it can be left with the domesticated horses without fear of its trying to escape.

"Horses are classed, according to the rearing and training they have received, in two chief groups—saddle horses and draft horses. The first serve as mounts for riders, the second draw loads in vehicles. Among saddle horses the most celebrated are the Arabian, remarkable for their mettle, intelligence, docility, fleetness of foot, and ability to endure long abstinence from food and drink. The Arab steed is medium-sized and has a delicate skin, small head, slender frame, a spirited bearing, finely modeled legs, stomach little developed, and small, polished, very hard hoofs.

"Draft horses, whose function it is to draw heavy loads in wheeled vehicles at a walking pace, have quite opposite characteristics. They lack lightness and mettle, but patiently exert their strength, which is considerable, as might be inferred from their more massive build and from the great quantity of feed that their maintenance demands. They have a stout body, heavy walk, thick skin, large head, wide chest, broad rump, capacious stomach, strong legs, and hoofs of no delicate proportions. France possesses in the Boulogne breed the most highly prized of draft horses. This vigorous animal, usually dapple-gray, plays the laborious part of shaft-horse. Having its position next to the cart or wagon, it is placed between the two shafts. It is the one to pull the hardest on up-grades, the one that eases with its enormous weight the jolts on street pavements and checks the dangerous momentum of the vehicle on down-grades."

CHAPTER XXXIX

THE ASS

"YOUR UNCLE'S partiality, you have already been able to see, my friends, is for the weak, the ill-treated, the unfortunate. I did not try to eulogize the horse, the valiant animal commending itself sufficiently to our esteem without that; but very gladly will I enumerate the good qualities of the ass, sad victim of our brutality despite the service it renders us. To give my words more authority I will add Buffon's testimony to my own.

" 'The ass,' says the illustrious historian of animals, 'is not a degenerate horse, as many imagine; it is neither a foreigner nor an intruder nor a bastard; like all animals it has its family, its species, and its rank. Although its nobility is less illustrious, it is quite as good, quite as ancient, as that of the horse. Briefly, the ass is an ass, nothing more, nothing less.

" 'This initial fact is of no slight importance. In considering the ass as a degenerate horse we are led to compare it with its assumed origin, and the comparison is not favorable to it: the long-eared donkey makes but a pitiful showing beside the brisk and noble courser. But as it is in reality a separate animal let us expect of it only the qualities of its species, the qualities of the ass, without depreciating the animal by comparisons with others that are stronger and better endowed. Do we despise rye because it is not so good as wheat? We thank Heaven for both, the first as the valued crop of the mountains, the second as that of the plains. Let us not, then, despise the ass because it is inferior to the horse. It possesses the good qualities of its species, and cannot possess others. We fail to recognize that the ass would be our foremost, our finest, our best made, our most distinguished domestic animal if there were no horse in

254

the world. It is second instead of first, and for that reason seems as nothing to us. It is comparison that degrades it. We look at it and judge it, not on its own merits, but relatively to the horse. We forget that it has all the good qualities of its nature, all the gifts belonging to its species, and remember only the beauty and merits of the horse, which it would be impossible for the ass to possess.'

"Buffon asserts that the nobility of the ass is as ancient as that of the horse. I will venture even further than the master and maintain that it is certainly more ancient in the sense that the ass was domesticated before the horse. It was the first to serve the Asiatic shepherds in their migration in quest of better pasturage. It carried the folded tent, the dairy utensils, the new-born lambs, the women and children. What animal did the ancient patriarchs ride? What did Abraham ride on his journey into Egypt? The ass, my friends, the peaceful ass. On nearly every page of Genesis the ass is mentioned; the horse does not appear there until Joseph's time."

"The ancient origin of the ass could not have nobler credentials," said Jules.

"Why then, asks Buffon, such scorn for the ass, so good, patient, sober, useful? Should men scorn, even among animals, those that serve them well and at so little expense? We educate the horse, take care of it, teach it, train it; while the ass, left to the rough handling of the lowest servants or to the mischievous pranks of children, far from improving in quality, can only deteriorate. If it were not fundamentally of excellent character, it would lose all its virtues from the way in which it is treated. It is the laughing-stock and the drudge of boors who beat it, overload it, and wear it out without consideration."

"Oh, how many of these poor donkeys I have seen," Jules exclaimed, "overwhelmed with their loads and beaten unmercifully because they hadn't strength enough to go on!"

"What can become of the poor animal thus degraded by bad treatment? An intractable, brutalized, bald-headed, mangy, weakened creature, object of pity for any one who has not a heart harder than stone. But let us consider the ass as the Orientals know how to raise it in all the comfort and content of careful home treatment. We shall find an animal of fine appearance, gentle looks, glossy coat, distinguished and spirited bearing, trotting briskly along the streets of the large towns, where it is habitually used as mount for going from one quarter to another. Its gait, without fatigue for the rider, makes it preferred to the horse; the greatest ladies, in making their calls, do not disdain its richly ornamented pack-saddle. The city of Cairo alone, in Egypt, uses some forty thousand of these graceful trotters. In such society would our shameful donkey dare to show itself? Ah! let us pity the poor creature: its wretched lot has made it what it is."

"I should willingly agree with the people of Cairo," said Emile. "I should prefer the donkey for a mount. At any rate, if one gets a fall the danger is not so great."

"The donkey is just the mount for invalids, children, women, and old people; it is naturally gentle, as quiet as the horse is spirited, mettlesome, and impetuous. Since, by endowing it with a patience that is proof against everything and with a small size which makes a fall from its back not at all dangerous, Heaven has created the donkey expressly for you, show the good beast by your care that you are not forgetful of your servant.

"The ass is patient; it suffers punishment and blows with constancy and perhaps with courage. This fine virtue is, as it were, written on its coat. You will often see on the donkey's back a long black stripe and another shorter one crossing the first on the shoulders. The two dark bands form the image of the cross, divine symbol of resignation to suffering. I know very well that this peculiarity in the animal's coat has not the least significance in itself; but still it is worthy of remark that the donkey, the innocent victim of our brutality, bears the cross on its back.

"The ass is temperate in both the quantity and quality of its food. It is contented with the toughest and least palatable pasturage, which horses and other animals disdain to touch. Along the roadside it browses the prickly tops of thistles, branches of willows, shoots of hawthorn. If afterward it can roll on the grass a moment, it counts this as the very summit of earthly happiness. But it is very dainty about water: it will drink only the very clearest and from streams that it knows. It drinks as temperately as it eats, and does not plunge its nose into the water, from fear, as they say, of the reflection of its ears."

"That's a funny sort of fear," said Jules.

"Therefore I don't believe the saying is well founded. The ass is not so silly as to be frightened by the reflection of its ears. If it drinks merely with its lips, without plunging its nose into the water, it is because, like the cat, it fears getting wet. It does not, like the horse, wallow in mire and water; it shrinks from even wetting its feet, and will make a detour to avoid mud. Hence its legs are always dry and cleaner than a horse's. Its aversion to wet explains sufficiently its manner of drinking, without attributing it to any silly fear of the reflection of the animal's ears."

"Why do people speak of that fear, then?"

"Simply for the malicious pleasure of adding one more example of stupidity to the donkey's account. Is it not agreed that the unfortunate beast has every possible whimsicality? Has not its very name become the favorite term to denote stupidity? All this is pure calumny; far from being the idiot it is called, the ass is a cunning beast, prudent, full of circumspection, as is proved by the care it takes in not drinking except from known springs already tested by use."

"Why make such a fuss about drinking?" was Emile's query.

"Why? Alas, my friend, evil sometimes befalls us for not exercising the donkey's prudence in the choice of our drinking-water. The unknown spring whence we draw water may be too cold, unwholesome, full of injurious substances. Better advised than we, the ass will put its lips only to water known by experience to be wholesome."

"And the ass is a hundred times right," Jules declared.

"If I dared to, I should blame the ass for the passion it has for rolling on the ground, sometimes, alas, without any thought of the load it carries. But is it really the animal's fault? Since nobody takes the trouble to curry the ass, to relieve the itching of its skin, it rolls on the grass and seems thus to reproach its master for neglect. Let the curry-comb and the brush keep its back clean, and the donkey will cease trying to rub itself, all four legs in the air, against the prickly foliage of the thistles. It is the accumulation of dust and dirt that torments it, not parasites, for of all hairy animals the ass is the least subject to vermin. It never has lice, apparently on account of the hardness and dryness of its skin, which is in fact harder than that of most other quadrupeds. For the same reason it is much less sensitive than the horse to the whip and to the sting of flies.

"When overloaded, it lies on its stomach and refuses to move, determined to let itself be beaten to death rather than get up. 'Oh, the stubborn brute! Oh, the stupid ass!' cries the master; and down comes the stick. Is it stubbornness on the animal's part to refuse to work? Listen first to a short story. In the old days of the Roman Empire a man of profound wisdom, Epictetus, was a slave in the house of a brutal master. One day the latter beat him unmercifully with his cane. 'Master,' said Epictetus to him, 'I warn you that if you keep that up you will break my leg and your slave will lose in value.' The brute struck all the harder, and a bone broke. With sublime resignation the slave uttered no reproach except to say: 'I told you you would break my leg.'

"To return to the ass laden beyond its strength, if it could speak it would certainly express itself thus in imitation of the sage: 'Master, I assure you very humbly the load you are putting on me overtaxes my strength and I cannot carry it.' But the man inconsiderately continues augmenting the burden until at last the animal's back bends under the weight. The donkey first inclines its head, lowers its ears, and then lies down. That is its way of saying, 'I told you I couldn't carry such a heavy load.' Any one but a boor would hasten to lighten the load, instead of unmercifully beating the animal, and the donkey would get up as soon as the weight became suited to its strength."

"They won't make the donkey any stronger by beating it," was Jules's comment.

"And, what is more, they will turn a docile animal into an obstinate, ill-tempered one. In its early youth, before it knows the hardness of life, the donkey is gay, playful, full of pretty tricks; but with the sad experience of age, with crushing fatigue and ill-treatment, it becomes indocile, slow, obstinate, vindictive. Is not that, however, our fault? How many injuries has not the unfortunate beast to avenge, and what a host of good qualities must it not have to remain in the end as we find it? If the donkey harbored ill-will for blows received, its master would become an object of hatred and it would be constantly biting and kicking him. On the contrary, the animal becomes attached to him, scents him from a distance, distinguishes him from all other men, and can if necessary find him amid all the confusion of a fair or market.

"With passable food and, above all, with good usage, the ass becomes the most submissive, faithful, and affectionate of companions. Let it be saddled or harnessed, loaded with pack-saddle, panniers, farm tools, or what not, it shirks no labor. If there is any fodder for it, it eats; if not, it crops the thistles by the side of the road; and if there are no thistles it goes hungry without letting its fast diminish in the least its good will. It is a philosophical beast, neither humiliated by bearing the poor man's pack-saddle nor puffed up by the rich man's elegant housings, and anxious only to do its duty everywhere and always.

"The ass has good eyes, keen scent, and excellent ears. From the quickness of its hearing and the length of its ears the inference is drawn that the animal is timid. I am willing to assent to this, the ass never having earned a reputation for prowess or daring. Moreover, its quickness of hearing and length of ears are shared by many other animals that do not surpass it in courage, as, for example, the hare and the rabbit, which are even more richly endowed than the ass in respect to length of ears. Their weakness and defenselessness expose them to a thousand dangers and make their life a continual state of alarm. To be warned in time of peril and save themselves by speedy flight, their surest dependence is the excellence of their hearing, which is partly due to the enormous size of the external ear, movable in every direction so as to receive sounds from all sides.

"Merely because the ass has the long ears indicative of timidity shall we charge the animal with poltroonery? That would be unfair, for if it does not court danger it at least knows how to face it when peaceful means of safety are out of the question. The horse is warlike, the ass prefers the gentle ways of peace and consents to the arbitrament of force only when no other course is possible; but then its courage rises to meet the danger. If in its wild state it is surprised by an assailant, it hastens to rejoin its companions of the pasture; and, all grouping together as do wild horses in their war tactics, they begin to kick and bite with such fury that the enemy decamps as quickly as possible, with jaw-bone fractured by a flying hoof."

"After such an exploit," said Jules, "let no one tell me the donkey is a coward."

"I fancy," put in Emile, "that after routing the enemy the donkeys do not fail to chorus a song of victory."

"It is not to be doubted that, to congratulate one another and to celebrate their triumph, the donkeys sound a few clarion notes, such as they so well know how to give. The horse neighs and the donkey brays, the latter cry being very loud, very pro-longed, very disagreeable, and composed of a succession of discords ranging from sharp to grave and from grave to sharp."

"And the last notes," added Emile, "are hoarser and gradu-ally die away."

"I see Emile is well acquainted with the donkey's voice. Let us go on to some of its other peculiarities. From time immemo-rial the ass has had the reputation of being stupid: its very name is synonymous with stupidity. There is a whole vocabulary of abusive epithets that we bestow on the ass, and these epithets nearly always allude to its stupidity. We call it a numbskull, a ninny, a jackass, a wooden-head, and I don't know what all; and, as a crowning slander to the animal, the dunce of his class at school is made to wear a cap with donkey's ears. Never has calumny been more flagrant. The donkey a dunce? By no means! Is it not the donkey that, with a prudence worthy of imitation, refuses to drink from unknown springs? Does it not, when lost in the crowd at market, know how to find its master almost as easily as the dog, and does it not begin to bray with joy at sight of him? But there is something better than this to prove its intelligence. Recall to mind the wagoner's long team of horses on the highway. There are four, six, eight of them, sturdily tugging at the enormous load. Between the two shafts, the most arduous position of all, is the massive shaft-horse, while at the head of the team proudly marches a donkey, harnessed very lightly. What is this little creature doing at the head of those robust companions? First, it pulls with vigor, so far as its strength will admit; and, secondly, it has a still more important function to fill. Its part is to guide the equipage and keep it in the middle of the road, to avoid ruts, get around difficult places, and, in general, pick the way. While the heavy horses work only with their shoulders to draw the load, the donkey, to lead the way, works at the same time with its head. This post of honor, this position as leader of the file—would it be assigned to the ass if the animal were not recognized as the most intelligent of the team?

"I should like to show you also the donkey traveling in mountainous countries in company with horses and mules. It is the one to direct the band, showing the others the turnouts to take to avoid a dangerous place. If the path gets too bad, the donkey foresees the peril with an astonishing sagacity; it turns aside a moment from the beaten track, finds a way around the difficult spot by a cleverly calculated bend, and takes the regular road again farther on. Any mule or horse that disdains to follow the donkey's intelligent leadership runs the risk of getting into trouble whence it will be very hard to get it out."

"As far as I can see," said Jules, "the donkey is more intelligent than the horse, since it acts as the horse's guide."

"That is my opinion, too, in spite of the reputation for stupidity that it has acquired, I don't know why. The donkey walks, trots, and gallops like the horse, but all its movements are within a smaller compass and much slower. Although it can start out at a brisk enough pace, it cannot cover great distances or continue on the road for a long time. Whatever gait it takes, if the animal is urged to go faster it is soon exhausted. It is especially suited to mountainous countries. Its small, hard hoofs enable it to follow stony paths with the greatest ease; its prudent gait and firm and circumspect step give it access to rough places and the steepest slopes.

"The donkey is very robust. In proportion to its size it is perhaps of all animals the one that can carry the heaviest load, but as its body is small the burden placed on it ought not to exceed moderate limits. What a useful servant would one not have in an animal having the qualities of the donkey and the vigorous development of the horse! Such a creature does not exist in the natural order, but man has obtained it by the intervention of his art.

"The species of the horse and that of the ass are unmistakably distinct from each other and never cross in the wild state. Nevertheless, since they are very nearly related, as their close resemblance in form proves, cross-breeding between them is possible with careful management. From this unnatural union comes the mule, of which the father is the ass and the mother the mare. The mule then is not a separate species of animal having its own independent existence; it is not an ass nor a horse, but a bastard creature intermediate between the two. To its father, the ass, it owes its large head, long ears, narrow and hard hoofs, thick skin, rough coat, generally dark in color and sometimes ornamented with the two black stripes in the form of a cross on the back. To the ass it also owes its temperate habits, its tenacity in work, its robust constitution, and the sureness of foot so necessary in mountainous countries. From its mother, the mare, it gets its powerful equine frame, its quick gait, its freedom of limb. Its rude strength, moderation in supplying its animal wants, power of enduring the utmost fatigue, indifference to extreme heat, make it one of the most useful animals, especially in hot climates where there are long spells of drought."